Dear Romance Readers,

Finally, just in time for those long and lovely summer afternoons, your romance wishes have all come true. The BOUQUET line launches with four stories that will leave you begging for more—and four more will be coming your way every month!

We're celebrating the Bouquet debut with a delicious story by award-winning romantic favorite Leigh Greenwood. Leigh is a thoroughbred racing fan, and **The Winner's Circle** features a Kentucky bluegrass horse farm . . . and a sizzling love story. The heroine of Patricia Werner's **Sweet Tempest** is a meteorologist who flies into the eyes of hurricanes to collect data, but finds the stormiest passion in the arms of a charismatic storm chaser.

We wouldn't dream of launching a new line of romance without a story about a baby, and Kathryn Attalla, well known to Silhouette® and Precious Gems readers, has crafted a fetching one to grace the Bouquet debut lineup. Heroine Caitlin is forced to strike a hard bargain to hold onto her baby . . . (but can she hold onto her heart?) in **The Baby Bargain.** And we welcome newcomer Karen Drogin to the Bouquet list with **Perfect Partners**—two lawyers, first adversaries, then lovers, who learn that partnership means much more than billable hours.

Treat yourself to the bouquets that never wilt—sparkling romances you'll want to treasure on your keeper shelf. The kind of romance novels you read, then sigh and say, "Finally. Exactly the kind of book I really love."

The Editors

LOVELY LIBERTIES

Courtney deftly cut a bale of hay in half with her pitchfork, lifted it without visible effort, and tossed it into the next stall.

"From the way you handle that pitchfork," Seth said, "I would hazard a guess no one has dared take liberties with your person."

"Until I met you, no one dared take liberties with me in any manner."

"Does that mean you'll let me take liberties with your person?" Seth asked. "You're quite a temptation, you know."

"Make one move and I'll pin you to the wall," Courtney threatened, but she didn't raise her eyes for fear Seth would see the hungry expression in them. She moved the wheelbarrow to the next stall . . . but before she could retrieve the pitchfork, she found herself swept up into Seth's arms.

"I'm glad you warned me," he said, his face lowered until it was close to hers. "Pitchfork holes would ruin my shirt."

"Let me go."

"Do you really want me to? It feels very right to have you in my arms."

Her protest was smothered by his lips. It was useless to tell her arms not to encircle his neck, or to order her lips not to kiss him back.

It would be so easy just to give in to this man . . . and let him take care of her forever. . . .

THE WINNER'S CIRCLE

Leigh Greenwood

Zebra Books
Kensington Publishing Corp.
http://www.zebrabooks.com

ONE

"If you don't come up with some money from some-where, we're not going to be able to keep this place afloat."

Her farm manager's words haunted Courtney as she leaned against the top rail of the white fence, her gaze on the yearling colt frolicking in the large field, her chin resting on her hands, her hair blowing unhindered in the breeze. The weather was unusually hot for October, and her normal outfit of jeans and boots was completed by a sleeveless tank top.

She had been looking for more boarders ever since her grandfather's death three years ago, but most owners weren't willing to quarter their horses on a debt-ridden farm owned by a twenty-four-year-old woman. Her grand-father had spent ten years training her to take over, but most people said she was too young and too inexperi-enced.

"I've worked everything out to the last penny," she had told Ted, trying to sound confident. "If we're careful, we can make it until Gus starts racing."

Her experienced eye noted every detail of the colt's movement as he showed off for her, trotting toward her, then wheeling and galloping back down the field. His red chestnut coat, very close to the color of Courtney's own hair, gleamed brightly in the sun. His muscles rippled as he moved effortlessly into full stride.

"You're going to win so many races I'll never have to worry about money again," Courtney said aloud, so used to talking to the colt it never occurred to her to leave her thoughts unspoken.

As though he understood, the colt headed across the field at a full gallop, dodging butterflies and dragonflies as if they were thousand-pound horses straining to beat him to the finish line. After running half the length of the field, he turned and stopped, tossed his head, then trotted back to receive his praise and the treat hidden in one of Courtney's pockets.

"You're spoiled, Gus. You know that, don't you?" she crooned, as she patted his beautifully arched neck with one hand and fed him sugar from the palm of the other. "I probably won't be able to find a trainer who can do a thing with you, and I'll end up watching you chase butterflies for the rest of your life."

A shudder ran through Courtney. She knew if Gus didn't win races, she would lose him. She didn't think she could endure that. She'd bred him, been present when he was foaled, helped him stand the first time he nursed. He was *her* horse, *her* baby, and he would be a great champion. He had to be!

"He's a superb animal."

Courtney whirled at the sound of an unfamiliar voice. A giant of a man, looking like Atlas with clothes on, stood not three feet away, smiling at her in a way that threatened to deprive her mind and body of their ability to function. Impeccably dressed in a wine-colored blazer, club tie, and brown slacks, his wavy blond hair combed neatly in place and his mahogany-colored leather shoes newly polished, he just stood there, watching her with a boyish grin advertisers would have paid a fortune for.

"Who are you?" Courtney mumbled, too stunned to remember her manners.

"Seth Cameron." His extended hand engulfed her own. "I couldn't help noticing your colt as I drove by."

Although she was still dazzled by the presence of this enormous man, her eyes narrowed. "You can't see this pasture from the road." How could anyone so huge look so cuddly? Well, perhaps not cuddly exactly, but there was definitely something of the teddy bear about him. And then there was that smile. Courtney allowed her slim body to lean against the fence.

"I meant your farm road," he explained, pointing to where a Jaguar, the same shade of gray as his eyes, was parked.

"What were you doing on my farm?"

"Looking at your colt."

"Who told you about him?" It was hard to carry on a sensible conversation with this man.

"I'm afraid I can't answer that. It's a trade secret."

"What are you, some kind of reporter?"

"Nothing like that," Seth assured her with a deep, rumbling laugh. "Though there is a good deal of research involved in what I do."

"And what is that?"

"I buy and sell horses. I was hoping I might talk to you about selling this colt."

Courtney came off the fence with a lunge. "He's not for sale," she snapped.

Seth blinked at the unexpected change, but all he said was, "What's his pedigree?"

All that provocative male attractiveness, all that delectably seductive charm, and he was a horse salesman. She felt betrayed, and her mouth twisted angrily. "What difference does that make? I'll never sell Gus!"

"Gus?"

"Yes, Gus," she repeated irritably. "You can't expect me to go around calling him that Deputy-Minister Spring Sunshine colt, can you?"

"I suppose not, but Gus?"

"He's a real country cousin," she explained, the sharpness leaving her voice. "There's nothing he likes better than rolling in the dirt. He thinks God made mud especially for him."

"A lot of personality, huh?"

"I've spoiled him if that's what you mean," Courtney said, her features relaxing into a smile. "He thinks I have nothing to do with my day but ooh and aah over everything he does, and he expects a treat every time he performs."

"His action looks good."

"He can reach a flat gallop in half a dozen strides," declared Courtney, incensed her colt should receive such lukewarm praise from this brash intruder. But what could she expect from a horse merchant who couldn't see anything but dollar signs whenever he looked at a thoroughbred. It was a shame, too, she thought, because he had a positively impish twinkle in his eyes, and his mouth turned up at one corner in a lopsided grin. If she hadn't known better, she'd have sworn he was teasing her—and enjoying it.

"I take it you intend to race him?"

Courtney nodded.

"Do you have a trainer?"

She shook her head.

"Are you sure you won't consider selling him?"

Courtney couldn't keep nodding her head. It made her

feel like some kind of trained animal. Neither could she sustain her irritation at this behemoth, not with his twinkling eyes and crooked grin. At twenty-four she was no innocent schoolgirl, but she might as well have been for all the good her years were doing her now.

"Grandpa always raced his horses," she said.

"You won't find it as easy as he did."

"And just what do you mean by that?" Why was it that every time she started to think she might like him, he said something to provoke her?

"It's nothing personal, but horse racing is pretty much a man's game. There are a few women in it, but usually in partnerships."

"So you don't think I can handle it?" The fact that the owners who refused to board their horses at her farm felt the same way only made her more irritated with him.

"I don't know what you can do. I don't really know you."

If she hadn't been sure he was trying to be obnoxious, she would have sworn there was an open invitation in his words instead of a challenge. The twinkle in his eyes had turned to something soft and bluish gray, and there was the faintest suggestion of a pucker about his lips.

"I'm not exactly without friends," Courtney stated defiantly, and earned another of those rumbling laughs that so effectively undermined her animosity. This man didn't play fair.

"I'm sure you aren't, but I took your flame-and-daggers look to mean you'd be damned if you'd call on any of them for help."

Courtney swallowed her reply. Not only could this man demolish her resistance with nothing more than a twisted grin, but he could read her mind as well.

"What I intend to do is really none of your concern,"

she replied, trying to sound indignant rather than breathless. "Actually, nothing I do is your concern."

"It doesn't have to stay that way."

Why couldn't she stay angry with him, Courtney thought, as she tried to calm her racing pulses? The sooner he left, the better. "If there's nothing else you wanted to say . . ."

"Sure I can't interest you in selling that colt? I could have buyers from both sides of the Atlantic bidding for him."

"No!" Why did he persist?

"I could enter him in a winter sale, or one for two-year-olds in training."

"How many times do I have to tell you he's not for sale?" A true salesmen never gives up, Courtney reminded herself, and this Seth Cameron was showing every sign of being a *bona fide* salesman, right down to his size fourteen Gucci's.

"Why isn't he?"

"That's also none of your business," Courtney snapped, her temper flaring at his unrelenting pitch. His faintly amused grin increased her irritation until she blurted out, "He's going to be a champion. I'll be buying horses soon."

"Buying?"

Courtney had to give him credit. Neither his face nor his voice betrayed the surprise he must have felt at her announcement.

"Yes, buying," she repeated, glad to have the upper hand for once. "Idle Hour was once the finest farm in Kentucky. I mean to see it is again."

"If you sell the colt, you'll have capital to buy new stock. That way you could hedge your bets, spread the risk over several horses instead of one. That's what most people would do."

"I'm not most people."

"It can be mighty tough in this business going it all alone."

"I'm not *all alone* yet, but I intend to be quite soon," Courtney snapped. "I want you off my property in five minutes."

"Now, that doesn't sound very hospitable. I thought southern women were supposed to act neighborly toward visitors."

She didn't understand how the whole time he was trying to steal her horse he could appear so downcast that she wanted to console him. His look of wounded sensibilities would have done justice to the world's most talented beagle. "We're always courteous to *gentlemen* but we're a good deal more circumspect when it comes to *men.*"

"Ouch! A southern belle who bites."

Courtney couldn't repress a reluctant smile. "Your accent's a dead giveaway, so stop pretending you're not as southern as I am. Though why any self-respecting Kentuckian would want to sell horses when he could race them is something I'll never understand."

"Well, you just think that one over for a little while. It'll give us something to talk about when I come back."

"I don't want you to come back," Courtney said a little too slowly. She had to stop looking into his eyes. She couldn't think with him watching her as though she were a cream pastry and he was having an attack of the sweet tooth.

"I'll tell you what. If you'll work on your attitude toward salesmen, I'll work on mine about women in racing. A person should always strive to be open to new experiences. I'd sure hate to think a fine-looking woman like you was close-minded."

"Leave!" Courtney commanded, so sharply that Gus snorted and bounded away from the fence only to stop a short distance off and stare at her. "Now see what you've made me do," she said, furiously rounding on Seth.

"Now, how could an easygoing fella like me make a lady like you lose her temper?"

Courtney longed to tell him, but she couldn't think of any way that didn't involve using at least a half dozen four-letter words. Besides, what right did he have to call her a fine-looking woman! "Just leave."

She spun on her heel and started toward the barns, but she couldn't resist a look over her shoulder. That annoying man was still standing where she left him, gazing after her with his lopsided grin. He touched his fingers to his forehead in a salute before heading toward his glistening Jaguar, which was about as quietly expensive as everything else about him, she thought rancorously. With an angry toss of her head, she turned back toward the barns; but her heart was beating as though she'd just finished running, and she was strangely agitated.

She didn't know why she had allowed him to upset her. He was exactly the kind of high-pressure salesman she loathed. It seemed no one could resist them. Every time she opened the paper, another family farm was up for sale, some breeder was putting his yearlings on the market for the first time, or a promising young race-horse was being rushed off to stud—all because these smooth-talking con men couldn't wait to sell Kentucky's heritage to the highest bidder.

He'd probably breed a knock-kneed mare to a three-legged unicorn if he thought the resulting foal would bring a high price on the auction block. She didn't know why he bothered about Gus. The colt didn't have the kind of flashy pedigree that was currently fashionable with the big spenders. Maybe Mr. Cameron was just learning.

No, whatever his reason for fancying her colt, Seth Cameron was no neophyte. Everything about him, from his expensively tailored clothes to his silver-and-gray Jaguar, spoke of confidence and success. He had probably put his own parents in a nursing home and sold the family farm to some Greek shipping magnate. She could picture him having grown up on a tobacco farm, or maybe beef cattle. He probably played football in college, maybe even professional football. He was certainly big enough to push full-grown men around. Now he was trying to act like he was nobody special. Someone ought to tell him that smooth-talking con men with more muscles than the Jolly Green Giant were definitely not ordinary.

Still, there was something boyishly disarming about his twinkling gray eyes and sandy blond hair. If he hadn't mentioned selling Gus, she'd probably still be talking to him. He might even be quite handsome, but who could tell? Trying to get a good look at his face was like trying to look at Mount Rushmore from somewhere underneath George Washington's nose. At five feet, eight inches, Courtney was used to thinking of herself as a tall woman, but five-eight didn't feel like much next to Paul Bunyan's twin brother.

Courtney kicked at a clump of grass and mumbled a curse she was glad nobody overheard. Why was she wasting her time thinking about someone like Seth Cameron? If he set foot on her farm again, she'd sic Hamlet on him.

She was so deep in thought she nearly collided with her manager as he came out of the farm office. Ted Bassett looked like an accountant—short, balding, with a slight paunch, and thick glasses—but there wasn't anybody in Kentucky who knew more about how to run a horse farm. Without even stopping to think of the incongruity of the situation, she asked, "Ted, do you know a man by the name of Seth Cameron? He's a big man, must be six-four. He's some kind of sales agent."

"Sure. Why?"

"He was here just now."

"What for? He only handles the really expensive horses."

"He was trying to get me to sell Gus. He asked a lot of questions, but I got the feeling he already knew the answers."

"Cameron would. He never wastes time going to a farm unless he knows pretty much what he's going to see when he gets there."

"But how could he find out about Gus?"

"Good Lord, Courtney, every farmhand in Lexington brags about the new colt on the farm. Did he offer cash?"

"No. One of the sales."

"Did he mention a price?"

"You know I won't sell Gus," Courtney said, giving Ted a particularly penetrating look.

"I was just wondering."

"Men like him are destroying racing. They were always at Grandpa whenever he bred something good, always trying to pick his bones. As long as they could keep making money, they never cared that they were destroying him."

"Courtney, you've got to realize things are never going to be the way they were when your grandfather was young."

"I know, but things wouldn't be so bad if we didn't have people like your precious Mr. Cameron ready to stuff people's pockets with cash if they'd sell their best horse. He'll never get Gus." Courtney spun on her heel.

"Courtney, could I talk with you a minute?"

She stopped and looked back. Ted's face was constantly furrowed by worry these days, and she knew she was the cause. She entered his office and settled into the chair in front of his desk. She knew what he was going to say, but she would listen to him anyway. She owed him that much. He worked as hard for the farm as she did.

"I know you're going to hate what I'm about to suggest, but hear me out."

"Don't try to soften me up. Just tell me what you have in mind."

"I want you to sell the northeast corner to Valley Enterprises."

"No!" Courtney rose from her seat, her voice leaping an octave.

"For what they're willing to pay, you could run the farm for ten years."

"I wouldn't care if they offered a million dollars an acre. We only have to hang on for less than a year. Gus is the kind of horse my grandfather dreamed about his whole life."

"Do you know what the odds are against that? It's twenty thousand to one he'll be a champion—more like a half million to one he'll be the kind of horse you need."

"We'll make it—I know we will. He'll be faster than anything else on the track. I've timed him in the field—"

"You're not going to sell any land, are you?" Ted asked, defeat in his voice.

"No."

"I don't know how to tell you this, Courtney, but I've put it off too long already."

Something in Ted's voice warned Courtney this wasn't about another stopgap measure.

"I'm going to start looking for another job."

Courtney was too stunned to speak. Ted had been the farm manager since she came to live with her grandfather. He was as much a part of Idle Hour Farm as she was. It had never occurred to her he wouldn't always be here.

"I'll be sorry, but I have to think of my family. I still have the youngest boy in school, and you know about Edna's heart. I've got to have something I can depend on."

"You can't leave."

"I don't have any choice."

Courtney left his office in a daze. Ted's decision had shaken her badly. She wandered over to her favorite bench under one of the enormous oaks that shaded the office. She couldn't survive without Ted. Even if she could do everything as well as he could, managing the farm was too much work for one person. If she was going to spend several hours a day getting Gus ready for serious training, she would have to hand over still more of her duties. She was too upset to think right now, but she had to figure out a way to keep Ted. Later she'd block everything out of her mind and concentrate. That was one of the differences between them. Ted liked to see all the way to the end. She was satisfied to solve one problem at a time.

Seth settled into one of the deep, leather-covered chairs in Clay Marchmont's study. After a day like this, it was a real treat to be invited to eat with Clay and his wife. Nothing to do but dig into one of the best cooked meals in Lexington and sample the finest bourbon money could buy while he waited. It was tempting to put all thoughts of work out of his mind; but there was something about this day that wouldn't let him alone, and that something was Courtney Clonninger. "I was out at Idle Hour Farm today," he told Clay.

"You mean Courtney Clonninger's place?"

"Do you know any other farm by that name?"

"No, but you're still in one piece. If you went there for what I think you went for, I'm surprised you're alive."

"She didn't cotton to the idea, but she didn't shoot me."

"If you go out there again—and I can tell from the determined set of your chin that you're going to do just that—you might not be so lucky. There's the small matter of her dog."

"Dog?"

"You obviously haven't met Hamlet. She says he's a dog, but I maintain he's a small horse with very sharp teeth."

"You don't think she'll change her mind?"

"Can you give up whiskey, horses, and women?"

"I've already given up one of them." Clay cocked an interested eye. "Temporarily," Seth added with a sheepish grin.

Clay burst out laughing.

"Tell me about her," Seth said.

"Half the eligible men in Lexington have tried their hand with her and been turned down flat. Her grandfather left her two thousand acres of prime Kentucky bluegrass, but it's mortgaged to the hilt."

"I'm not interested in her land. I want to sell that colt."

"I'd give up on that if I were you. Just the mention of a salesman is enough to start her foaming at the mouth. I'm surprised she didn't go after you with a shotgun."

"Why is she so dead set against salesmen?"

"You'll have to ask her, but salesmen pretty much

picked her grandfather's bones when things started to get rough."

"What happened?"

"Mostly a combination of bad luck and a man who couldn't—or wouldn't—change with the times."

"My figures tell me she's in deep trouble, but she doesn't act it."

"Courtney's a proud woman, but she's down to her last nickel."

"Then, you can imagine how shocked I was when she said she'd soon be buying horses. I'm sure I could talk her around if she wasn't convinced her colt is the second coming of Secretariat."

"Who told you that?"

"She did, in so many words."

"Then, you know why she won't sell. If you owned Secretariat, would you sell?"

"Hell no. I'd syndicate him for the best price I could get and buy myself a half dozen top brood mares."

"Okay, cancel the part about syndication—Courtney doesn't believe in selling anything—and you know where she stands."

"Good God!"

"I'm the closest thing she has to a financial adviser, and I can't get her to listen to anything I say."

"Can she make it?"

"Possibly."

"Damn! I just missed the chance to syndicate one of the best horses of the decade."

Clay's gaze narrowed. "Do you think that horse is *really* good?"

"Yes, I do. I didn't see Secretariat as a yearling, but I've never seen anything to match this one. I watched him one day with a group of other yearlings. Several times they tried to gang up on him. He would sprint away, just flat-out leave them standing, and he wasn't even trying."

Clay was quiet for a while. "I'm glad she's got a good horse, but it's my guess that unless Courtney is mighty lucky, she's going to need some help from her friends."

"Can she get it?"

"I don't know. A horseman may be a millionaire several times over, but his money is tied up in horseflesh. What Courtney needs is cash."

TWO

Seth slowed his Jaguar as he neared the pasture; but Courtney was not at the fence, and the colt was nowhere in sight. He continued down the tree-lined road past fields and paddocks lush with ungrazed grass until he came to a fork in the road, the right going off to the barns and the left up to the main house, an enormous white structure he could just make out through the foliage of the gnarled oaks that lined the driveway. Pausing for only a second, he turned his car to the right and pulled up in front of one of the barns.

He probably shouldn't have come back. Courtney had made it plain she had no intention of selling Gus, but something kept bringing his mind back to the colt. Well, maybe it wasn't the colt so much as it was Courtney. Her tall, slim body had made a strong impression on him, despite the fact he'd never been particularly drawn to redheads. They were often capricious and temperamental, and Courtney showed every sign of running true to form. Add to that a strong dose of Irish blood, and you had a perfect combination for disaster.

Courtney didn't strike him as the kind of woman who was indifferent to men. He wondered if her temper was the reason none of the Kentucky lads had succeeded with her. He could easily see her looking down her turned-up nose at some cheeky guy—it was even easier to see her belting him—but he couldn't imagine her going to bed alone for the rest of her life. She had too much fire, too much life to stay on the shelf forever.

Seth gave himself a mental shake and let out a soft chuckle. Sentiment always ruined business, and it was going to require cool thinking to handle this woman. He picked up the folder of information he had compiled on Courtney, her farm, and her colt, but didn't look at it. He didn't need to. He had it memorized.

He wasn't giving up on the colt, but he might have to wait a few months. Meantime, he might try talking her into selling part of her farm. It was worth more than a dozen horses, and she couldn't possibly need two thousand acres with so few horses.

He laughed to himself again. If Courtney had any idea what he was thinking right now, she probably would shoot him. He'd never tried to pressure anyone into selling anything, but he doubted she'd believe that. She seemed to think a salesman was only marginally better than Attila the Hun. He doubted she credited those in his profession with any more refined feelings than a primitive instinct to go for the jugular.

He tossed the unread folder aside and got out of the car. After the unseasonable heat, the crisp breeze felt good. The quiet was eerie, but the aromas of hay and manure told him there were horses about. Even though farms tended to be quiet after lunch, he had expected to see some signs of activity. He walked over to the office and opened the door. There was no one inside. The air-conditioning being off told him no one was coming back, either.

He stuck his head inside the first brick-and-timber barn he came to, but the dry, dusty smell told him the barn was not in use. It was the same for the next; but the third barn greeted him with the familiar medley of smells, and he stepped inside. The ceiling was high and open, and light and air flooded in through the open doors at the opposite end. One stall door stood ajar with a wheelbarrow parked just outside. As he watched, the end of a pitchfork emerged to toss manure and wet straw into the wheelbarrow. Seth was unprepared to find Courtney, her russet hair in a blue bandanna and the bottoms of her jeans tucked into her boots, knee-deep in straw.

Even now, he found it impossible not to stare at her. She was a lovely woman with a stunning figure, but it was her energy and intensity that commanded his admiration. If he had any doubts before about wanting to help her, he had them no longer.

"If you keep standing there with your mouth open, I'm liable to unload my pitchfork over your head," Courtney threatened without pausing in her work. "Haven't you seen a woman muck out a stall before?"

"Often," Seth replied, gathering his wandering wits, "but not, that I can recall, when she was the owner of the stall." She hadn't lost a drop of vinegar from yesterday, and she didn't look any the worse for having a piece of straw sticking out of her collar.

"I'm not as rich as the people you're used to. We don't have too many horses here at present, so we cut corners when we can." She finished the stall, closed the door behind her, rolled the wheelbarrow to the next one, and began mucking it out.

"If you'd let me sell that colt, you'd never have to muck out a stall again."

Courtney ignored him, and Seth moved closer. He liked looking at her.

"I could get at least two or three million, maybe more if the right people bid against each other."

Still Courtney didn't respond.

"I know you can use the money. A place like this must cost a fortune."

Courtney flashed him a look of burning reproach.

"I take it from your less than enthusiastic response you still don't want to sell the colt. Have you considered a private sale? You wouldn't be at the mercy of an open auction. You could invite only the buyers you want. You could sell a half interest. Even a third."

She still refused to speak. He'd talked to empty space plenty of times before, but with Courtney he liked it less than usual. She didn't even look up when she changed stalls, just started pitching manure in his direction.

"Look, I'll syndicate him for you. That way you can sell as few shares as you like." Courtney continued to work in silence until Seth couldn't stand it any longer. "Hell, aren't you going to talk to me?"

"Not as long as you talk about selling Gus."

"You sure are one stubborn woman," Seth said, wondering if that wasn't a trait best admired from a distance. It would probably be easier to make up with his old girl-friend than to keep after this stubborn redhead, but Seth had discovered about five minutes earlier that his favorite hair color was no longer blond. He had unexpectedly developed a strong liking for burnished copper comple-mented by hazel eyes.

Courtney stopped her labors and looked him straight in the eye. "If you were in my position, would you let some smooth-talking shyster talk you into selling Gus? Let me rephrase that," she said, putting her hand up to fore-stall Seth's indignant protest. "If this colt were the most important thing in your life, would you let some smooth-talking shyster talk you into selling him to a perfect stranger?"

Seth decided Courtney was growing on him, though God only knew why, but he hadn't expected to be so upset over running second to a horse. Even a horse like Gus. Hell, he was a man. He could talk, drive a car, count without having to tap his hoof, and no one had to muck out after him. "I was hoping you would eliminate the bit about a *smooth-talking shyster,*" he said.

"Perhaps shyster wasn't the right word."

Seth's relief was short-lived.

"Confidence man sounds a little trite, and con man has been overused, but I do think crook is going a bit too far."

"If that's what you think of me, I'm surprised you haven't called out the dogs," Seth said, feeling unreasonably warm. For a man who was supposed to be able to handle women, he had wasted no time striking out with Courtney.

"I thought of that; but I have only one dog, and he's off with Ted. Now, get back in your dual-exhaust chariot and get out of here. I have work to do."

Okay, he'd forget the hard sell. If he left Gus alone for a while, maybe she wouldn't treat him like scum. Having reached that decision, he was a little surprised to feel himself relax. He smiled. "I won't mention selling Gus again. How about showing me around the place?"

Courtney stabbed her pitchfork into the ground, and while leaning on the handle and resting her left foot on the bottom, she cocked a skeptical eye in his direction. "If you think flattering me about the lovely place I have here is going to change my mind, you're sadly mistaken. I don't trust you and your kind. I don't even like most of you. I wouldn't let you sell a mule."

"I don't know what happened to you in the past," Seth said, more than a little irked, "but I had nothing to do with it. Besides, it's not fair to assume all sales agents are alike."

"Why not? You assumed I was like all the rich females you know who think it might be fun to own a horse or two."

Okay, two could play at this game. He'd see how she liked being on the defensive. "I apologize if I sounded like I was lumping you with the rest of your gender. I still have reservations about your being able to succeed in this business, but it's becoming increasingly clear you're not like any female I've ever known."

"Good."

"Not necessarily. The others may have certain short-comings in common, but they also share several very desirable traits. After the way you've treated me, I'm beginning to wonder just how different you really are."

"Now, look here, Buster . . ."

Just what he thought. She didn't like it at all. "We'll never get to know each other better if you rip into me every time you open your mouth. Why don't we call a truce and you show me around the place? I have a feeling it may be the only thing we can talk about without my being afraid you'll stop using that pitchfork on manure and start using it on me."

"Is there a difference?"

Seth didn't pause or hesitate, or stumble. "I thought we called a truce?"

"You called it. In your typical male fashion, you assumed I'd go along."

"Okay, okay. Could we please call off the war? I'd like to see the farm."

"I have to give you credit for one thing," Courtney

said, stripping off her gloves. "You're persistent. Ted said you were very successful. I guess it's part of your technique to hound people until they're ready to pay any price to get you off their backs."

"If this is your idea of a truce, I want a three-day head start before you declare war," Seth said. Good God, this lady had built a defense perimeter around her that would repel an armored tank. She was dug in for the duration.

"Okay, I withdraw that statement," Courtney said, an apparently reluctant grin banishing her frown. "I promise not to make any more references to the truth without warning you first."

"Is fighting a habit with you?" Seth asked, his exasperation beginning to take over. "You may not like me or what I do, but can't we agree to a cease-fire?"

"I didn't mean to say that—truly I didn't," Courtney apologized. "I promise, word of honor, not to let another unpleasant thought pass my lips."

But you'll let plenty of them cross your mind, Seth thought to himself. His blood was up now. No woman had ever flatly rejected him on a personal *and* professional basis at the same time. Okay, he wasn't Tom Cruise, but he wasn't cold grits either. He'd started off on the wrong foot, but this lady was going to know a lot more about this particular sales agent before he got into his "dual-exhaust chariot" and rode off into the sunset.

"I don't know why you want to see the farm," Courtney grumbled as she led the way toward a barn built around a courtyard. "None of the other salesmen ever did."

"Humor me. Having denied me the chance to make an indecent profit on the sale of your colt, you can tell yourself you're trying to raise my morale by giving me an intimate tour of all that's yours."

The green faded from Courtney's eyes, and they narrowed dangerously, but Seth met her brittle gaze with his most innocent smile. Her mood changed when they emerged from the barn, and a huge Great Dane bounded up to her.

"The small horse with very large teeth," Seth observed dryly.

"What?" Courtney inquired, as she averted her face to keep Hamlet from covering it with his long tongue. Standing on his hind legs, he was taller than Courtney.

"Just mumbling," Seth replied.

"This is Hamlet," Courtney told him as the dog dropped on all fours and turned his attention to the visitor, a low growl rumbling in his throat.

"Am I remaining here at the risk of my life?" Seth asked when the growl continued unabated. "Do you keep him as a pet or to devour—probably in one gulp judging from the size of his jaws—any salesman unwise enough to venture down your farm road?"

"I think you'd take at least three gulps," Courtney replied, an amused smile on her lips.

"Dutch comfort."

"He'll be fine unless he thinks you're going to hurt me."

"There's always the possibility he's complaining about his moniker. You do have a penchant for unusual names."

Courtney blushed. "He's really Hamlet II. I got the first Hamlet on my fifth birthday. When he died and Grandpa came home with this guy as a puppy. I just kept the same name."

"Why Hamlet?"

"Can't you guess?"

"Ah, yes. Hamlet was the Prince of Denmark. Ergo, Hamlet was a great Dane." Seth regarded Courtney with amusement. "Pretty good reasoning for a five-year-old."

She blushed. "We'd better get going. I have a lot to do today."

Hamlet seemed to second her invitation. He had stopped growling and decided to wag his tail. When he later thrust his wet nose into Seth's hand, Seth knew he had moved one step farther inside Courtney's line of defense.

Seth quickly discovered the pillared stone gate and tree-lined driveway were just a prelude to the rest of Idle Hour Farm. Except for a couple of show places built by oil-rich Arabs, he had never seen anything like it outside Europe. The stables were constructed around a series of spacious courtyards, all tree-covered and lined with cobblestones, and containing stalls big enough for two horses. The stables themselves were of brick and oak with slate roofs and covered walks on all four sides. It was the most lavish display of wasteful extravagance he had ever seen.

"Why did your grandfather sink so much money into this place?" Seth asked. "The barns alone must have cost a fortune."

"Grandpa always said nothing was too good for his horses."

"Maybe, but he's saddled you with a great white elephant. You'd have room for twice as many horses if you divided the stalls and paddocks up properly."

"Grandpa wanted his horses to have plenty of room," Courtney informed him irritably. "This farm was the love of his life. Turning it into the kind of place he'd always dreamed of became his passion."

"What happened?"

"His luck turned sour. He had a champion go lame before the Derby and then come up sterile in the breeding shed. Another dropped dead on the race track."

"What happened to the rest of his horses?"

"He wouldn't let go of the land, so he had to sell his horses. For twenty years he kept trying to breed a horse that would put everything to rights again, but salesmen like you kept after him, badgering him to sell his best stock, until there was nothing left. All he really wanted was one more champion before he died."

"He may have got it."

"But he'll never see it," Courtney said bitterly. "Do you ever think of anything other than horses?"

"What's wrong with that?"

"Nothing, if you're a horse, but you look very human to me. You've certainly got the shape for it." Seth hadn't meant to let that slip out, and he almost laughed at Courtney's reaction. She didn't appear to know whether to be pleased or to hit him. She compromised by pretending to ignore his remark. It was the first sign of uncertainty he had seen, and he took heart at once.

"I knew he would leave Idle Hour to me someday, so it seemed reasonable to learn as much as I could about running it."

"You could let your manager, or your husband, do that for you."

"I don't have a husband."

"You might not always be single." He couldn't understand why some guy hadn't snapped her up, red hair and temper not withstanding.

"Why not? Is having a husband and children all that important?"

"It is to most people."

"I'm not like most people. Gus is all the family I want. At least he can't walk out on me."

Courtney hurried ahead. Obviously she had said more than she intended, but Seth was more concerned about the look of sharp pain he had seen on her face before she quickened her steps. Somewhere, sometime, someone she loved very much had hurt her deeply, and she was still feeling the pain. Seth wondered if that was why she had been so abrupt with him. She didn't seem so hard and sharp-tongued anymore, just a lonely woman trying to keep him from seeing the ache in her heart.

"I have to get back to work. You've already thrown me a couple of hours behind." She was dismissing him; clearly she meant to say no more.

"Thanks for the tour," Seth said. "In spite of what I said, this is a beautiful place and I enjoyed seeing it. If you ever need anybody to help you figure out how to run it more efficiently—"

"You'll be happy to tell me how, right?" Courtney said, firing up again, her moment of weakness obviously past.

"As a matter of fact, I probably wouldn't have done as well as you. I sell horses. I don't raise them. I was going to recommend a friend. I won't bother you now, but if you ever want some advice—"

"I'll call you."

"Do you always finish people's sentences?"

"Only when they're predictable."

"I'll work on that. Right now I'm late for an appointment, so I'd better be going. Think about what I said. I'll be back."

"It's a waste of time."

"It's Indian summer. Besides, aren't all southerners allowed to waste a little time?"

"Maybe, but the first frost can come without warning."

"You've given me plenty of warning," Seth said, with a rueful chuckle. "Just about every time you opened your mouth."

"Now who's breaking the truce?" Courtney challenged.

"I am," Seth admitted, "but I'm also beating a hasty retreat. See you."

"I hope not," Courtney called after him, but her reluctant smile contradicted her words. "Hold up, there's something I forgot to ask."

Seth turned, surprised, and waited for Courtney to approach him.

"How did you learn so much about farms? The salesman who came to see Grandpa never knew anything about barns, pasture rotation, or stall size, and they didn't care to learn."

"Didn't I tell you? Until the bank sold the farm out from under him, my father made his living by breeding and racing horses."

Stunned, Courtney stared after Seth as he hurried off to his Jaguar. How was she to know his father had lost their farm? He had descended on her without warning or invitation, had never once told her that her assumptions about him were unfounded, had kept after her to sell Gus, and had as much as called her grandfather a crazy Irishman.

Oh well, he'd asked for it, sticking his nose in where it didn't belong and refusing to take no for an answer. Anybody who did that should expect to have his feelings hurt once in a while. She didn't want him to think she was cruel or thoughtless, but she didn't want him to think she couldn't take care of herself either. Mr. Seth Cameron was going to discover that Courtney Clonninger was one woman who could succeed in this business, and she was going to do it without his help.

The sound of a backfire caught Courtney's attention, and she looked up to see a devil red Austin tear up the road and make the left turn toward the house at a perfectly insane speed. Marcia Ribbesdale, Courtney thought happily to herself and immediately headed for the house at a run.

Emerging from a tunnel-like path between towering rows of hollies, she reached the driveway to find Marcia—a stunning blonde dressed in the latest fashion—leaning against the car, unmindful of the damage dirt or snags could do to her pastel silk print.

"My God, isn't that the same bloody pair of jeans you were wearing when I was here six months ago?" Marcia exclaimed, pretending to be horrified as she came forward to give Courtney an enthusiastic hug. "They must have grown to you by now."

"They aren't, and they haven't. Besides, not everyone can marry a filthy rich English lord who encourages his wife to fill her closets with designer originals."

"Now, darling, don't be jealous. It's so unworthy of you. If I had your figure, I'd never wear another diaphanous frock. Do you have any idea how loathsome it is to be forever billowing like a bloody parachute? I feel rather like Isadora Duncan, always trailing things. Now take me inside and give me something to drink. I don't know why I decided to come home in the middle of this bloody awful heat wave when I could be in Scotland instead.

"But I do know," she said, taking Courtney by the arm and heading her toward the house. "I grew lonesome for the sound of a decent southern accent. Bloody hell, I'd even take a Boston accent, anything to be spared cockney for just a few weeks, not to mention Scottish brogue. You'd think those people could speak English. After all, they're supposed to have invented the bloody language."

"They probably think we're the ones who can't speak it properly."

"They do, but you only have to listen to them to know they haven't a clue."

They paused in the wide hall that ran through the center of the house to allow their eyes to adjust before entering the library, Courtney's favorite room—dark, cool, and full of books and leather-covered furniture.

"Thank God for air-conditioning." Marcia sighed and flopped down on one of the sofas in a most unladylike fashion. "They never air-condition anything in England. According to them it never gets bloody hot."

"If you'd stop talking for one *bloody* minute, I could ask you what you want in your *bloody* drink."

"I do say it rather a lot, don't I?" Marcia said with a giggle. "It's Gerald. He can't put together two sentences without saying it at least three times."

"You weren't doing much better. Now, what would you like?"

"Milk."

"What?"

"I said milk."

"I know what you said. What I want to know is why?"

"Oh, I didn't tell you, did I?" Marcia said, suddenly looking rather pink and pleased with herself.

"You haven't told me anything, and you *bloody* well know it."

"Okay, okay. I won't say it again. As for the milk, well, the doctor says I ought to."

"Why? You don't have an ulcer, do you?"

"Silly, they don't use milk to treat ulcers anymore."

"I never had one, so I wouldn't know. Now, what is it you haven't told me?"

"I'm pregnant."

"But you were afraid you couldn't . . ."

"I know, but I can. I mean, I did."

Courtney plopped down on the sofa and gave Marcia a hug. "So that's why you came home during the hottest October on record."

Marcia nodded.

"Do your parents know? What did they say when you told them?"

"I couldn't wait until I got home. I called as soon as the doctor was sure. Mom was ecstatic. Can you believe it? Dad met me at the airport with tears in his eyes. I guess a heart does beat somewhere in that ironclad chest."

"That man is crazy about you, and you know it. He was just strict because you were his only child, and a girl to boot."

"Strict!" Marcia squeaked. "He was positively medieval. Given his choice of a locked tower or a chastity belt, he'd have demanded both and then asked for an armed guard. I almost didn't get to talk to Gerald long enough to find out whether I liked him or not. Fortunately Gerald had the brilliance to hint that Dad's prize two-year-old was about to buck his shins. By the time the trainer, the groom, two veterinarians, and the farrier had convinced him the colt was only sore, Gerald and I were practically engaged. Tell me," Marcia said, suddenly breaking off, "wasn't that Seth Cameron I passed coming in?"

"Probably," Courtney admitted. She didn't know why she should feel vaguely embarrassed, especially not with Marcia, but she knew she was blushing.

"What was he doing here? Don't tell me you've finally given up this ice-maiden routine and gotten interested in a real man?"

"I'm not an ice maiden," Courtney declared. "Running this farm doesn't leave me time for dating, but I wouldn't be chasing after Seth Cameron if I were a certified vamp. Besides, the only reason he was here was to talk me into selling Gus."

Marcia sat up. "You're selling your colt?"

"Of course not, but I can't get your Mr. Cameron to believe that. That's the second time he's been here, and I'm sure he'll be back again. I've never seen anyone so persistent."

"Or so big," Marcia said. "Doesn't he give you a tingly feeling all the way down to your toes?"

"Why should he?" She hadn't felt exactly tingly, but she had no intention of telling Marcia what she had felt. She wasn't sure she wanted to admit it to herself.

"Come off it," Marcia said rudely. "You're a female. Unless you're dead, you can't be completely unaffected by that man's charm."

"Not completely," Courtney admitted with a guilty grin. "He's got a smile that melts my bones, and no matter what he says—and he says far too much—I can't stay mad at him."

"Nobody can. It's a treat to see all those cool English lassies flipping their stiff upper lips over him when he comes over for the fall sales."

"And I'll bet he doesn't mind one bit." She could see him now, smiling in a way that could reduce a woman to mindless surrender.

"I won't say he's never accepted an invitation, but Seth's no philanderer. He may do a lot of shopping, but he's looking to settle down." She paused, a frown puckering her brow. "It's all over between him and Cynthia, but I can't see him falling for you. You've got a spectacular figure—I ought to know; I've been jealous of it since we were fourteen—but you're not his type."

"And what's wrong with me?"

"Nothing, love."

"And how do you know so much about Seth and what he likes?" Courtney demanded, her self-control dangerously tight. "You've only been in town a day or two."

"Three to be exact. I'm an incurable gossip, just like my mother, and I don't bury myself on a farm mucking out stalls. I was just trying to warn you. You can't expect a freckle-faced redhead in jeans to succeed in capturing his interest where any number of devastating blondes have failed."

"Well, you don't have to worry. I don't want to captivate him any more than he wants to be captivated. He thinks my attitude—correction, *all* my attitudes need changing."

"I've been telling you that for years."

"Especially about Kentucky and the horse business."

"I've told you that, too. Gerald's family goes back for centuries—it seems like thousands of centuries from the number of gloomy pictures he has hanging all over the place—but he's started breeding for the market. He had to, or give up horses altogether. We're not as rich as everyone likes to believe."

"I guess I could see it if you only did it in a small way and still tried to race as many of your horses as you could, but Mr. Cameron seems to be interested in nothing but selling."

"That's why he's the best. He's an expert judge of horses. He won't buy or sell anything for more than he thinks it's worth, and he's never broken his word to anyone. The man is just twenty-nine. If I weren't already married to Gerald, I'd go after him myself."

"Not to mention carrying Gerald's baby."

"That, too," Marcia said with a self-satisfied smile. She bounded up from the sofa. "I've got to be going. I want to do a little crowing to a certain brunette who said some very unkind things when she heard I was marrying an

English lord who would naturally expect an heir. I also want to get home before Mother begins to imagine I've wrapped my car around one of your seventy-five-year-old oaks and starts calling every hospital emergency room within a radius of a hundred miles."

They walked outside together, and Courtney watched her friend roar down the driveway as though it were Daytona Beach. Maybe her mother had reason to have nightmares about hospital emergency rooms, but Courtney's thoughts didn't stay with Marcia's terrible driving very long. She found herself mulling over what Marcia had said about Seth and was unable to repress a tiny smile of satisfaction. She had attracted his interest. He had already come back once, and she knew he'd come back again.

Don't let him fool you, Courtney warned herself. He may want to flirt a little, but all he really wants is your horse.

THREE

Seth drove back to Lexington very slowly. He was hardly aware of the passing cars or the rolling countryside liberally splashed with the red-gold, brown, and yellow of fall. In spite of the extravagance of Idle Hour Farm, in spite of the fiscal insanity of not selling land or horses, he had decided—rather quixotically he had to admit—to do what he could to help Courtney Clonninger hold onto her farm.

He had never forgotten how he felt when his father told him they had to sell their farm and move into Lexington. They hadn't suffered financially—his father had made an even better living selling equine insurance—but his father had never gotten over a lingering feeling of defeat. For years Seth had hoped his father would buy back the farm. But he never did, and Seth had finally given up thinking about it.

Or had he?

Losing her farm would be difficult for Courtney, but losing her horse would be much worse. She had no family to turn to for support, and no job to give her a much-needed feeling of accomplishment. Apparently, she hadn't thought about anything but Gus for so long she couldn't think of herself as separate from him. Probably everything for her was tied up in his success, even her self-esteem.

His first impulse had been to shrug and say no one should value themselves according to their success, but he was honest enough to admit he judged himself by his successes. He didn't know Courtney's reasons—they probably stemmed from some deep, psychological scar—but she had cut herself off from the world for the sake of her goal. As much as Seth wanted to help her keep Gus, there was something in Courtney Clonninger even more worthy of preservation, and he couldn't stand by and see it destroyed.

Seth sank into his favorite chair in Clay's study. He was going to have to ask his friend where he'd bought it. He wanted one like it when he built his own house. "She showed me over the whole layout," he told Clay over another bourbon, a sour mash this time. "Whatever possessed the old man to buy such a showplace?"

"He bought the house. He *built* the rest."

Seth let out a long, low whistle.

"Exactly. It was nearly forty years ago, but I remember my father saying it must have taken nearly everything he had. He had to buy three farms to get the land. He demolished the existing buildings, pulled up fences, tore out roads, and started over. He even dug that lake—it used to be a stallion paddock—diverted a creek to fill it, and had the trees lining the main road brought in from the Appalachian Mountains. Dad said for a while people couldn't talk of anything else. After he sold his stallions, nobody had much reason to go there, and folks gradually forgot about it."

"Are you sure Courtney can last until that colt races? I haven't given up trying to sell him, but she's so sure he's the reincarnation of Pegasus she won't even listen to me."

"I think she can."

"I don't want to know what you think. I want to know facts and figures, everything you can tell me about her financial situation."

"That kind of information is confidential. I couldn't give it to you if I had it, which I don't. Courtney doesn't deal with me alone."

"Look, my father had another line of business he could step into when we lost our farm, but Courtney doesn't seem to know anything except horses."

"She won't starve."

"Only if she sells up. Kentucky bluegrass doesn't exist anywhere else in the world. Once it's paved over, it's gone forever. You figure out how to stave off her creditors, and I'll come up with ways to increase her income. She can board hundreds of horses on that place, not the handful I saw. She doesn't even have enough to keep the fields nearest the house grazed down."

"We should all be so lucky."

"She can worry about building up her fields after she's got something to wear them down. Can you do that, without the whole world knowing about it, I mean? I have the feeling she'd buck hard if she thought she was being turned into a community project."

"You bet she would," Clay said with a hearty laugh. "I wouldn't give a plug nickel for your life if this ever leaks out."

"Thanks. Just make sure you keep a still tongue in your head. I'd rather get my kicks in the sales ring."

"Or in bed?"

"Precious little chance of that these days. My love life gets worse the more successful I become. I thought money was supposed to attract women, not drive them away."

"Not the kind of women you're interested in. They only fall for the real man."

"I didn't find her when I was poor, and I didn't find her when I was in between. I guess this *real* man doesn't have what it takes."

"Don't sell yourself short."

"Sell, hell! I can't even give myself away."

The blaring horn of an oncoming car brought Seth out of his abstraction. He ignored the angry glare of the driver, a man he'd known for years, and pulled his car back into his own lane. If he didn't soon get his mind off Courtney, he was going to get himself killed.

He was on his way to meet one of his clients at Idle Hour Farm, a man who was looking for a new place to board his mares, and he was going to have a fight on his hands to convince Courtney to accept him. It seemed all he had to do was recommend something, and she was ready to turn it down. It had taken only a five-minute telephone call to convince Sid Phelps that Idle Hour was tailor-made to his needs. It had taken nearly thirty minutes of carefully wielded salesmanship to talk Courtney into just meeting Sid.

Seth had talked over the idea with Courtney's farm manager before he mentioned it to her. He hadn't liked talking to Ted behind her back, but he had been certain Courtney wouldn't listen to anything he proposed. She seemed convinced every salesman was out to destroy the thoroughbred industry in general and her in particular.

"I'd like to bring a client over to see your farm," Seth had said when he finally broached the idea with Courtney.

"He's not happy with his boarding arrangements, and he's looking for a new place."

"Why did you think of me?" she had demanded, suspicion sounding in her voice. If she took it into her head he'd engineered this visit, she'd probably refuse pointblank to meet Phelps.

"I didn't right off, but yours was the only place with enough land to handle his horses. It's not just anybody who can take on a hundred horses at a moment's notice." It wasn't exactly the truth, but it was close enough.

"I'd have to hire more men."

"With the money you'll get from Phelps, you can hire as many men as you want."

Ted had told Seth that the chance to hire back the men she had laid off would probably be the only reason Courtney would agree to any plan of Seth's. But finding additional boarders was only a bandage. Idle Hour Farm had been depleted of its stock—that was still a puzzle no one had explained to his satisfaction—and that meant plowing millions of dollars back into the farm, not just going along with a comfortable surplus each year.

The only way he could see to come up with the investment capital was to sell the colt or have him turn out to be the kind of champion she expected. But while the rational side of Courtney's mind might tell her she had to sell, the emotional part of her shouted it down. Not even Ted had been able to bring her around. Why did Seth think he could?

Seth knew his interest in Courtney had moved from the professional to the personal, but that didn't simplify the situation. In fact, if his instincts were correct—and they usually were—it would complicate things rather badly.

Coming back so soon wasn't a particularly intelligent

thing to do. Courtney had made it clear she didn't want to see him. In fact, there didn't appear to be anything about him she did like. He laughed. There must be a bit of the medieval knight errant in every pragmatist, or at least a romantic desire to root for the underdog.

But why had he chosen Courtney? There were lots of other lost causes, most of which offered him a challenge without the threat of personal abuse. He had already admitted he liked her—that was the only way he had gotten to sleep last night—but he hadn't been able to figure out why.

He couldn't dismiss her looks, but even though her figure was right up there with the best and he had a particular fondness for her turned-up nose, she'd never be considered a great beauty. He appreciated her stubbornness, but that wasn't a particularly endearing quality. Neither was her tendency to liken him to something that crawled out from under a rock. He admired her willingness to do her own work, but that wasn't it either.

Seth wandered too near the center of the road twice more before he concluded it was Courtney's indomitable spirit that made her special, her refusal to accept what everyone else said was the only way, her refusal to give up her dream or lose faith in her colt. To a man who had built his business and reputation by cold-blooded evaluation of his product, a shrewd knowledge of his customers, and a no-nonsense perception of his business, this should have been anathema. But packaged inside this tempestuous redhead, Seth found it exciting.

"It's just a juvenile desire to live dangerously," he mumbled to himself as he turned into the farm road.

He nearly swallowed his tongue when he saw Sid Phelps's Mercedes parked in the pull-off by the farm office. He heaved a sigh of relief when he realized the portly man wasn't accompanied by a lava-spewing red-head. He needed a few minutes alone with Courtney to calm her down. She had sounded pretty annoyed over the phone.

Getting out of his car quickly and offering his hand to Phelps, Seth said, "I wasn't expecting you until later."

"My wife's attending some kind of reception. If I don't show up before it's over, she'll have my head."

"I guess there's really no need for you to see more than a few barns and maybe a pasture or two," Seth said. If he could send him on his way before Courtney appeared, things might go a little easier.

"Do you approve of what you see?" The unexpected voice startled them both. Seth took one look at Courtney's expression, and his hopes plummeted. All her defenses were up. Even her clothes were calculated to raise hackles—and temperatures.

She wore a red halter top with her boots and jeans. Seth hadn't thought of her as particularly busty, but he found it difficult to ignore that red top. It was like a challenge.

"This is a beautiful place," Sid remarked. "I've never seen anything like it."

"There isn't anything like it," Courtney replied, a little too sharply for politeness. "My grandfather wanted only the best for his horses."

"So do I, and this is it."

"Is that all you have to say?" Courtney asked, surprised out of her icy disdain. "What about the costs, the quality of my help, the reputation of my vet?"

Seth groaned. She wasn't going to make this easy.

"Seth wouldn't have recommended you if everything wasn't top flight. Now, as I've already explained to Seth,

I'm on my way to meet my wife. I'll notify Hilltop Farm I want my horses sent over first thing in the morning."

"I'll take care of that," Seth offered. He accompanied Phelps to his car, all the time half expecting Courtney to say something that would throw the whole deal into the ditch. He offered a prayer of thanks to the god who kept her silent until Sid's car started down the road.

"Is that the kind of ignorant fool you have for clients?" Courtney demanded when he turned back to her.

"That statement is an insult to your intelligence," Seth said sharply.

"That man wouldn't know a horse from a jackass."

"Don't parrot your grandfather's words."

"I'm parroting them because you've made me so angry I can't think for myself," she snapped. "Men like him have no business in horse racing. They would be just as happy owning greyhounds, or camels."

"What right do you have to deny Sid the pleasure of his money just because you know more about horses than he does? Does he deny you the use of his tractors, which by the way is what he makes, because he knows more about them than you do?"

"Grandpa was against people like him coming into racing," Courtney said, recovering quickly. "He said they would buy a horse by its pedigree and not even look to see if it had four legs."

It's a pity the old man hadn't cared as much about people as he had about horses, Seth thought. If he had, maybe his granddaughter wouldn't be more comfortable with horses than humans.

"That may be true of some owners, but it's not true of Sid," Seth snapped. He was tired of hearing her grandfather's prejudices on Courtney's lips. "Besides, think of the money he'll bring in every month."

"I don't need his money."

Seth lost his patience. "Let's find Ted," he said, taking Courtney by the arm. "I want to hear you tell him that."

"Take your hands off me," Courtney ordered, attempting to wrench her arm from Seth's grasp. "I can walk by myself."

Just then Ted rounded the corner with Hamlet at his heels. "Has Mr. Phelps arrived yet?" Ted asked.

"Yes," Seth said before Courtney could open her mouth, "but Courtney has decided he's an ignorant fool, and she's going to refuse to take his horses."

"What?" Ted exclaimed, turning so sharply he almost stumbled over Hamlet.

"I said I *wanted* to turn him down," she defended, giving Seth a ferocious glare. "I didn't say I would."

"Thank God for that," Ted said. "For a moment I thought you'd lost your mind."

"It goes against everything Grandpa believed," Courtney said. "He'd rise up and haunt me if he knew I was boarding for a man who bought his horses at auction and who chose our farm because he likes the look of our barns."

"You act like you're afraid to do anything your grandfather wouldn't approve of, even when you know it's the thing to do." Seth's rising level of frustration was causing him to be a little rough on Courtney, but it didn't cause him to miss the look of pain at the back of her eyes. "Sid chose Idle Hour Farm because he has faith in my judgment. When you get to be as successful as he is, you don't have time to do everything yourself."

"I wouldn't care if Phelps chose the farm because of our holly bushes," Ted said. "I can put up with any amount of ignorance as long as he pays his bills on time."

"If you want the farm to be prosperous, you've got to start making more money," Seth said in a softer voice.

"I don't want to do it by violating everything Grandpa believed in."

Courtney knew Seth couldn't have any idea how important her grandfather had been to her. Even now, three years after his death, she found it hard to accept that he wouldn't suddenly round a corner, his flame red hair tousled, shouting orders at the top of his lungs.

But what made her absolutely furious, what had set her teeth so on edge she could hardly remain civil, was that Sid Phelps had turned her down six months ago when she had approached him about boarding his horses at Idle Hour. He had said he knew things were in pretty bad shape, that he didn't think she could hold the farm together.

Well, things hadn't changed a bit, but here he was, not only ready but eager to hand over his horses on nothing but Seth Cameron's say-so. She would have sicced Hamlet on Seth if she hadn't been positive the dog would have been more likely to lick him to death. Only Gus shared her distrust of the universally loved Mr. Cameron.

Ted started to slip away to his office. "Don't go," Seth said. "I want you to tell Courtney whether or not I'm making sense."

"She knows you're right." Ted turned to Courtney. "I went along with your grandfather because he paid me to run the farm, not give him advice, but he always knew I disagreed with him."

"Do you want to hold onto Gus?" Seth asked.

"You know I do," Courtney answered impatiently.

"Then, you're going to have to forget a lot of what your grandfather taught you and approach this problem with a little realism. You may have to sell a small part of your land."

"I'm not selling one foot," Courtney said, angry at having to explain things she considered none of his business. "Grandpa didn't want to leave this place to me. He didn't think I could handle it by myself, so he ruined himself trying to bring the farm back before he died. But I'm going to set Idle Hour on its feet, and I'm going to do it by myself."

Both men stared at her, startled by the vehemence of her speech.

Seth recovered first. "Then, you're going to have to consider selling at least part of Gus."

"When will you understand?" Courtney asked, brittle anger in her voice. "I'd sell every square foot of this place before I'd sell the smallest piece of Gus."

Seth felt like a fool. Why hadn't he seen it before? It was right before his eyes. The petting, the games, the hours spent together, the understanding between them. It wasn't just the farm and her grandfather. It was Gus, too.

"I've got land, barns, and help," Courtney said. "Even I can tell the obvious thing to do is go after boarders."

"You also have your own training track. Why not break yearlings, too?" It made Seth feel a little better to recommend something she might like. Maybe it would make her look a little happier.

"Why not?" Ted asked, a note of excitement in his voice. "You're really good with young horses. John and I can take care of the brood mares and foals."

"I don't know anybody who wants me to break their yearlings."

She didn't sound unwilling, and Seth started to hope he had found a weak spot in her resistance. "As soon as people find out what you've done with Gus, they'll start lining up," Seth said.

"I won't have you asking for me," Courtney said, adamant again.

"I won't have to. They'll ask me. That's what I do, remember: give advice for a fee."

"I thought you only sold horses."

"Once I've sold a horse, the client needs somewhere to board it, someone to break it, someone to train it. Who better to ask for advice than the man he has already worked with and trusts?"

"How convenient for you."

"For my clients, too. It would be easier if I could stick to selling, but you have to give the buyer what he wants, or he'll find someone who will."

"That's why I'm determined to always be my own boss."

"I, however, not being my own boss, must go see that Mr. Phelps's horses are ready to move as soon as possible."

"We can't possibly be ready by tomorrow," Courtney protested.

"I know. How about a week?"

"Perfect," Ted said. "We'll be ready."

"Good. And dust out those yearling barns. I know some people who've been looking for just the right place. I'm about to give them the happy news I've found it."

"Seth, don't you dare . . ."

But he was gone, with Hamlet trotting alongside. Courtney was left to watch Ted stare after Seth's retreating form in admiration. It filled her with helpless fury. It wouldn't matter if Idle Hour was saved if Seth did it. *She* had to do it.

"I think that man could sell coal heaters to the Arabs," Ted said.

"I'm sure he could. He's railroaded me into doing one thing after another I didn't want to do. I don't know what made him come here in the first place, but things haven't been the same since. And nothing I say makes him believe I don't want his help."

"Mr. Phelps's horses will mean we can rehire most of the men we've let go," Ted said. "It also means we'll be able to pay the taxes on time."

"I'm still tempted to tell Phelps I won't take his horses." It was a last, futile attempt to strike out against the necessity of doing something she didn't want to do. Courtney knew she didn't mean it.

"Make up your mind," Ted said. He was more abrupt than Courtney could remember him ever being before. "I've got people to hire."

"Go make your calls. Mr. Phelps can bring his horses as soon as you and Seth get everything arranged."

"It won't be so bad," Ted said. "It'll be good to have the place busy again. And with the extra money, maybe you can look around for a good horse or two."

"Gus is going to make all the money I need."

"If he's that good, you'll need mares to breed with him. You can never start looking for good brood mares too soon. You think about it. You'll see." Ted turned back toward the office, and Courtney wandered over to her bench under the tree. She picked up a handful of acorns and idly arranged them in designs.

Now if she could only stop feeling guilty. It wasn't hard to remember what her grandfather was like when he was angry. He would stare her straight in the eye, his finger pointed dangerously close to the end of her nose and his voice raised to a thunder pitch, as he shouted out the lesson he wanted her to learn. He always finished by making her swear on her grandmother's grave to do exactly what he asked until the day she died. She had just ignored twenty years of such promises, and she owed it all to Seth Cameron.

Hamlet trotted up and flopped down next to the bench, but she ignored him. He was a traitor, just like she was. One by one, she dropped her acorns on his head. He snapped at the falling missiles. It served him right for running off with Seth. She gathered up another handful.

Why had Seth suddenly turned up on her farm anyway? Somebody must have told him about Gus. People talked, but she knew there weren't many who would believe Gus was destined to become a champion after just one look.

He hadn't tried to convince her to sell the colt today, so why had he come back? Had he given up, or was this just a clever maneuver to get her off balance, then spring it on her again?

Was he really interested in her? He certainly didn't act like it. She was sure it was Gus, that he'd disappear the minute the colt was sold. That was okay. She could handle that, but she wasn't sure she could handle his being interested in her.

She started pitching the acorns to a squirrel, which disdainfully refused her offering for acorns of his own choosing. Even rodents were turning their noses up at her these days.

Courtney had to admit there had been more excitement in her life these last few days than at any time during the past several years. Now all of a sudden things were going too fast for her to keep up.

No one except her grandfather had ever been able to talk her into doing anything she didn't want to do, and yet she had let that mountain of determination scoot a hundred horses right past her. Why had she let him get away with it?

She knew why.

She didn't mind if Seth didn't like her—she wasn't completely sure she liked him—but it had become terribly important to her that he not think she was stupid.

She picked up a dried twig and began to break it between her fingers.

But she must like him a little. She could hate sales agents all she wanted, but she would be disappointed if Seth didn't come back with Phelps's horses. In fact, she had taken it for granted he'd deliver them himself.

In some ways he reminded her of her grandfather. Of course, they didn't look the least bit alike. Her grandfather had been short, thin, and wiry with an unruly shock of red hair. Seth was huge. She doubted his shoulders could fit through half the doorways in Lexington. His sandy blond hair was always a carefully controlled riot of curls, and he had some barely perceptible freckles. Her grandfather had favored jeans like she did, but she'd never seen Seth without a coat and tie. He never seemed to perspire or be uncomfortable. The man was coolness personified, totally, totally assured. That's why he reminded her of her grandfather. Both were absolutely certain of what they were doing.

Courtney picked up another twig.

She wondered if she would ever develop that kind of confidence. She had it when she was on a horse, but when it came to sums of money that ran into the millions, she was glad to depend on Ted. Her grandfather hadn't, and she doubted Seth would either.

What would she do if Ted left? She was ashamed and shocked to admit her first thought had been of Seth. No woman could resist the temptation to rely on someone so powerful. There was something about his size that gave her a feeling of safety instead of bigness, of warm security rather than brute strength. She could fight her own battles, and she never backed down from confrontations, but she couldn't deny the appeal of a safe haven when all the scrapping was done. She had a very disturbing feeling that such a place for her was somehow connected with Seth.

She angrily dashed the broken pieces of twig into the fallen leaves.

Damn! She *was* interested in him.

Courtney headed toward the house even though she hadn't done the chores that were her part of her daily schedule. She knew if she didn't do her work now, it would make things more difficult later, but her thoughts were occupied by a very large man who had pushed his way into her life and who threatened to dominate it entirely before he was done.

FOUR

Courtney hummed as she changed the bedding in Gus's stall. Ted had surprised her by asking her to give the yearling barn a good cleaning. With so many men on the place, she guessed he was trying to get her out of his hair, but she didn't mind. She liked to keep busy, and it made her feel closer to Gus.

The future of Idle Hour was riding on his back.

She spent long hours every day training him to accept the bridle and saddle and to tolerate every part of his body being handled. She'd had a time teaching him to stand still while she picked up his back feet. He wanted to see what she was doing, and in trying to turn around so he could watch, he always moved. But now he was so accustomed to everything she did that even though his eyes still followed her with keen interest, he stood still.

But she hadn't ridden him yet.

She would sit on his back in the stall for a few minutes every morning, but she had decided to wait for cooler weather before she took him outside under tack. She had walked him through the starting gate until he paid no attention to it. She knew many races were lost because horses were afraid of the gate or didn't know how to relax and were left behind when the bell rang.

Gus was developing rapidly, but she didn't want to race

him before the middle of next summer. She held firmly to her grandfather's belief that a horse shouldn't run until his body was physically mature enough to stand the strain of training. But in spite of what Seth Cameron might think, she had enough business sense to know the farm couldn't wait two more years. Gus had to start winning races soon. The Triple Crown was her objective, but he needed all the racing experience he could get before then.

Courtney started on the last stall. She had to get back up to the brood mare barns to see how Ted and the men were getting along. They had been working double shifts for three days to be ready for the Phelps horses. Today was Monday. The boarders were scheduled to arrive on Wednesday. Courtney wondered if Idle Hour would be ready.

It seemed that every time she turned around she was confronted by Seth or something he had done. She had hardly known the man for a week, and already no part of her life remained untouched. He had made her question just about everything she did, but never once had she questioned her determination to hold onto Gus or the farm. They were the tools of her trade. No one would ask a plumber, electrician, or mechanic to sell his tools. She couldn't do her work without horses and land. The sooner a very big man with twinkling gray eyes understood that, the better they would get along.

She tossed the pitchfork into the wheelbarrow, closed the stall door, and headed for the compost pile between the barns.

And she did want them to get along. It had been too long since anyone had wanted to look after her. Her grandfather had done it, but she was the only child of his only child. Seth had no reason to help her, but he had. And he'd overcome her opposition to do it. Obviously he wasn't as bad as she thought, certainly not as bad as the salesmen she remembered. Just thinking about some of the things she had said to him made her cringe. It was a wonder he was even speaking to her.

Courtney had no sooner emptied the wheelbarrow, and leaned it and the pitchfork against the wall, than she heard the unmistakable groan of a loaded horse van. They weren't ready for the mares! Half the stalls hadn't been cleaned or spread with fresh straw. There were no buckets, halters, hay, or oats, and the feed still hadn't arrived. She raced outside. To her utter astonishment, instead of continuing on toward the brood mare barns, the van pulled to a halt in front of the yearling barn. Seth, his Jaguar already parked between two large trees, came toward her as two men got out of the van and started to let down the ramp.

"You told me the horses wouldn't get here until Wednesday," she said, the tone of her voice accusing him of willful treachery.

"These are yearlings. Are the barns ready?"

"Y-yearlings?" she stammered, utterly confused. "I thought Mr. Phelps already had someone to break his yearlings."

"He does. These horses belong to several of my other clients."

"Do you mean you're about to unload twelve horses on me unannounced!"

"Twenty-four. A second van will be here by the time we get this one unloaded. I thought you had bigger barns."

"No, you didn't," raged Courtney. "You brought those horses here to give me a nervous breakdown. I can't possibly break that many yearlings by myself."

"I never thought you could," Seth replied as he directed the men to lead the first of the yearlings into the barn. "You'll have to hire some riders to help you. Four ought to be enough."

"So you think you've got it all worked out, do you?" demanded Courtney, just as aware as Seth of what needed to be done.

"I don't see any problem."

"Then, I'll give you one. There's a pitchfork and wheelbarrow around the corner. You can take them and start working on the other barn."

"Only if you'll help. I try to be a gentleman, but the facade breaks down when it comes to having healthy young women watch while I do their work."

"I never expected you to do any work at all," Courtney barked. She charged around the side of the barn and jerked the wheelbarrow and pitchfork from against the wall. "I'm just angry." She rolled the wheelbarrow to the second barn. Seth had already opened the door and removed his coat and tie.

"Do you want to haul in the straw or spread it out?"

"Neither until I get rid of some of the dust and cobwebs," Courtney answered as she opened the doors at the far end to let the breeze blow through.

"Find me a broom and I'll help."

"You may want to tie something over your face," Courtney said as she handed him a broom. She had a bandanna conveniently around her neck, but Seth whipped out his handkerchief, as large an example of its kind as Seth was of the human male, and tied it over his nose and mouth. Courtney thought it made him look ridiculous, like a little boy pretending to be a bandit, but she decided against telling him.

For the next several minutes the air was so full of dust

it was impossible to talk. Courtney was thankful the strong breeze would soon clear the air. There were at least a dozen things she wanted to say to Mr. Cameron.

She was angry he would drop a load of yearlings on her out of the clear blue. She would have sent them back, but she figured Ted had asked her to clean the barn because he'd known they were coming. She'd have to talk to him about that. He was doing what he thought was best, but she couldn't have him collaborating with Seth behind her back. That was treason, and people used to be hanged for that. Of course, Seth's repeated invasion of her life could be seen as a prolonged siege, and they tortured people for that!

She didn't want to torture him exactly, but she might be able to stomach his help a little better if she could find a few minutes of breathing space. Every time she thought she had recovered from his last assault, there he was again with something else to throw her off balance. The man was obsessed, but Courtney couldn't decide whether he was obsessed with her, the farm, the colt, or his own benevolence.

"Why are you helping me?" she asked once the dust had settled and they could begin spreading straw in the stalls.

"Because you'll never get the barn ready by the time the next van arrives. I don't like turning yearlings out into a strange pasture until they've had time to settle down."

"I don't mean the barn," Courtney answered, her irritation showing in her short, clipped syllables. "Why are you so determined to help? Is it so I can keep the farm?"

"I'm not sure I know what the real reason is yet."

"Oh." Courtney tried, but she couldn't keep the disappointment from her voice. The next thought that occurred to her kept her silent for several minutes, even though Seth started talking again.

"I've asked myself the same question, especially after the times when your welcome has been less than enthusiastic, and all I've been able to come up with is that I admire your indomitable spirit. I don't want the farm to be lost, I don't want Gus to be sold abroad, and I don't want to see another horseman—excuse me, *horsewoman*—forced to find a new way to make a living. Most of all, I suppose I hate to see you lose your struggle after you've held on so long.

"Besides, now that you're boarding horses for my clients, I have a perfectly legitimate reason for wanting you to stay in business."

Seth stopped for a moment, puzzled by the silence from the next stall. Courtney rarely appreciated what he had to say, even when he was complimenting her, but she never listened to his explanations in silence. He found that more troubling than anger. "You still there?"

"Yes," she muttered in an oddly detached voice, and he could hear her start to spread the straw again. "I was just thinking."

"About what I said?"

"Yes," Courtney said absently. "You may be the most irritating and insensitive human I've ever met; but you're not stupid or intentionally unkind, and I do think about the things you say, even though you don't believe I have the intelligence to run this farm by myself."

"I've never said a word against your intelligence," Seth protested. Then, forever willing to put his head on the chopping block, he added, "It was just your business sense I questioned."

"After just saying you admired my resolution, I find that an odd statement even for you."

But Courtney's tone carried none of its usual sting, and Seth walked to the door of the stall where she was working. "You sure you're not coming down with something? You're not acting right."

"I'm fine," Courtney declared, pushing through the door past him. "If you don't get a move on, we won't have the rest of these stalls ready when the van arrives." She deftly cut a bale in half with her pitchfork, lifted it without visible effort, and tossed it into the next stall, where she spread it out with a few practiced strokes.

"From the way you handle that pitchfork, I would hazard a guess no one has dared take liberties with your person."

"Until I met you, no one dared take liberties with me in any manner."

"Does that mean you'll let me take liberties with your person? You're quite a temptation, you know."

"Make one move, and I'll pin you to the wall," Courtney threatened, but she didn't raise her eyes for fear Seth would see the questioning expression in them. She plunged her pitchfork into the bale of straw and moved the wheelbarrow to the next stall, but in the split second after she released the handle bars and before she could reach for the pitchfork, she found herself swept up into Seth's arms.

She had no idea such a big man could move so fast. She had underestimated him.

"I'm glad you warned me," he said, his face lowered until it was close to hers. "Pitchfork holes would ruin my shirt."

"Let me go," Courtney said, but her voice was unsteady, and her eyes betrayed her nervousness.

"Do you really want me to let you go?"

Courtney had a feeling he wasn't asking a question. "Someone might see us."

"I don't care."

"But I do."

"No, you don't. I've never met anybody who cared less what other people thought, but you are afraid of what Courtney Clonninger will think of you."

"Don't be absurd," Courtney said, desperately wanting to say something that would put him in his place. His nearness was making it hard for her to think. She had never been held by arms like these. She realized she'd let very few men hold her, but none of them had been Seth's size. His mammoth dimensions made her feel positively petite and feminine, something Courtney realized she had never felt before. It was a feeling she liked very much.

"For days I've been wondering how it would feel to hold you, if you were as cold and unyielding as you pretend."

"And your verdict?" Dammit, why did his opinion mean so much to her? She had a sickening feeling in the pit of her stomach, as though she were about to fall off the edge of the world.

"It's better than I had imagined," Seth replied. "You're warm and pliable. It feels very right to have you in my arms. Now I have an undeniable urge to kiss you."

"I don't imagine many people are able to deny anything to someone as big as you." Courtney knew right away that had been an unbelievably stupid thing to say. She might as well have given him permission to do anything he wanted.

"You have, for much too long," Seth said.

Then he kissed her.

Courtney hadn't thought about being kissed by Seth

until just minutes earlier, but nothing could have prepared her for the feeling that swept through her from top to bottom and back again. She had been kissed before, but never like this. Her muscles deserted her completely, forcing her to melt into Seth's arms, even though her brain was telling her she didn't want to.

The lips that covered her mouth were firm and insistent. There was no avoiding their assault, no denying their intent. Courtney felt Seth's hands below her shoulders and in the small of her back, pressing her close to his body, lifting her off the ground and into his kiss.

Courtney knew she ought to struggle, to angrily remove herself from the prison of Seth's arms, but an equally compelling desire to return his embrace held her there. Seth, the treacherous man, continued to hold her suspended while his lips traveled from her mouth to her nose to her eyes. No one had ever kissed her so thoroughly, so possessively. The shock of feeling her body pressed tightly against Seth's hard muscles detonated every nerve ending in her body, and suddenly Courtney felt something inside her let go.

Somehow, she really didn't know how, she found her arms around Seth's neck, and she was returning his kiss with an abandon that only moments ago she would have flatly declared was impossible.

"I wondered where you two . . ." It was Ted's voice, and he was inside the barn.

Courtney and Seth fell apart, but their gazes remained on each other, Courtney's eyes wide open and staring.

"Excuse me." Ted was already backing toward the door before the words left his lips.

"Is the van here yet?" Seth asked as he picked up his pitchfork.

"It's coming down the road now. That's why I . . ."

"It won't take us more than a couple of minutes to finish up. Why don't you show them where to unload."

"Sure," Ted said and disappeared. Courtney didn't look up as she took up her pitchfork and began to spread straw.

"I didn't mean for anyone to see us," Seth said.

"Don't say a word," Courtney managed to say, certain she would break into tears any minute. "Haven't you done enough already?"

"No. I wanted to go on kissing you."

"No doubt having an audience wouldn't have bothered you at all." She knew she was reacting unfairly, but she couldn't help it.

"Yes, it would, but it wouldn't have stopped me."

Courtney couldn't tell him she was ashamed of herself. Knowing she had responded eagerly to his kiss made her so angry she wanted to stab something. And she wanted to stab it hard.

"I don't know what got into me, but I don't allow just any man to kiss me." It was a difficult admission, and the sound of her voice made Seth look at her curiously. She was standing there with this stunned look on her face, spreading and respreading the same straw.

"I never thought you did. Until you put your arms around me, I kept expecting to feel that pitchfork between my ribs."

Courtney tried to take comfort from knowing he hadn't expected her to give in, but the mere fact that she *had* given in robbed her of any solace.

"I just don't want you to think that because I continue to let you railroad me into doing things for the farm, you can railroad me as well. In fact, now's a good time to tell you to stop. I appreciate what you've done for me, but it's enough."

"Courtney, it's me, Seth Cameron, you're talking to, the man who just kissed you, the man you just kissed back."

She froze. "I know."

"Then stop. You sound like you're talking to a state delegation intent on banning pari-mutuel wagering."

"You're just as dangerous." Courtney quickly changed stalls and started tossing straw furiously in all directions.

Seth paused in his work. "Take it easy, Courtney. Just because you kissed me back and it scared you half to death is no reason to talk like a fool. It was a perfectly normal thing to do. We're adults. I can't imagine either of us talking the other into something we don't want to do."

Courtney jabbed at the straw. "I've let you sweet-talk me into one thing after another since you set foot on this place. There's no telling what you've still got up your sleeve."

"Come on, that's not fair to either of us."

"Maybe," Courtney said as her pitchfork slowed down and her gaze became more unfocused, "but I don't trust myself anymore. I never had this trouble before you came into my life."

Seth stabbed his pitchfork into the ground. "What do you mean by this *came into my life* bit?" he asked.

"I don't know," Courtney answered. "All I know is I want to get away from you."

"No, you don't. You're just afraid of yourself." Seth spread the last of his straw with a swift sweep of his foot and marched over to where Courtney was working. "You're afraid of losing absolute control. Look at me," he commanded when Courtney kept working and refused to raise her gaze from the stall floor. "Look at me and deny what I've said."

Her pitchfork stopped. "I can't, but neither will I be bulldozed into something I don't want."

"You mean something you're afraid of."

"That, too. I don't want to get involved with anyone. I don't have time."

"Do you mean because of Gus?"

"Because of Gus, you, the farm, me, everything." Forcing her features into a blank expression, Courtney looked up at him. "I don't want to, I haven't got time, and I'm not ready."

"Which one, or is it all of the above?"

"Does it really matter?"

"Yes."

"Why?"

"Because you're lying to yourself." Seth took her by the arms. "I want to know what I have to fight. I won't let you go without a struggle."

"You don't have that right. You've got to let me go if I want you to."

"No, I don't. It's not just you, Courtney. It's my feelings, too."

"You can't force me into a relationship I don't want."

"No, but I won't let you keep running away from yourself."

"What makes you think refusing you is running away from myself?"

"Your kiss," Seth said persuasively. One arm encircled her waist and drew her close. "No woman kisses like that if she doesn't mean something by it. Trust me."

Courtney felt powerless to drive him away. Her mind might be saying she wanted him to leave her alone, but her body knew it was a lie. "I don't trust you, or myself. Now let me go. I've still got one stall to go."

"Not until you admit you're trying to run away from yourself."

"I won't have you putting words into my mouth."

"Not for me, Courtney. For yourself."

How could she continue to hold him off if she admitted she desperately wanted him to kiss her again?

Just then Ted reappeared at the barn door with Hamlet, who came bounding toward them. Now she wouldn't be forced to answer any of Seth's questions. In less than two seconds she would be protecting him from Hamlet's lethal jaws.

But things didn't go as she expected. True, Hamlet came bounding toward her with his gigantic stride. True, Seth kept a hold on her guaranteed to convince the dog she was being attacked. But when the enormous beast bounded up to them, it was not to tear Seth's throat out, but to lick them both with his enormous tongue. Instead of a murderous growl, the treacherous animal wagged his tail so vigorously it almost threw his rear end off stride.

Seth released his hold on Courtney and took the big dog's face in his hands, roughhousing in a way Courtney never did. Hamlet loved it. With a delighted growl he jumped up and clamped his enormous jaws about Seth's arm. The two of them began to wrestle, Hamlet standing almost as tall as Seth. Moments later, much to Courtney's chagrin, both of them were down on the floor of the barn, Hamlet uttering the most spine-chilling growls of his whole life, Seth laughing with a deep chuckle that brought a smile to her lips, even though she wanted to brain them both.

"Looks like he's made a friend," Ted said, just as surprised as Courtney. "I've never seen him take to anyone so quickly."

"That dog is a snake in my bosom," Courtney said.

"Aren't you mixing your metaphors?" Ted asked, unable to hide an appreciative grin.

Courtney stalked out of the barn.

* * *

For two weeks Courtney avoided Seth. Once, nearly caught in the yearling barn, she hid in the loft until he left. She knew it was pure cowardice; but she also knew what Seth could do to her self-control, and she wasn't taking any chances. Judging by the way she'd felt when he'd kissed her, she was certain he could talk her into virtually anything he wanted, and her panic turned into a cold, abiding fear.

Courtney had never had anyone to love except her parents and her grandfather, and all three had been taken away from her. After her grandfather's death, she had made a solemn vow to devote all her energies to the farm, but now she realized she'd really been saying she wasn't going to let anyone get close to her again. Love didn't last long, and it hurt too much when it stopped.

But that one embrace had shown her how vulnerable she was, how close she had come to letting down the barriers and allowing herself to care again. It terrified her. She didn't want to lose control of her life or her feelings ever again.

The next time she saw Seth, she was in the paddock behind the barn with the four riders she had hired to help her break the yearlings. She had given them strict orders not to leave her alone even if it meant keeping the yearlings out all night. She wanted to stay safely occupied so she would have an excuse not to look at him, not to stop and talk with him. The one time Ted asked what was wrong between her and Seth, she cut him so short he never mentioned it again.

But she couldn't ignore a telephone call from Marcia. "If you don't come out of hiding, I swear I'll come over and break your bloody door down myself."

"But there's nothing for Seth and me to talk about," she had protested.

"Hogwash! You're acting as nervous as a cat in a dog pound, and Seth is looking like the IRS has found his secret bank account."

"Don't be ridiculous."

"I may be fanciful," Marcia had replied hotly, "but you're the one who's being bloody ridiculous, hiding behind that wall of horses, pretending Seth Cameron's being interested in you hasn't bloody well scared you to death."

"You're just imagining th—"

"Good God! When I think of the women in this world who would gladly endure a face lift, a fanny tuck, breast enlargement, even lipo suction to have a man like Seth Cameron follow them around, I could choke you."

Courtney couldn't help but smile. "I'm not that desperate yet."

"More's the pity. If you weren't so bloody well built, maybe you'd be more thankful for a little male attention."

"If you think Seth Cameron has any concept of what it means to stop at a little attention, you don't know the man."

"All the more reason to stop acting like a bloody nun and reward the man for his persistence. I'm giving you exactly one week to climb down out of your tree, Courtney Clonninger. If you don't, I shall drag Seth over to Idle Hour and personally ram him down your throat."

But before Marcia could make good on her threat, her husband became impatient for her return. When she didn't respond to his transatlantic pleas to come home immediately, he flew over and collected her in person.

Marcia's departure meant there would be no one to

force Courtney to confront her fears, and her mood turned still more gloomy. Even the fact that Gus's training was going better than expected failed to lift her spirits. She had more than enough work to keep her mind off Seth, but she still found herself feeling low.

During the daytime, she could keep the bedeviling thoughts at bay, but during the long, lonely hours of night, Courtney came to admit she was shutting herself off from one of the most important parts of life. In the dark she could almost forget her parents had abandoned her and just think of Seth. She tried not to, but she couldn't help herself.

She imagined the wonderful days they could spend in each other's company, the hours working with the horses, the evenings spent enjoying the coolness of the outdoors, the nights she could spend in his arms. She imagined all of this, then cried herself to sleep because she knew she would never have it. For no matter how strong her desire was, her fear of being abandoned again went even deeper.

Seth paced impatiently up and down in front of a barn at Eden Farms. He'd come to evaluate a yearling, but the owner was late and had left instructions to her groom not to show the horse until she arrived. The yearling in the stall regarded Seth out of sleepy eyes. The groom eyed Seth with increasing nervousness.

"How much longer is your boss going to be?" Seth demanded irritably. "I can't spend all morning waiting."

"I don't know, sir. She just told me to tell you she'd be a little late."

"You might as well bring the horse out. At least I can look him over while I wait."

But Seth's mind wasn't on Mrs. Alice P. Ball or her horse. It was on Courtney and her refusal to see him. His feelings hadn't grown to the point where it was impossible to walk away, but he wasn't ready to give up yet.

Seth knew Courtney needed time to come to grips with her own demons before their relationship could develop beyond the point of uneasy friendship. He had declined Marcia's offer to help him storm the house. He knew enough of Courtney to know that such an assault could cause her to lock him out of her life forever. He had gained a foothold, but it was precarious at best.

The colt he was looking at was a flashy golden chestnut with a blaze and four white stockings. He had a excellent pedigree and splendid conformation, but there was something about his movement that bothered Seth.

"Trot him," Seth ordered the groom before sinking back into his abstraction.

Seth asked himself again and again why he was knocking himself out over Courtney, why he accepted repeated rejection from her when there were plenty of other women ready to give him their full attention. Maybe that was it, the challenge of the inaccessible.

That thought forced him to pass his intentions under some rather searching scrutiny. It wouldn't be right for him to pursue Courtney for the satisfaction of capturing her affections. She was fighting her feelings for him with everything she had. He didn't like it, but she had the right to repulse him if she wished.

Yet, if she conquered her fears and fell in love with him, it would mean real commitment on her part. She couldn't just like him a lot any more than she could blithely engage in an affair that would last a few months before they both stepped away from it without pain. Seth owed it to Courtney to be certain of his own intentions before he set about demolishing her resistance.

Rousing himself, Seth studied the colt very carefully.

There *was* something about the animal that made him uncomfortable. Acting purely on intuition, he said, "Put a saddle on him and take him down to the paddock. I want to see him gallop."

"Mrs. Ball said I was not to take him out without her being here."

"Saddle up now, or I'm leaving," Seth snapped irritably.

Funny, he had never worried about his intentions with any woman he'd dated before, and it wasn't because he was insensitive or took advantage of them. Somehow his other relationships had developed naturally and slowly from acquaintance to friendship. On the whole, he was disappointed that nothing more permanent had developed, but he was glad he could say he'd broken no hearts, made no promises.

That wasn't how it would be with Courtney. Intuitively he knew to pursue her now would be the same as a declaration of love, a promise of a lasting relationship, a vow to remain faithful to her. Seth didn't think he could give her that.

Seth followed behind the yearling as it walked down to the field, his eyes never leaving its actions, his thoughts never leaving Courtney.

Still, he couldn't let her go. She had a hold on him like no other woman. At times it felt almost as if he was two people. One of him was in touch with his feelings and knew they were too underdeveloped to support the kind of relationship Courtney would require. The other was a separate person, existing outside his body, from where he could see both himself and Courtney. He knew they were going to fall in love and that it was only a matter of time before they would realize it. At the same time a tiny voice buzzed about his head like a gnat, frantically whispering warnings Seth couldn't understand. He waved the annoying voice away.

Seth needed only one look at the colt in full gallop. Without interrupting his thoughts, he motioned for the groom to bring the horse in.

Unfortunately, the person outside himself couldn't convince the person inside. Neither could dismiss the annoying little voice, and Seth continued to be bedeviled by uncertainty. He felt as though he were standing with one foot in each of two separate personalities and they were trying to pull him apart.

Seth held the gate open for the groom. As soon as he dismounted, Seth bent down and picked up the yearling's foreleg. He rubbed the hair backward all along the lower leg until he found what he was looking for—a small, thin scar. Now he knew why the groom had been given orders not to show the horse under saddle.

"Tell Mrs. Ball her horse might be worth a hundred thousand dollars, but not a million and a half. I would have sold him for her if she'd been honest with me about that left foreleg. I won't touch him now."

FIVE

Seth shivered and pulled his coat more securely around him. The cold penetrated his ears and made the inside of his head throb. He should have worn a hat if he wanted to watch Courtney exercise the yearlings. The biting edge of winter had come to the bluegrass at last, and the threat of snow hung in the air.

Courtney no longer went into hiding the minute she heard his car turn into the farm road, but she wouldn't allow herself to be alone with him. He had seen a haunted look in her eyes, and he made up his mind to do something to make her eyes shine bright and clear once more, even if it meant she'd argue with him again.

The riders were working the yearlings in sets of four, Courtney calling out instructions from the rail. Nearby a groom walked Gus, a heavy blanket draped over him.

"Is it cold enough for you?" Seth asked, hoping the ordinariness of the question would put her at ease.

Courtney jumped at the sound of his voice. "Too cold," she said, giving him a strained smile. She didn't back away, but Seth could feel the effort she was making to face him squarely. "I don't like to work horses in weather like this. It's too easy for them to become overheated and get sick."

"They're in excellent condition," Seth said, indicating

the set just finishing up. "You've done a good job with them."

"It wasn't difficult," Courtney said, beckoning to the groom who was walking Gus. "They were fit when I got them. All I had to do was get them used to the routine and tone up their muscles."

"Is that all you've done with Gus?" Seth watched the groom strip off the blanket. Gus had lost his baby fat and was beginning to take on the look of a greyhound. "He looks like he's way ahead of the others."

"He's a January foal and can stand a little training. See for yourself." She allowed the groom to give her a lift into the saddle, and the prancing colt moved out onto the track. Seth knew Gus wouldn't be put into serious training for another six months; but already his muscle development was apparent, and the spring in his prancing stride gave promise of abundant and easy power.

Courtney allowed Gus to break into a canter and then a slow gallop once around the half-mile track. They began a second circuit at the same speed; but Seth noticed that on the backstretch Courtney let out a notch on the reins, and Gus began to lengthen stride. It wasn't his speed as much as the ease with which he ran and the fluid motion of his stride that impressed Seth. No one could be certain just how good he was until he began to race, but Seth couldn't remember seeing a yearling that impressed him half as much.

But he was just as impressed with the rider. Some might think Courtney was too tall, but her skintight jeans made it easy to see she didn't carry an extra ounce of weight. There wasn't a more perfect figure in all of Kentucky.

"What do you think of him now?" Courtney asked as she slid from the colt's back and turned him over to the groom. The next set of yearlings was already stepping onto the track.

"You have him in excellent condition."

"I know that. What do you think of him?" Her flush of excitement was the first purely pleasurable response Seth had seen in weeks, and he experienced a pang of jealousy that he wasn't the cause of it. For God's sake, don't start being jealous of a horse, he told himself, but he knew there was nothing ordinary about Gus's importance to Courtney.

"He's the finest looking thoroughbred I've ever seen at this stage. He shows every sign of being an outstanding horse."

"Is that all you can say?"

"I can't tell you he'll be the champion you're hoping for, but I can say I haven't seen anything half as good in his crop. By the way, don't forget to increase his insurance policy."

"He's not insured." She said it like it was the most ordinary statement in the world, but to Seth it was nothing short of blasphemy.

"You're joking. You just said that because my father sold insurance." That had to be the reason. No sane person would leave a horse like Gus uninsured.

"No, he's uninsured."

"You've got to be crazy," he nearly shouted at her. "What if something were to happen to him?"

"I can't afford to insure him for his real value, so what's the point of insuring him for a hundred thousand? The money wouldn't be enough to help the farm. Anyway, Grandpa never insured his horses."

Seth repressed a strong desire to shake Courtney until her teeth rattled. He knew she couldn't insure Gus for what she thought he was worth—no insurance company on earth would be willing to write such a policy—but that was no excuse for leaving herself completely unprotected. After hearing his father talk about insurance for as long as he could remember, it was impossible for Seth to think of horses without thinking of insurance at the same time.

"You're going to have to insure him, or no trainer will touch him. Have you picked one out yet?" Seth asked. The mutinous look on Courtney's face had warned him it was time to change the subject.

"No. I broke him myself because I didn't trust anybody else, and now I'm beginning to feel the same way about trainers. I know I can't train him, and I don't intend to try," she said before Seth could voice the objections hovering on his lips, "but I can't turn him over to just anybody."

"You'll never find anybody who'll give him the kind of care you have. The best you can hope for is a trainer who'll do what's best for him."

"That goes without saying," Courtney replied, "but I'm worried that none of the top trainers will accept him. What if I can't pay his training fees until after he wins a race?"

"I thought the farm was doing better."

"It is, but there are taxes and nomination fees and monthly payments on all Grandpa's loans. Gus must have the very best."

"I'll give it some thought and see what I can come up with," Seth said.

"It's my problem, not yours," Courtney said. Even though some the old sharpness was in her voice, Seth was surprised to see the haunted look return.

"Okay, hands off," he agreed, unwilling to do anything that would deepen that look. This was the longest Courtney had talked to him since that day in the yearling barn, and he didn't want to jeopardize his progress. "I do have a favor to ask of you, however," he said. Courtney looked at him suspiciously. "The Keeneland bloodstock sale is coming up soon, and I want you go to it with me."

"Why?"

"I want to buy some mares, and I don't know anybody who knows any more about brood mares and their bloodlines than you do."

"Now you're trying to flatter me."

"No, I'm not. When it comes to predicting the racing success of anything on four feet, I'm as good a judge as you can find, but I can't do the same thing with brood mares."

"I don't believe you," Courtney said, "but I'll go anyway."

"What time shall I pick you up?"

"I'll meet you there."

Seth was prepared to argue, but something about the brittle glitter in Courtney's eyes warned him not to. "Meet me for breakfast?"

"I'll have coffee and a sausage biscuit on the way."

Seth accepted his defeat gracefully and headed back to his car, wondering what he could do next to speed up the thaw in their relationship.

Courtney felt invigorated as she walked down the aisles between the stalls of the horses that were to be sold later that morning. Even on a freezing November morning, the medley of smells was warm and familiar, and Courtney found herself smiling with pleasure. She took a sip of her coffee and popped the last bite of her sausage biscuit into her mouth. She had never realized the extent of her self-imposed exile until this morning.

It had taken Seth Cameron to draw her out of her

cocoon. Seth, who couldn't understand that not everyone in the world considered insurance as vital as their life's blood; Seth, whom she couldn't get out of her mind even when he was out of her sight; Seth, who caused her heart to ache as painfully as it had when her grandfather died. He was back in her life again, and she knew she wanted him to stay.

It had been a last-minute decision to arrive at the sales arena an hour before she was to meet Seth, but she was glad she had. She felt more like her old self than she had in weeks. Maybe it was the excitement of being around people and horses, but she felt more confident than she had since before her grandfather died.

Courtney took a last sip of coffee, tossed the cup into a trash can, and began thumbing through one of the five catalogs it took to list the horses offered for sale. Someone was always having a tax year, or reducing their holdings, or merely culling their stock, and it was usually possible to make some good buys if you knew your bloodstock and were very lucky.

She wasn't completely sure Seth meant what he said about her ability to judge brood mares, but she took pride in her knowledge, even though it wasn't as extensive as her grandfather's had been. His library was one of the best private collections of breeding records in the state, probably the whole country, and she devoted several hours each night to studying the contents of those thick volumes.

She wouldn't buy anything for herself this year because she didn't have the money, but Gus would start winning races next year. She would need every bit of her knowledge to buy the best possible brood mares for him.

She didn't need Seth to tell her she had to buy new stock if she wanted to rebuild her farm. She had figured that out even before her grandfather died; she had known it as she watched him sell off his horses year after year; she had worried about it every time she looked at an empty barn; she had planned for it every night as she studied her books.

But now, almost three years later, she was no closer to her goal than she had been the day her grandfather died. Though she devoted every moment of her day to the farm, doing the work of a hired hand in the morning, pouring over loan repayment schedules and payrolls with Ted during the afternoon, and studying pedigrees at night until her eyes grew red and irritated, she was making little progress toward being able to restock the farm. Could she save Idle Hour by herself, even if Gus did become a champion?

Courtney pulled herself up short. There would be plenty of time during the months ahead to worry about that. Right now she had to study her catalogs. Evaluating brood mares was apparently one of the few things Seth Cameron thought she could do without his help, and she was determined he would have no reason to doubt her abilities.

Thirty minutes later she was approaching the sales arena.

"I wondered where you'd be," Seth said when Courtney materialized out of the crowd milling around him. "I saw your car in the parking lot."

The Keeneland sale of brood mares was the major sale of its kind and attracted buyers from all over the world. Even though seats could only be had by reservation, the parking lots filled up early.

"I got here early so I could look at some of the mares. If I didn't think Ted would quit on the spot, I'd be tempted to bid on one or two myself."

"I don't want you as competition. I want you to direct all your talents toward finding a few hidden nuggets for me."

They were forced to delay the rest of their conversation while they made their way into the sales arena. A sharp wind added urgency to their steps. Once inside the pavilion, it was some time before they were done greeting old friends and being introduced to new ones, but Seth could see that Courtney was bursting with eagerness.

"I've found two mares you should buy. I particularly like one of them."

"Okay, convince me."

Seth listened carefully, but he was more struck by Courtney's attitude than what she was saying. Except when she was talking about Gus, he'd never seen her so excited, so relaxed. She was leaning over to point out something about the mare's pedigree, and her shoulder was thrust against his body as she held the catalog for him to see. She was completely unconscious of the contact, but it nearly blew his concentration. For a long time he'd been strongly attracted to her trim, well-formed body, and now she was touching him, transferring her warmth and excitement to him.

He could also smell her perfume, the first time he could remember Courtney wearing any scent. In the multitude of heavy odors that surrounded them, it was light, even faint, exactly what he would have expected from a woman who wasted no time on feminine arts. Still, he found it alluring. She leaned her head toward his, and he smelled her hair, almost imagined touching it. Under the artificial lights it was a dark coppery red, showing none of the carotene highlights that shone so brilliantly in sunlight.

"But the one I really like is this one by Nijinsky."

"But she didn't do anything as a racehorse, and neither did her first two foals," Seth pointed out as he struggled to bring his mind back to the problem of chasing brood mares.

"That's what everybody else will think, too, so you may be able to get her for less than half what she's worth."

"I saw her first two foals run. I think. I could beat them both."

"Everybody knows Nijinsky's offspring tend toward stamina, grass racing, and maturing late. Their fool trainer ran them early, short, and on dirt."

"What about the mare herself and the stallion she's in foal to?"

"The mare was hurt in training and never fully recovered. The stallion's first crop was foaled this year, and they look great. The foal she's carrying will be a yearling when they race. The price will triple by then."

"You like the stallion that much?"

"So much I bred my twin mares to him."

"I didn't know you had any mares."

"They're half sisters to Gus by Mr. Prospector."

"Two in-foal mares out of Spring Sunshine must be worth a fortune. How come you never even mentioned them?"

"Why should I? They're no more for sale than Gus himself. Now stop talking. I want to see what they're going to bid on this mare. I'll bet she goes for more than a million."

Seth could have told her the mare in question had a reserve of one and a half million dollars, but his mind was on Courtney's mares. He wondered how much more there was she hadn't told him.

But he wasn't at the sales to worry about Courtney. He had come to lay the foundation for the reestablishment of his own farm. This was a huge step, one he'd thought about but hadn't seriously considered doing just yet. He knew why he'd suddenly made up his mind. It was Courtney and her fanatical devotion to Gus and her farm. He ought to tell her, but he was reluctant to admit it. To be frank, he was actually embarrassed.

But having made the decision to start his own farm, he had to be certain he bought the very best mares he could afford. He wasn't sure whether he would race the foals or sell them at auction—in his business he couldn't afford to tie up large amounts of capital for long periods of time—but the mares he bought at this sale would form the basis of his own brood mare band. They had to be good.

The mare sold for one million, eight hundred thousand dollars. The next several animals were all excellent individuals, but the cheapest of the quartet sold for three-quarters of a million. Then the Nijinsky mare came into the ring. Her looks attracted the notice of several bidders, but when they consulted their catalogs, their interest died. They began to talk in hushed whispers, biding their time until a more interesting prospect entered the sales ring.

"What do you think?" Courtney asked, whispering so no one would catch the excitement in her voice.

"She looks great, but no one is interested. It's got to be the race record of her first two foals."

"I broke those colts," Courtney said fiercely. "I *know* what they could do. If you don't buy that mare, you'll miss the greatest bargain of your life."

Despite Courtney's recommendation, Seth couldn't force himself to bid on the mare. If he was in this much doubt, he preferred to save his money. The sound of Courtney's voice jerked him abruptly out of his abstraction. She had her hand in the air to make a bid of fifty-five thousand dollars.

"Why didn't you tell me you wanted her?" Seth asked in a tight under voice. "I wouldn't have bid against you."

"I'm bidding for you."

"You can't do that!" he said, his voice a strangled whisper. That was a gross understatement, but what did you say to someone who had just broken the cardinal rule of an auction by making a bid she had no intention of honoring?

"I had to. While you were trying to make up your mind, that Mr. Dowling was going to steal her right out from under your nose. See, he's bid fifty-six thousand. Bid sixty immediately, and he'll pull out. If you hesitate, he'll keep going, and she'll cost you an extra fifteen thousand."

Seth forced himself to make the bid and had the doubtful satisfaction of seeing Dowling withdraw. Oh well, he told himself fatalistically, if he had made a mistake, at least it was a cheap one. Even with her record, this was a ridiculously low price for a mare of her breeding. With luck he could keep the foal and sell her next year for a better price.

"You've made the best buy of the day," Courtney said, obviously delighted with herself. "Now we can sit back and wait for the Damascus mare, but you're going to have to pay a lot more if you want her."

He didn't buy her. He would have had to pay too much.

"I'd better go around and inspect my purchase," he said when the session came to an end. "Want to come with me?"

"I can't. I have a thousand things to do at the farm."

"Will you meet me again tomorrow?"

"Okay, but I doubt I'll turn up anything this fabulous again."

"You really like that mare, don't you?"

"If I thought she was right for Gus, I'd beg, borrow, or steal the money to buy her. You just wait until you find yourself with a champion. You'll have me to thank." With that she hurried away and was soon lost in the crowd, leaving Seth bemused and wondering how he, the best known salesman in Kentucky, could have allowed himself to be buffaloed into buying a mare he didn't want.

"Well, that's it," Seth said, rising to his feet and stretching his stiff body. "In three days we've watched more than five hundred brood mares go through that ring."

"And you've bought three for extremely good prices."

Seth had bought two more mares on the third day, both on Courtney's advice.

"You don't have to hint so strongly that it's all your doing. I know it, and I'm prepared to admit it by buying you the fanciest dinner in Lexington."

"Thank you, but I can't."

The haunted look was back. Surely he couldn't be the cause of it. Only something she cared about a great deal could cause such unhappiness. "Everybody has to eat."

"I'll put a Lean Cuisine in the microwave."

"You ought to have a balanced meal once in a while."

"I do. Lunch."

Seth was determined she wouldn't avoid him this time. He had suffered the tortures of the damned sitting next to her for three days and having to behave as decorously as a brother. It wasn't like he was inviting her to his apartment or some roadside café. Besides, there was new urgency in his need to be with her. For the last three days he had seen her in a new light. She had been animated, excited, open, cheerful, even sparkling. He was jealous that her work could make her come alive in a way he couldn't.

"You need to get out. You spend too much time working. It'll be good for you to relax for one evening."

"I've just spent three days away from the farm. It'll be spring before I catch up."

"In that case, you might as well enjoy yourself."

"I'm sorry, but I really can't."

"Not even for one night?"

"No."

"Don't you mean you won't because you're afraid?" Seth knew he was taking a risk, but he wasn't going to make it easy for Courtney to slip away.

"No, that's not what I mean."

Courtney looked annoyed, but Seth increased the pressure. "You're afraid to be alone with me."

"I've been alone with you for three days," Courtney replied hotly.

"Hardly, with nearly three thousand chaperons. You wouldn't let me pick you up or take you home. We won't be alone in the restaurant either. If you're afraid to get in the car with me, you can meet me there."

"I'm not afraid to be alone with you," Courtney insisted, but she wouldn't meet his gaze.

"Yes, you are. You're afraid I'll kiss you again, and if I kiss you again, you're afraid you'll lose control and kiss me back."

"I am not," Courtney replied angrily. "I don't *want* you to kiss me."

"What you mean is you don't want to take a chance that you might like being kissed. You've decided there isn't any room in your life for anything but Gus and work. You don't have time to be human, to be a woman, to give yourself a chance to discover there's more to life than horses."

"The most important thing in my life is the farm."

"Why?"

"Because it is," Courtney sputtered.

"Why?"

"I've just told you why."

"If you had told me the most important thing in your life would be your children or your husband because you didn't feel complete without them, or your career because you needed to feel you were contributing to society, I could believe you. But you told me nothing. That makes me believe you're hiding behind the farm because you're afraid of life, afraid its real passions and feelings might touch you. What are you waiting for, someone to come along and make the sky light up, bells ring, birds sing, flowers bloom?"

"Of course."

"How are you going to find him if you stay hidden?" He meant to continue his attack until she couldn't accept any more slights without fighting back.

"And I suppose you think you're the man to make the skies light up and bells ring?"

"You'll never know if you always duck behind a horse when I come around."

"Okay, Mr. Seth Cameron, I'll go to dinner with you, but I don't think your methods are very sportsmanlike."

"Being persuasive isn't such a terrible thing," Seth objected. "If it makes you any happier, you can call it a business meeting to pay my debt for your help in buying those mares. But the truth of the matter is I just like being with you. I miss talking to you." Forcing her to meet with him against her will wasn't the best way to help her get over her fears—it could even make them worse—but he couldn't help it. He had to see her.

Courtney's body was taut with excitement. She had spent the ride home angrily berating herself for giving in to Seth's arm twisting. He never seemed to think anything he did was unfair as long as he got what he wanted, and she was tired of being stampeded by him. She would show him there was more to Courtney Clonninger than a pair of jeans.

The minute she got home, she took the longest bubble bath within memory. Tonight she was determined there would be nothing of the stable about her. Seth Cameron was going to find she could be a totally feminine woman.

When she finally got out of the bathtub, warm and faintly scented, she covered her body liberally with moisturizing gel. She had washed her hair earlier, and now she brushed it until the dark copper glowed warm in the lamplight. The black highlights made it all the more striking. She brushed it back from her face, let it swirl about her head like a Russian fur cap. She penciled her brows a dark brown, then brushed her lashes the color of ebony. She added just a touch of color to her cheeks and put on a lipstick whose muted tone wouldn't clash with her naturally strong coloring.

It had taken her nearly an hour to decide what to wear. She finally chose a gold lame dress that fit her body almost as snugly as her jeans. She finished off with gold hoop earrings and two simple, thin, gold bracelets.

She stepped back and studied her appearance. She was pleased to find it combined a kind of expensive elegance with a barely understated sensuality. Not quite satisfied with her lipstick, she replaced it with a color that gave her lips a moist luster. The dress was strapless, but she looped a scarf of the same gold over one shoulder and attached it at the waist on the opposite side. She experimented until she found the angle that provocatively covered only one breast and shoulder. She couldn't resist the temptation to tease Seth just a little.

She completed her outfit with a pair of high-heeled gold shoes and then turned her attention to a wrap, finally settling on a blue fox that had been her grandmother's. It gave her just the touch of outrageousness she was looking for. Elegant and sensual she would be, but she wanted everyone to know she was playing a role.

Seth could hardly keep his eyes on the road. When he had asked Courtney to dinner, he had been trying to force her to stop hiding behind her farm and come out and have a little fun, even let herself get to like him.

He had been knocked speechless when she opened the door. As she stood there in all that formfitting gold with the light from behind throwing her spectacular figure into a stunning silhouette, he had felt the breath catch in his throat; the next moment his heart was pounding like he had run a mile.

He had always thought Courtney was attractive, but he'd never seen the bold, sensual, beautiful woman who stood before him. The fact that it was Courtney made it all the more staggering.

"My God, you're beautiful."

Courtney laughed a Marlene Dietrich laugh, a low sound deep in her throat that made her seem like a mature, sophisticated woman. It made him feel like a schoolboy.

"Thanks for the compliment, but it's probably the shock of seeing me in something besides jeans. Or didn't you think I owned a dress?"

"I never thought about it. I mean I didn't know. I just assumed . . ."

She laughed again, and Seth felt utterly foolish.

"I hope you're not taking me to McDonald's. Not after I went to the trouble to dress up."

"Not McDonald's," Seth had said, beginning to recover his presence of mind. "I have reservations at a real restaurant."

They rode in near silence, Seth discovering that all his conceptions about Courtney had suddenly gone off kilter. There was nothing casual about his attraction to this woman. It was strong and vital. It was suddenly much more than he wanted it to be.

What had he gotten himself into?

They talked of many things during dinner, but Courtney guessed Seth's thoughts were as far from the subjects of their spoken words as her own. Her plan had backfired. True, she had achieved the desired effect, but it had been on the other diners and the waiter, who was at their table every five minutes. The one time she got up to go to the ladies' room, every man in the restaurant stopped eating.

If Seth's face hadn't been a mask of imperfectly concealed physical hunger, she might have laughed at her predicament. As it was, one look at his taut features and she felt any minute she might become the main course. Finally, their table was cleared, coffee and liqueurs placed before them, and the waiter was mercifully forced to turn his attention to his neglected customers.

"Well, you got me back," Seth said, an uneasy smile on his lips. "But I have to admit if I had known you could look like this, I would have twisted your arm a lot sooner."

"I should apologize," Courtney said, making no false

pretense of ignorance about what she had done. "I thought it would be a good joke."

"And it wasn't?"

"No."

"Why not?"

"I thought it would be funny, something we could laugh about tomorrow."

"Courtney, you can't lie worth a damn. You meant to do exactly what you've done: bring me to my knees by proving what a stunning, desirable woman you are. Now that you've done it, you're unhappy about it. You're even a little scared."

"I admit I wanted to prove to you I was something other than a tomboy, but I did mean it as a joke."

"Only now you've discovered there's something more between us, something we can't shrug off and forget."

Courtney nodded. She didn't trust her voice.

"What are we going to do about it?"

"Nothing," Courtney replied, a trace of desperation in her voice. "What I mean is, I like you a lot more than I thought. I didn't mean most of what I said about your selling horses. I still don't like salesmen, but I can separate what you do from what you are." She stopped, looking frustrated. "Now you've gotten me confused, and I'm getting off the subject."

"Maybe you're trying to say you realize you like me, that I'm becoming more than a casual friend, and you don't want that to happen."

"That's close enough," Courtney admitted. "I don't want a serious relationship. I knew when you kissed me things were out of hand. That's why I avoided you for so long. I thought I had myself under control, but I was wrong. It took only five minutes for me to decide you were the most handsome man in the room. Then before

I could stop myself, I was wanting to know what you were like as a little boy, what your favorite desserts were, if you liked baseball. I don't want that. I don't have time for it."

"It caught me off balance, too," Seth confessed. "I've been attracted to you for some time, only this evening I discovered I liked you in a whole different way than I thought."

Courtney hoped he wouldn't tell her.

"I think I'm in love with you, and that scares me just as much as it scares you."

Courtney didn't think that was possible. She felt the panic rising in her throat. If she had driven her car, she would have left right then. She was flattered, but love was something she couldn't allow, not even the possibility. She almost had to grip her chair to keep from running away.

"You said you found yourself wanting to know what I was like as a kid," Seth said. "Well, I found myself wanting to have kids. And as much as I admire you and like you and find you terribly attractive, you're not at all what I thought I wanted in a wife."

Courtney hardly knew how to take that, but it piqued her vanity. "What's wrong with me?"

"Nothing," Seth said, reaching out to take her hand. "I suppose every man thinks he wants to marry someone like his mother. When he finds the woman he really wants, well, it's something of a shock."

"Am I that bad?" Courtney could have kicked herself. Not five minutes ago she was declaring she didn't want a serious relationship, yet now she was upset because he had said she wasn't exactly his type. Good Lord, she'd better make up her mind before she got herself into real trouble.

"You're one of the most amazing females I've ever met.

You're also one of the most stubborn and contrary, but I don't think it would be hard to learn to live with you."

"I don't have a lot of experience with this sort of thing,"— that's a joke, she thought to herself, you don't have *any* experience—"but that seems like a funny way for a man who thinks he's in love to talk."

"You've knocked the air out of me. I've had relationships, but I've never been in love. I had no idea it would be so completely different. Hell, it's not the same thing at all. This is going to take a little getting used to."

"You make it sound like a terminal condition." Courtney was definitely piqued now. How dared he say he loved her and then say the experience had practically turned him into a broken man.

They spoke very little in the car on the way home, but when they reached the steps, Courtney made it clear Seth wasn't going to be invited in for a nightcap, coffee, or anything else.

"I didn't think I would be," Seth said, still a little bemused by the revelations of the evening, "but I'm giving you fair warning. It may take me a little while to get my mind straightened out, but when I do, I'll be back." Courtney tried to slip through the door, but Seth was having none of that. "I'm not that confused," he growled as he swept her up in his arms.

Courtney's protest was smothered by his lips. She was overcome by the same weakness that had attacked her that morning in the barn. It was useless to tell her arms not to encircle his neck or to order her lips not to kiss him back. For the first time in years she felt free of all the ghosts that flitted through her nights. It would be so easy just to give in to this man and let him take care of her forever.

Seth's kiss had all the tenderness and intensity Courtney would have expected of a man in love. His arms cradled her in an easy embrace; his mouth took her lips gently, kissing them lightly, brushing them lightly, nibbling them lightly. It was as though she was the most valuable thing in the world.

Then with an involuntary upsurge of passionate energy, Seth crushed her mouth with his own; his tongue pushed its way between her lips, thrust past her teeth, and forced her mouth open to his assault. Her body was pressed against him, making Courtney stingingly aware of the power of his muscled limbs, even more aware of the throbbing energy of his body. His tongue explored her mouth, seeking, probing, demanding. She clung to Seth, afraid he would never let her go, half afraid he would.

Then almost as suddenly, it was over, and he was gone.

His kisses left her breathless, but once her brain started working again, she decided the idea of giving in to Seth wasn't so unacceptable as she had previously thought. True, she'd have to wait until things were settled with the farm, and she supposed she'd have to tell him about her father, but it might not be so bad if she let herself fall in love. She didn't think it would be very hard to do.

But something told her Seth wasn't one to wait on another person's convenience, especially where his own happiness was concerned. She'd started something tonight. No matter how superficial her reason for wearing that dress, she had a feeling the consequences of doing so were going to be momentous.

SIX

On a bitter January morning, Courtney watched the yearlings-turned-two-year-olds as they came around the far turn. They were still working in sets, but she was giving them enough hard work to toughen their muscles. They would soon be going off to trainers in Florida and California. Then she'd be able to turn her attention to Gus and the two mares who would be foaling during the early winter.

But right now her mind wasn't really on the two-year-olds, Gus, or the mares. It was on Seth.

He'd been by the farm half a dozen times since their dinner date. While they had enjoyed several long talks and he continued to show a keen interest in the farm and the progress of the yearlings, he'd treated her like an ordinary business partner. She told herself it was probably best that he'd mistaken his feelings toward her, but she found herself unaccountably irritated.

You're just like a child, she told herself. As soon as you can't have something, it's exactly what you want. If you don't have any more sense than to do the one thing you shouldn't, it's a good thing Seth has enough sense for both of you. You know it's impossible for the two of you to be more than friends. You disagree about everything.

What do you think would happen if you did fall in love and get married?

Within months, probably weeks, you'd be arguing across the breakfast table, the dinner table, at bedtime, and probably five or six times in between. He wouldn't be able to see why you sink time and money into land and horses that might never pay off at the race track, and you'd never understand why he sells horses with no more emotional involvement than selling cows.

She supposed there were people somewhere who felt as strongly about cows as she did about horses, but she couldn't imagine how.

"When are you shipping them out?"

The pounding of the horses' hooves had drowned out Seth's approach, and his unexpected presence made Courtney jittery. It had gotten so she couldn't be around him without her whole nervous system setting up an alarm.

"The first ones go out in two days. They should all be gone in two weeks."

"Will you miss them?"

"A few, especially the bay filly in this set and a blond chestnut out earlier. I think they have a chance to be something special."

She wondered if he would come around as often after the horses were gone. She was boarding over a hundred mares for his clients, but he didn't take much interest in a horse unless it was unraced and its potential still a matter of speculation. She wondered why he liked to gamble so. She preferred a sure thing.

"Any of them as good as Gus?"

"No, and that's no empty boast. I worked him with the sets twice last week, and both times I had to practically choke him to keep him from running away." Would he come to watch her work Gus even though he knew she wouldn't sell him?

"When does he leave?"

"Probably not for another three months. I want to keep him as long as possible." The thought raced through her mind that she wanted to keep Seth with her as long as possible, too, but she denied that.

"What are you going to call him?"

"I've registered him as Red Phoenix."

"Have you found a trainer yet?"

"No." The set had finished, and Seth and Courtney strolled toward the barn.

"What will you do to keep busy after they leave?"

"The mares will soon foal, and I intend to give their babies as much attention as I give Gus."

Three months earlier he would probably have asked her to spend the time with him. What had gone wrong? Didn't he want to be around her anymore? He was looking at her as though he could devour her on the spot. That wasn't what she wanted from him, but she didn't know what she did want. She'd asked herself, but she wouldn't let herself answer. If she ever dared put her thoughts into words, she wouldn't be able to go on telling herself she didn't want anything at all.

"I almost forgot about your mares. When are they due?"

"In about four weeks."

"Who are you going to breed them to next?"

"I don't know. I don't have the money to breed both of them to a top stallion, and I don't want to breed to the wrong horse."

She wasn't really interested in talking about the mares now. She wanted to know what he was going to be doing, what he was thinking, why he wasn't in love with her any-more.

"There're a multitude of mid-priced stallions to choose from. What are you looking for, speed or stamina?"

She was looking for a little interest in herself, but apparently she wasn't going to get it. She'd always told Seth he ought to take more interest in his horses. Now, it seemed, he had finally taken her advice. It was ironic and she wasn't happy about it.

"A little bit of both."

"How about Spectacular Bid or Affirmed? They're both quite reasonable now."

"I want to breed them both to Unbridled, but his fee has gone too high."

"What are you going to do?"

"I don't know. What do you plan to do until the summer sales?"

Seth smiled. "What I always do, sell horses, though I won't bother to suggest any to you. Nothing I say ever pleases you as well as what you've already decided."

Courtney started to protest, but stopped when she realized she never received a suggestion from him without immediately rejecting it or telling him why her choice was better. "I don't reject your opinions without a reason. I've usually already thought through my decisions very carefully before I say anything to anyone. Besides, sometimes there's no right or wrong decision, just more than one possible choice."

"I didn't come to give advice. I want to ask for some."

"What about?" Courtney asked eagerly.

"It's a surprise. You have to come for a drive with me."

Courtney didn't hesitate. She didn't stop to remember she hadn't been alone with him in a car since the night they had gone to dinner or that she never wanted them to be any more than friends. All she could think about now was that maybe Seth wasn't completely indifferent to her, that maybe he still liked her. She didn't want him to fall in love with her, but she was honest enough to admit she had been unhappy when she thought he was no longer interested in her.

Seth wasn't like any of the men she had turned her back on so easily. Even if he had realized he didn't love her, she couldn't face the idea of not seeing him again. They might even be more comfortable that way. There wouldn't be anything wrong with seeing him two or three times a week, just to talk. She wasn't too busy for that.

She looked over at him now, silently driving them to some unknown destination. Didn't the man know how to talk and drive at the same time? Why didn't he say something, anything that would give her an idea of what he was thinking? She wanted to know what he was feeling, but he had ignored every hint she had thrown his way. She couldn't come right out and ask him if his feelings had changed. Maybe that was her answer. Maybe he hadn't responded because he wasn't interested enough to bother.

That idea didn't do much to lift her spirits. She sank down into the deep bucket seats of his Jaguar, wondering again why a man his size would want to squeeze himself into such a small car and wishing the winter landscape didn't look so dismal.

"I probably shouldn't have made such a big secret of it," Seth said, breaking his silence. "You'll probably think I'm getting excited over nothing."

"Since you haven't told me anything, I don't know what you're talking about."

"Never mind. Just keep your eyes on the roadside until you see something you recognize."

Courtney did as he asked, but wondered what could be so important about the miles of fences they were passing. She was just about to tell him she didn't recognize any names when she saw a newly painted sign that read: *Hill & Dale Farm, Owner Seth Cameron.*

"You bought a farm!" she exclaimed. "You never told me you wanted one."

"We all have our secrets. I swore the day they took Dad's farm I'd buy it back. It's nothing like Idle Hour, but it's mine."

Courtney couldn't explain why suddenly the landscape seemed more friendly and her mood lightened. Seth's buying a farm didn't necessarily mean his feelings for her were still strong, but it might. It might also mean that his ideas about horses were changing.

"It's barely a hundred acres, but it's some of the best land in the county."

"Can I see it?"

"There's no way I'd let you back in this car until you've gone over every inch," Seth said. His face reflected a different kind of pleasure from anything Courtney had ever seen before, and abruptly she realized it was pride of ownership, a deeply ingrained pleasure in the ownership of land that only another landowner could understand. He might be the smoothest salesman in all of Kentucky, but it was obvious Seth Cameron had never outgrown his love of the land. Courtney was pleased. Somehow she felt she had won a small victory.

They went over the whole farm. Courtney would have sworn there wasn't a square foot they missed, and she was forced to agree it was a fine piece of property. The buildings were still in excellent shape, the fields in superb condition.

"Are you going to be able to run it yourself and keep selling?" she asked as they headed back to the car.

"I'll have to hire a manager, at least until it begins to pay for itself, but if I can get a few more mares like the ones you picked out for me, maybe that won't be too long."

"It'll be at least four years."

"Two. I plan to sell everything I raise as yearlings. That way I don't have to invest much more than the cost of the mare and the stallion's fee. That's the most cost effective way to raise horses."

"That's not raising horses," Courtney shot back, unable to keep silent. "You have to race the results if you're going to be a horseman. I thought you had finally begun to understand."

"And I hoped you had finally started to realize there was more than one way to look at the horse business," Seth replied. "You've got this notion that if people don't agree with you, they're wrong. Nobody is right all the time, not even you. You said yourself there weren't always right and wrong decisions, just different solutions. Well, consider this a different solution. Maybe it's not the one you could accept for yourself, but you have no right to reject it for me. You most certainly have no right to reject people just because they disagree with you."

Suddenly it seemed the most important thing in the world for him to know she hadn't rejected him. "It's not what I would do, and it's not what I want you to do; but I'm not rejecting you. Why do you think I came with you when I didn't even know what you were going to show me?"

"Then, why does it always sound like a rejection?"

"Maybe it's because if I accept your opinions, I'll begin to question my own. I don't think I could carry on if I weren't totally convinced I'm right." Suddenly Courtney felt very vulnerable, and she didn't like it. "Sometimes I don't want to have to give up everything for the farm. It's frightening to have that much responsibility, but I have no choice. No matter what it costs me, I have to."

She felt like she was going to cry, and she nearly cursed out loud. She hadn't cried since her grandfather died, and she wasn't going to cry in front of Seth Cameron, especially not over something like this. "I think you'd better take me home. I promised Ted I'd help with the feeding."

But she couldn't hide her glistening eyes from Seth, nor the faint tremor in her lips.

All Seth's anger was replaced by an almost overwhelming urge to blow Idle Hour Farm into outer space—Ted, Gus, and the pregnant mares along with it. "They can manage the feeding without you this once," Seth said as he stepped in close and took her clenched hands in his. "Your grandfather wouldn't want to see his farm become a success at the cost of your happiness."

"Yes, he would," Courtney stated vehemently, her swimming eyes quickly upturned to his. "As far back as I can remember, that's all he ever thought about. He planned for it, worked day and night for it. It's all he ever dreamed about."

"He did it out of choice. You don't have to do it if you don't want to."

"Yes, I do," Courtney insisted desperately. "You don't understand, but I do."

"Why should you have to commit your whole life to someone else's dream?"

"I can't tell you. I wish I could, but I can't." She hiccupped, but she resolutely held back the tears.

"You've got to tell someone. You can't keep carrying such a secret all tied up inside. Don't you trust me?"

"It's not that. I just can't tell you."

Courtney was in his arms, her warm body pressed tightly against his chest, but Seth could feel her withdraw from him, shrinking back behind the protective walls she had built for herself. He wished he could destroy them, but it was no more possible to free her from this prison than it was to lift the burden of the farm from her shoulders. Until she was willing to share it with him, she wouldn't give him her heart.

"You don't have to do it all by yourself, you know," he said and kissed her gently on the lips. "Whenever you want to tell me, I'll be here."

She held him more tightly.

Just the feel of her in his arms was enough to make him forget every piece of his strategy. She was warm and soft, and her body yielded suggestively to the contours of his own body until it awoke yearnings he found hard to control.

The taste of her lips was intoxicatingly warm and sweet. The touching innocence in her kisses held a freshness, a feeling that she was discovering something for the first time.

Seth didn't think he was going to be able to keep up this pretense of indifference much longer. For the first time she had shown her vulnerability, had admitted she didn't always want to limit her life to the farm, had admitted doing so would cost her something important. As soon as she admitted Idle Hour Farm and Red Phoenix weren't all she wanted in life, he had a chance.

All he had to do was pretend his interest in her had cooled. That hadn't seemed like much, but it had proved to be just about the hardest thing he had ever done. If he hadn't worked so hard over the years to develop a poker face so his competition couldn't tell what he was thinking, he'd never have been able to fool Courtney.

But Marcia had insisted. He would never have done it without her badgering him. He hadn't been able to disguise his surprise when he had answered the phone one afternoon and recognized her voice.

"I'm in the last months of a bloody long pregnancy," she had announced without preamble, "so you can't say anything to upset me. And you've got to do exactly what I tell you without a lot of questions."

"What do you want?" he had asked, totally lost.

"Do you love Courtney?"

"Courtney who?" he asked, nonplused.

"How many Courtneys do you know well enough to be asked such a question?"

"One."

"Then, I guess that's the one I'm talking about."

"First, tell me whose side you're on."

"Courtney's, and yours if you love her. If not, I'm taking a contract out on you tonight."

"Okay, I confess I'm falling in love with her, but I don't think she cares very much for me."

"You haven't been going about it the right way. You've been too bloody polite. And for God's sake, stop following her around like a hound dog. That girl's as stubborn as a twenty-year-old mule. If you don't get yourself a bloody big stick, you're going to find your carrot's all gone and she's right where she was when you started."

"I take it you mean I must change my tactics."

"Of course. Isn't that what I just said?"

"I suppose so," Seth agreed, smiling to himself. It certainly was hard to picture Marcia as Courtney's best friend. They were like ice and flame. You would have sworn one would destroy the other.

"You've got to find some way to make her think you're going off her. Not too quick, mind you. Maybe you can act like you're having second thoughts. And don't do something bloody stupid, because Courtney's sharp as a tack."

"And . . ."

"Call me when you come up with the idea. I'll tell you what to do after that."

During the subsequent weeks, Marcia had made several transatlantic calls to check on Seth's progress and give him his required dollop of encouragement. "Gerald can stand the cost," she'd said. "He owes it to me for dragging me back to this bloody pile of rocks."

The minute Seth saw their strategy was beginning to work, it took all Marcia's threats to keep him from throwing himself at Courtney's feet and declaring his undying love on bended knee.

"It would be the worst thing you could do," Marcia had said to him in exactly the same tone of voice he expected she would have used addressing an imbecile. "Courtney has made up her mind to be a martyr, and there's nothing you can do to talk her out of it. But if she finds living like a bloody nun isn't all it's cracked up to be, she might change her mind. On top of that, she's got some problem about her parents she's been stewing over for years."

"What is it?"

"I don't know. Courtney doesn't tell me about all her misfortunes, thank God, but whatever it is, you're going to have to get past it before she'll admit she's in love with you. Courtney's a stubborn woman. She can withstand almost any kind of frontal attack, but I don't think she'll like losing something she wants badly. Even if she could, she'll be more vulnerable, and maybe you can slip past her bloody defenses."

It had happened just as Marcia predicted, but Seth felt ashamed of using subterfuge. It hadn't taken him very long to know he loved Courtney. What did worry him was the chance he might never conquer her fixation about the farm. He couldn't live with that ghost. He could spend the rest of his life helping her achieve her goals, but there would have to be no barriers between them.

He also knew that even if she could be talked into marrying him now, and in her weakened condition that just might be possible, she would be marrying him with only half her mind and half her heart. That wasn't acceptable to him. As frightening as it sounded, if she couldn't give him all of herself, he would have to do without any.

But he wasn't willing to concede defeat yet. He knew how to plan and wait. He'd made his plans. Now it was time to wait.

Seth saw the light streaming through the windows of the brood mare barn and lengthened his stride. Ted had promised to call him when Courtney's mares were ready to foal. Thirty minutes earlier Ted had phoned to say one mare was down and Courtney was at the barn.

"There's almost enough to have a party," Seth announced as he walked up to the stall. Courtney was kneeling over the mare, her back to him; but she turned quickly, and a sudden smile lit up her face. Seth had to hold onto the side of the stall to keep from dashing in and sweeping her into his arms.

"I've heard of a salesman's nose for a horse," Courtney said, a welcoming twinkle in her eyes, "but I never knew they could smell out a foal before it was born."

Even with the strong smells of the barn, Seth could detect the subtle fragrance of Courtney's perfume. She had started wearing it all the time now.

Despite the cold, Courtney wore jeans and a formfitting sweater which made him think of the night in the restaurant and the gold dress that shimmered with her every breath. He had never stopped thinking of that dress. He dreamed of it. The very color had become a virtual alarm which could cause him to remember with burning accuracy every physical and emotional reaction he had experienced that night.

"How's she doing?" he asked.

"Fine." Courtney patted the mare's neck to soothe her anxiety. The action emphasized the curve of Courtney's body, the swell of her breast.

"You expecting the other mare to foal, too?" He had to say something to take his mind off Courtney.

"Not for another six or seven days. She's just here to keep Dixie company." Courtney stood up and stretched, and any doubt Seth had about his sensitivity to her physical presence was erased. He pulled his coat more closely about him.

"I'm tired," she said. "I hadn't counted on the foal coming so soon."

"Come sit down for a bit," Seth said, quickly stacking three bales of straw into a chair. "I imagine your man can handle things for a while."

"John's been foaling mares for more than forty years."

"Then, what's keeping you up?"

"Trying to find a stallion I can afford. I've been studying pedigrees into the small hours for weeks."

Seth had a mental image of her sitting before the fire in a robe open almost down to the waist, one tempting foot peeping out from under the edge of the robe. He could see the firelight dancing in her hair, and he had to physically stop himself from reaching out to touch the dark, coppery waves that clustered in a riotous mass about her head.

"Ted says I can't have a penny more than fifty thousand, and I can't find anything I want for that price."

Seth settled himself down next to Courtney, and she moved over to make room for him.

"The more I think about it, the more I'm certain Unbridled is the best possible choice, but his fee is seventy-five thousand." She turned eyes that were sapphire blue to look squarely into his. "What do you think I ought to do?"

Seth was floored. Courtney had never asked his advice or opinion on anything. He hoped it was a sign she was softening toward him. But that thought had barely registered before he was body slammed by her gaze. At that moment he would have mortgaged his soul to buy those two seasons to Unbridled if by doing so she would have continued to look at him like that for the rest of her life. "I told you once, but you didn't like my advice."

"I just didn't like the stallions you mentioned."

"There are dozens more. Take your pick." He was prepared to spend the whole night discussing each of the hundreds of stallions that stood in Kentucky. His arm rested on the bale at Courtney's back, and he could already feel the heat of her body, imagine the slight give of her flesh. The look in her eyes said she was aware of his closeness and was not afraid. Yet the message was so at variance with everything that had happened between them until now that he doubted he could trust her eyes. Her body was inclined slightly toward him, her slim shoulders held erect, causing her breasts to point directly at his chest. "Is there any one you particularly want to talk about?"

"I wondered what you would think of shipping the mares to England. I can get much better prices over there."

Seth's fingers found an errant curl, twisted it around his fingers. It felt alive in his hand. "The shipping and boarding costs would probably take everything you saved," he said, relinquishing the curl to allow his fingertips to caress the softness of her shoulder. It was all he could do to keep his fingers relaxed and his touch light. Every instinct, every nerve in his body, screamed *attack!*

"I was afraid of that." Her reply was dreamy. She was paying no more attention to the conversation than he was. The mare in the adjacent stall nickered insistently.

"The foal's coming, Miss Courtney," John called from where he was kneeling beside Dixie. "I can see the front feet."

It was almost like tearing off a part of his own body when Courtney removed her shoulder from under Seth's fingertips. He fought down an impulse to pull her back down next to him.

"Looks like it's going to be an easy foaling," John said as he grasped the front legs and slowly pulled the foal from the mare's body. "You'd think she had done it a dozen times before. He'll be out any minute now."

Seth lunged to his feet, walked over to the stall, and leaned over the top rail. Courtney and John were kneeling beside the mare, her head of flaming copper contrasting with his salt-and-pepper gray, the riotous freedom of the curls on her uncovered head at variance with the untidy ends escaping from under his tight-fitting cap. They were bent over the quivering newborn foal, rubbing its coat dry, making sure its nose, eyes, and ears were clear.

"It looks mighty fine," John said.

A bittersweet smile bent Seth's lips into a slight curve. It was a fine-looking colt indeed, but it was just one more thing to come between him and Courtney. He wondered if she would ever have time for him. His fingertips still burned from the feel of her. How long would it be before she allowed him to touch her again?

"He's beautiful, isn't he?" Courtney said, turning to Seth.

His doleful thoughts were banished by the brilliance of the smile she directed toward him. "He's almost as beautiful as Gus."

"That's high praise. Are you going to offer to sell him for me?"

"You plan to keep him, don't you?"

"Yes," she replied with the closest thing Seth had ever heard to real openness, a welcoming warmth.

Seth wondered what was so magical about this evening. It wasn't just the fact she was smiling or seemed pleased he was here. There was something different about her whole attitude. It was as though she had somehow managed to sidestep the wall that had always been between them and come to him as an ordinary woman comes to an ordinary man. For the first time he saw Courtney as she could be if she followed her heart. He would never ask her to give up the farm or sell Gus. All he asked was that she allow him to step within the circle of things she loved.

"Dolly's down!" There was alarm in John's tired voice. Courtney spun away into the adjacent stall. The mare was in distress. "It's turned wrong. There's just one foot showing."

No one had to tell Seth what that meant. If the foal

was turned the wrong way, its sharp hooves could tear up the inside of the mare before they could get it out. Or the pressure on the foal might be so great they would lose the foal before it was born. Worst of all, they could lose both the foal and the mare.

"I'll see if I can force it back in and turn it around," the old man said.

Seth entered the stall to share in the tense drama with Courtney and John, a participant in spirit if not in fact. He watched Courtney as she knelt by the mare's head, holding it down to keep the animal still, constantly patting her neck and talking to her to keep her quiet. He knew Courtney was scared, afraid she would lose the mare and foal.

"I got the leg back in, but I can't turn the foal," John panted. In spite of the cold, perspiration dripped from his face. He looked white with fatigue, exhausted.

"It's no use, Miss Courtney. That mare's pushing down so hard I can't move the foal."

"Let me try," Courtney offered, but John shook his head in defeat.

"Move over," Seth ordered, and suddenly he was kneeling next to the mare, his coat off, his sleeves rolled up to his shoulders. Carefully he reached inside the mare and gently pushed the leg that had reemerged back into the womb. The pressure was terrible. He felt as if his arm were being crushed. Then as the muscles of the uterus relaxed after a contraction, he took hold of the foal and turned it a little. Taking a breath he turned it a little more before another contraction clamped down on his arm and the foal and immobilized both.

Seth's face grew red with the exertion. He hadn't done anything like this in years, he realized as he struggled to position the foal so it would emerge from the womb with its head between the two front legs. At last, as the mare's muscles relaxed after still another contraction, Seth was able to move the foal into the natural foaling position. It slipped from its mother's womb with the next contraction.

"It's another colt," John said, "and he's even prettier than the first one." He started rubbing the newborn with a soft cloth.

Courtney's gaze was locked on Seth, a look compounded of surprise and pride in her eyes. "You said you didn't know anything about brood mares."

"Not how to pick them out," Seth panted, his breath coming in rapid gasps, "but I learned about foaling on the farm. I guess it's something you never forget." He washed his arms in a bucket of water and dried them with one of the many cloths John had draped over the stall slats.

"It ain't that simple," volunteered John. "You got a feel for things and a mighty strong arm to boot."

"I guess I owe this foal to you," Courtney said.

Seth rolled down his sleeves, picked up his coat, and put it on. "Consider it partial payment for the champion your Nijinsky mare is going to give me."

He searched Courtney's eyes closely, but she seemed to be drawing away from him. He remembered the moment of near intimacy on the bales of straw. Had he imagined the look of longing in her eyes? Had he seen it there only because he wanted to see it?

"It looks like I have two more champions," she said. "They'll be two years old when Gus is four. They won't have to race against him. I'm going to need even more mares when they retire."

"Come down to earth," Seth said with an exasperated edge to his voice. "Let the poor things nurse before you start pushing them down victory lane at Churchill Downs.''

There wasn't much reason for him to stick around. She was dreaming about her future with her horses, and there was no place for him in her dreams. There never had been.

"I know only one of them can win the Derby."

"Then, I'm surprised you haven't already entered the second one in the English Derby." Maybe she would follow the colt to Europe, and he would be released from the agony of having her so close but so utterly unattainable.

"I want them where I can keep an eye on them."

"Are everything you do and everybody you know going to take second place to these damned horses for the rest of your life?" Seth asked, frustration snapping the control he had on his temper.

The look in Courtney's eyes told him his outburst had shocked her. He'd probably agree with her tomorrow, but tonight he felt like taking her by the shoulders and shaking every thought of horses and Idle Hour Farm out of her head forever. He had almost reached the point where he didn't care about tomorrow if he could just have one night, even one hour, when he was the only thing on her mind. But that would never happen until she had rebuilt her farm to her satisfaction. He didn't know if he could stand to wait that long.

"It looks like I got here just in time for the hot chocolate," Ted called out as he entered the barn, his cheerfulness exploding into the tension of the moment.

"It'll be ready soon," Courtney said, stepping past the men with one last inquiring look at Seth. "You can come up in about five minutes."

"I'd better be going," Seth muttered.

"You can't," Courtney said. "If it hadn't been for you, we wouldn't have a reason to celebrate." She stepped out into the cold of the night.

"He turned Dolly's foal," John explained.

"Is the mare okay?" Ted asked.

"She's fine," John assured him. "He did a good job."

Courtney's in good company, Seth thought. None of them can think of anything but horses.

"Let's go to my office," Ted said to Seth. "You look like you need something stronger than hot chocolate." Seth would have gone home after he finished his whiskey, but Ted convinced him to go up to the house.

Within five minutes, Seth wished he hadn't relented. Ted and Courtney couldn't talk about anything except the two splendid colts. Ted was thinking in terms of paying off the debt. Courtney was thinking of buying mares.

"You ought to sell one of those colts," Seth announced abruptly. Courtney and Ted turned toward him in unison, the thread of their conversation snapped like a kite string. "You have two colts with the same breeding, so it only makes sense to keep the better one and sell the other."

"You know I can't sell anything that descends from Spring Sunshine," Courtney said, as if the reason for her decision was too obvious to need explanation.

"That's one way you could get the money to breed both mares. You'd still have Gus and one of the foals."

"No."

"I've got to be going," Seth said, rising to his feet. "I have an appointment early tomorrow. Some of us are more concerned with earning money than spending it." It wasn't a fair remark, and it certainly wasn't smart, but he was so irritated, so frustrated, so thwarted at every turn he hardly knew what he said anymore. "I'm sorry," he mumbled as he grabbed up his coat. "I'd better go."

"Seth."

The one word stopped him in his tracks. He didn't want to turn around, but he couldn't help it. Courtney was staring at him, a question in her eyes, but also a friendliness that made him want to drop his coat and sit back down.

"You saved that foal tonight, maybe the mare, too. Thanks."

Was there more behind that smile than mere gratitude? Was there finally a real interest in him as a man, not as someone who sold horses or brought her business?

Maybe, but he was too tired to try to figure it out just now. He nodded, returned an answering smile, and left.

SEVEN

All the warmth and brightness left the room with Seth. Courtney stared after him, unable to squelch the feeling of loss. Several times it had been on the tip of her tongue to tell him she liked him far more than she wanted, but she was afraid he might say he was no longer interested in her. She couldn't stand being rejected again, especially not after she admitted her need of him.

She realized that for nearly an hour she had thought of nothing but Seth. Not that she had any intention of forgetting Gus or the farm, but Seth had grown in importance until he was just as necessary to her happiness. The thought so shocked and stunned her she forgot to be angry at his abrupt departure.

"Did he really deliver Dolly's foal by himself?" Ted asked.

"Yes, and he did it like a veteran. John was exhausted. He'd already delivered Dixie's foal on top of being up the last two nights. It's time we got someone to help him."

"I'm not as young as I used to be either," Ted said, rising to his feet. "I think I'll be getting along to bed. You might consider Seth's suggestion," he added after a pause. "It could solve a lot of problems."

Courtney wanted to explain once again that she

needed to hang on only until Gus started winning, but she didn't bother. She had tried over and over, and neither Ted nor Seth could understand. "I'm not selling either of the colts."

"It's your farm," he said with a shrug. "But it could save our bacon if anything happened to Gus."

"Nothing will happen to Gus."

Courtney remained standing in the middle of the office for a long time after Ted left, staring at the huge picture of her father that hung over the fireplace. Their faces were so much alike he could have been her twin. The only difference was she had some of her mother's black hair in her russet tresses.

"I know where I can get the money if I have to," she said finally. "I swore I'd never see you, speak to you, or even write to you, but I'll break every vow I ever made to keep Gus." She stared a moment longer in silence, her eyes gradually growing cold and hard. "After all, money is the only thing you ever had to give."

She tried to remember the beautiful woman who had been her mother, but all she could clearly recall was the nanny who had taken care of her while her mother and father hurried from one social event to the next. She didn't suppose her mother actually disliked her, at least not after the socialite was able to resume her schedule, but Courtney's birth had been a mistake her parents didn't repeat. Courtney had been pampered and cared for like a valuable possession, but like all possessions, she had been kept on a shelf to be taken down for a few moments, then put back again.

It was impossible not to note the differences between her father and Seth. Never once had Seth offered her money. Instead he had offered her what no one but her grandfather had ever given her: time and himself. Why hadn't she realized how much time he spent with her? Of course, it was to his advantage to use one farm for all his clients, but he could have found excellent accommodations elsewhere. She also knew it was unusual for an agent to watch over his clients' horses as constantly as Seth did, but then she had thought he was watching over her as well.

And she did want him to watch over her. She had never known a man like Seth Cameron. Watching him save the foal tonight had brought everything into focus. If she wasn't already in love with him, she was falling hard. That frightened her. Her mother and father had turned their backs on her. Her grandfather had left her with a legacy of guilt. Every time she made a place in her heart for someone, they ended up hurting her.

She didn't know if she had the courage to try again.

But she didn't know if she could stop herself. Seth was everything she wanted in a man, even if he was also a few things she wasn't sure would be very comfortable in a relationship. He was thoughtful to the extreme. In fact, he would probably have gotten around her defenses a lot faster if he hadn't been so courteous. But he made up for it in persistence. Not for one minute since he'd first appeared at Gus's pasture had she been allowed to forget him. Nor could she forget the time he'd spent trying to ensure her farm's survival. And she had repaid him by ill-natured acceptance of his help and periods when she wouldn't even speak to him. Why had he kept after her? What did he see in her?

Maybe he felt differently now. Or decided she wasn't worth the trouble. But she hadn't been fighting him; she was only battling his insistence she sell Gus and his effort to insinuate himself into her life.

Why?

Because she had to save all her time and energy for the farm. She could only succeed if she gave it her single-minded attention, allowed nothing and no one to distract her from her chosen route. Once Gus was a champion, once she didn't have to worry about money anymore. . . .

For the first time in her life she found herself wondering if her goal was worth the struggle. What would she have if she succeeded? Would anyone offer to find her boarders then, to give her unasked advice, or save her foals in the middle of the night? Would anyone care about her? Or even know her? The greater her success, the harder it would be to distinguish the real Courtney from her property. That thought made her stomach churn.

A racking sob threatened to break the silence of the room, but she held it at bay by a single thought: as long as Seth was around, she wasn't alone.

"That's the colt I was telling you about," Seth said to the man who followed in his footsteps down the bridle path to avoid the snow that remained in patches on the grass. The man's height barely matched his girth. He was balding and had piercing black eyes; but his was an alert and intelligent face, and he spoke with the loud cheerfulness of a confirmed extrovert.

Gus's muscles moved smoothly under his skin as he glided around the turn and into the straight. Perched low over his back, Courtney kept him under a tight hold, refusing to let him out of the slow gallop she used to build his wind and muscle.

"He looks good from here," the man said, his expert gaze fully appreciative of the way Gus went about his work, "but you can't tell until they face the starter. How much does she want for him?"

"Miss Clonninger's not looking for a buyer," Seth replied, laughing easily. "Just a trainer."

"I don't like women owners. They're usually bitches."

Seth racked his brains for a way to introduce a man as brusque as Frank Slaughter to Courtney. He was one of the most successful trainers in the country. And one of the most tactless. Yet no matter how rude he was, people still clamored for him to train their horses.

Seth hadn't planned to bring him to Idle Hour. It just worked out that way. He wasn't excusing himself—he had been actively seeking a trainer for Gus—but he didn't know what she was going to say to his turning up with Frank in tow. Courtney didn't like being backed into a corner. Still, nothing was more important right now than finding a trainer for Gus. The whole future of Idle Hour could hang on that decision.

Seth knew he might lose all the ground he had gained by his course of feigned disinterest, but he couldn't sit around doing nothing. Besides, he didn't know how much longer he could go on pretending he didn't notice the gentle curve of her body or the full mound of her breasts. Maybe he was subconsciously putting their relationship to the test. If anything was likely to force a response out of Courtney, it would be Frank Slaughter.

He watched her as she rode, her lithe body poised in the saddle, the power and grace of her limbs equal to that of the magnificent animal beneath her. He felt awed and proud to think this woman was interested in him.

You're getting ahead of yourself, he told himself. She's interested, but you're hooked. Mere interest isn't good enough anymore. But he was still getting ahead of himself. Courtney hadn't accepted the fact of her interest in him—at least she hadn't admitted it to him—so he was looking at a lopsided relationship with himself holding the little end. He had to find out what was holding her back. Marcia had said he wouldn't get to first base unless he uncovered the secret that caused her to keep every man at a distance.

Gus swept by, and Slaughter's exclamation of pleasure intruded on Seth's thoughts.

"You didn't exaggerate," he said, never taking his eyes off the colt. "That's an exceptionally fine piece of horseflesh. And the girl's not bad either."

Seth looked at him sharply, but Slaughter only laughed.

"This is the only time I've ever known you not to look at a horse. It's got to be the girl."

Courtney jogged Gus back to where the men leaned against the rail. "You're Frank Slaughter," she said as she jumped down from the saddle. "What are you doing here?"

"How did you know my name?" Slaughter asked, preening slightly.

"My grandfather told me about you."

The words were spoken without warmth, and Seth felt the ground begin to tremble under his feet. This was going to be trouble. Courtney barely looked at him, but the swift glance was a question, almost one of surprised hurt. If he could have made Slaughter disappear in that instant, he would have gladly done so.

"Seth was telling me about your colt," Slaughter said without mentioning her grandfather's death. "He got me so interested I talked him into bringing me to see it."

"I'm not ready to let him go yet."

"You'll be looking for a trainer soon, though. Mind you, my barn is so full I have to turn people away all the time, but I still might consider taking him."

Courtney opened her mouth to respond. Certain her reply would be devastating, Seth braced himself. But much to his surprise, Courtney closed it again without saying a word. Baffled, he stared at her.

"As a matter of fact," Slaughter continued, his ego apparently a perfect insulation against the tension in the air, "I had one of those Arabs walk up to me last week and offer to pay me twice what I make to become his private trainer—and still keep ten percent of everything I won, mind you—but I turned him down."

"Thank you, but I'm not ready to decide on a trainer yet."

"You'd better not wait. I might change my mind."

Courtney's eyes started to turn slate blue, something Seth had never seen before, and he realized she was absolutely furious. But for some reason she was holding her anger in.

She's doing it because she doesn't want to hurt my feelings!

The realization caused his pulses to throb. He didn't care what she said. He didn't care if Courtney banished Frank Slaughter from their lives forever.

"A big, flashy colt like that ought to be running in everything available during the summer months," Slaughter said. "Let him clean up while he can."

Almost as though she sensed Seth's unspoken thoughts, Courtney's restraint vanished. "Gus is going to win the Triple Crown," she said, cold rage chipping her words like ice. "I have no intention of ruining him by racing too early."

"Are you saying I would ruin him?" Frank demanded, his own color fading as Courtney's rose.

"I don't know enough about training to make such a statement, but my grandfather did. He said you ruined at least two potential classic winners."

"Who the hell was your grandfather to criticize my training?" the enraged man stormed.

"A man who bred and raced more classic winners than you'll ever train, two of them Derby winners."

"See if I take your goddamned horse."

"I never offered him to you. I wouldn't trust you to train a goat."

Seth was certain his association with Courtney was causing him to go mad. Here he was watching one of the most powerful trainers in the world stalk away in a towering rage, and it was all he could do to keep the bubble of laughter inside him from erupting before Slaughter was out of hearing range.

"I can understand why you might not want Frank to train Gus—he's not the trainer for everyone—but did you have to add the bit about the goat?" he asked with an unsteady voice. "He'll hate me just because I heard it. He'll be sure I'll spread it over half of Kentucky."

"I'm sorry if I made things difficult for you," Courtney growled, her body still shaking with rage, "but that man is insufferable. He's the one who ruined your Nijinsky mare's first two colts."

"You've given him a kick in the pride he won't soon forget." They looked at each other and burst out laughing.

Seth held the gate as Courtney led Gus off the track. Her sudden nearness caused his laughter to wither and die in a quick intake of breath. He wanted to see her face, have her turn her gaze on him, but she occupied herself with Gus. She was the most exciting, compelling, frustrating, infuriating woman in the world, and he couldn't get her out of his system.

Whatever the outcome, he had to play this one out to the end. "You know you're a terribly difficult woman to help," Seth said, looking directly into Courtney's eyes, wanting very much to say something else. "Did your grandfather also tell you to bite the hand that feeds you?"

"My grandfather told me not to let anybody feed me," she said, heading back toward the barn slowly enough to indicate she wanted Seth to walk with her. "He said someday the hand might be withdrawn, and then I would starve to death because I hadn't learned to take care of myself."

"Do you believe everything your grandfather said?"

"Why shouldn't I? He was the only one who ever loved me." She flung the words at him like a challenge.

"Mind if I ask you what you mean by that statement?" Seth asked. Courtney had been walking around this for a long time. Maybe she would open up some now.

Courtney stopped and turned to face him. "As a matter of fact I do, but after all you've tried to do for this place and the abuse you've put up with from me, you deserve some explanation."

Courtney started toward the barn again. She didn't speak for several minutes. Seth remained quiet, allowing her to gather her thoughts.

"My father hated horses and Idle Hour Farm," Courtney began. "He and Grandpa never got along. Grandpa wanted him to stay here and learn to operate the farm, but my father wanted to go to business school before launching his assault on Wall Street. By the time he finished high school, my father hated Grandpa and everything he stood for. All he wanted was to get away. He left home at eighteen and never came back, not even for vacations. After graduation, he went to New York and married a woman exactly like himself. He didn't invite Grandpa to his wedding." Courtney was silent for a few moments.

"Grandpa got reports of them from time to time. My father received several rapid promotions, and my mother was a great social success. Then they made one big mistake. They had me. I was so much in the way they hired a nanny to take care of me. My mother died of a virulent fever when I was four. My father didn't have time for me before mother was ill. He didn't want me around after she died. When Grandpa asked if I could go home with him, my father offered to sell me to him."

"Sell you!" Seth's exclamation was so loud it caused Gus to half rear.

"My father agreed to give Grandpa custody in exchange for the five million dollars he needed to go into business for himself."

"Good God!"

"That's what happened to Grandpa's horses. He sold two of his best stallions to raise the money, and I arrived on the next plane from New York. My father only looked at Grandpa as a continual source of cash. After Grandpa's death, I found some of my father's letters. They were nothing more than extortion demands. For years he continued to extort money, always using the threat of reclaiming me to force Grandpa to sell more and more of his horses.

"I didn't know the true magnitude of my father's greed until I found the records of the special account Grandpa had set up so no one in Lexington would know what he was doing. The blackmail didn't stop until a federal grand jury investigated some of my father's deals. He would have gone to jail if he had been convicted, so he sold everything he had and left the country. By then Grandpa had nothing left." Twenty years of accumulated bitterness and guilt vibrated passionately in Courtney's voice. "Grandpa gave everything he'd worked for his whole life for me, but do you know what's the greatest tragedy of all?"

Seth didn't speak. He couldn't.

"I think the only thing in the world he really loved, I mean *really* loved, was his horses."

"Surely he—"

"He said he didn't regret it, that he would have done it over again. But I saw the look in his eyes when he gazed out over those hills where champions used to run, *his* champions, and saw nothing but empty fields. The memory of it haunts me every day of my life. I know I can't repay Grandpa—nothing could repay him for the years he spent watching the ruin of everything he loved—but that's why I swore to rebuild this place. I'm the reason it was destroyed. It's up to me to rebuild it."

Seth could hardly believe what he heard. His own family life had been so different it seemed inconceivable to him that people who proclaimed their love could wilfully destroy each other. Never had he dreamed that Courtney struggled under such a load of guilt. He could understand why she might blame herself, at least a little, but he couldn't understand why she should give up her future to atone for a debt she had no part in making. He didn't know where to begin, but he had to do something to make her change her mind.

"You can't ruin your whole life because of what your father and grandfather did," Seth said. This wasn't what he had wanted to say, but he was too nonplussed to think clearly. "Just because he wanted something doesn't mean you have to want it, too."

"Yes, it does. Do you remember when you took me to see your farm? You told me you vowed the day your family lost their farm you would have another someday. That's the way I feel; only my grandfather sacrificed his farm for me."

Seth started to protest, but Courtney cut him off. "I've never told anyone why Grandpa sold his horses. I could turn my back on this farm, and no one would blame me. I can't because I know why he sold them. It has eaten away at me for years. My whole existence is bound up in that vow. It's why there is no room for anything or anyone else. I know you don't understand. It isn't the way your mind works. But you don't know what it feels like to be sold by your father. That changes everything."

She stopped, visibly struggling to regain her composure. "Funny I should have told you all this instead of Marcia. I guess it's because she would never have understood my making the vow or being bound by it. You disagree just as strongly, but maybe you understand a little bit."

A sob shook Courtney, and she turned to Seth. He enfolded her in his embrace.

He still could hardly believe what she had told him. It put a different light on her loyalty to her grandfather, but it didn't explain her attitude toward the farm. At the moment, though, Seth was ashamed to admit he was having difficulty thinking about Courtney's grief or her farm. Having her in his arms, warm and willing, was playing havoc with his concentration and his sense of decency.

He had never felt more frustrated. After weeks of trying to get close to her, he was now holding Courtney, but he couldn't kiss her. As much as he wanted to, he knew it would be the wrong thing to do. His embrace, his presence, his sharing of her grief was the best thing he could do for her.

He castigated himself for his selfishness. The woman he had been trying to get to know better was sobbing out her heartache, and all he could do was think about kissing her. Didn't he have any human compassion and understanding? What was it about this woman that made him lose all sense of proportion?

Courtney stopped crying and tilted her head to look up at him. That was too much. He couldn't stand it any longer. Her eyes, still glistening with tears, pleaded for reassurance that there was at least a little bit of love in the world for her. He bent down and kissed her.

Her lips were salty, but he didn't mind. His arms closed tightly around her, and his kiss became more insistent. Courtney's response was tentative at first, but then her lips responded to his until they turned a kiss of consolation into a kiss of yearning. The taste of her mouth, the warmth of her body, the willingness with which she returned his kisses threatened to overheat Seth's sensory system.

It was hard to let her go when she withdrew her lips.

"Thank you," she said softly.

"What for?"

"For not running away. Men usually do when a woman starts to cry."

"But you cried because you wanted help." That was a mistake. He had said too much. He could see Courtney begin to withdraw from him.

"Well, I'm better now. I won't break down again. In fact, I don't know why I cried."

"Maybe you cried because you're lonely. Or because you don't want to be alone," Seth said.

"Perhaps, but you can't trust people. You never know what they're after."

"What makes you so sure you can put implicit faith in every word your grandfather uttered?"

"He may not have loved me as much as I loved him, but he did love me some."

A choking sob spilled out of her so suddenly it caught both of them by surprise, and Courtney turned and ran for the house. Seth's high school P.E. teacher would have been proud of the sprint it took to catch up with her. He grabbed her by the shoulders, forcing her to face him.

"I didn't mean that about your grandfather. I got mad when you said everybody wanted something from you."

"I didn't mean what I said either, but it's true just the same."

"What do I want?" Seth demanded angrily.

"I don't know. I thought you wanted Gus, or the farm. Once I even thought you wanted me, but now I don't know. I don't understand you at all."

Seth could practically hear Marcia's shouting it wasn't time to cave in; but he was only human, and he couldn't stand any more. He swept Courtney up in his huge arms and covered her face with kisses. "Does this help you understand me better?"

"I'm not sure," Courtney admitted, almost too breathless to talk, "but I like it better than your bringing trainers around to look at Gus."

"Is there anything I've ever done that you have liked?"

Courtney gave him a slightly quizzical look. "Go on with what you were doing, and I'll give it some thought."

"Termagant," Seth growled and kissed her ruthlessly. "You'd be well served if I threw you over my shoulder and made off with you."

"I'd dislike that," Courtney said, gently removing herself from his embrace and continuing toward the barn, "even more than your bringing Frank Slaughter down on me."

"He brought himself. Clay and I were talking about

Gus, and I mentioned I was coming out to see you. Frank must have liked what he overheard. He said he was coming this way, and he'd like to stop by with me. This is not my farm. I couldn't tell him no."

"This has to be the first time you've come by without a specific reason."

"Actually, I do have a reason. I have an offer for you." For a brief second Seth thought Courtney looked disappointed.

"You're turning into something of a Santa Claus. What have you got in your pack this time?"

"I'll have no slurs on my size," Seth said, hoping to lighten her mood.

"Santa Claus was short and rotund, hardly the description of a man who's ten feet tall with shoulders wide enough to fill a double door. Besides, your stomach is flat."

"That remark about my stomach is probably the only nice thing you've ever said about me; but I'm only six-four and I've never yet gotten stuck in a doorway."

They had reached the barn, and Courtney started to unsaddle Gus in preparation for hosing him down and cooling him out after his workout. She had plenty of men who could have helped her, but she always took care of Gus herself. Seth decided it might be better to give her his news while her attention was diverted, just in case she got angry.

"I found two seasons to Unbridled."

He might as well have dropped a bomb. Courtney leapt up from where she had bent over to check Gus's legs, turning in the process, and lost her balance. She fell conveniently into Seth's arms.

"But you know I can't afford them," she said, hope and fear of disappointment in her eyes. "I've talked to

Ted just about every day for months. He still insists I can't have a penny over fifty thousand."

"They're free."

"Free! What are you, some kind of wizard?" But Courtney's hopeful look began to fade. "There's a catch, isn't there?"

"I debated whether to tell you, but you ought to decide, not me. The owner will give you both seasons free if you agree to share foals. He tried to hold out for each of you owning a foal outright, but I insisted you each have half interest in both."

When Courtney didn't answer right away, Seth figured she was weighing her words so she wouldn't hurt his feelings. She shouldn't have worried. He never expected her to accept the seasons, not after she'd fought so hard to keep her horses. But he felt he had come out a winner. She'd never taken so much trouble to spare his feelings. She must care for him more than she knew.

"I appreciate your going to so much trouble, but I can't accept any arrangement that won't let me keep ownership of the foals. I know I've said this over and over again; but it was one of Grandpa's cardinal rules, and I can't go against it." She actually looked like she was sorry she had to disappoint him.

"Would you be surprised if I said I expected you to turn them down?"

"And you're not upset?"

"No"— Seth refrained from saying he thought it showed a lack of business sense—"but I think you owe me dinner. It wasn't easy to come up with that deal. What say I come by for you about seven-thirty?"

"You said *I* owed *you* dinner. I should pick you up."

Seth looked taken aback, but he recovered quickly. "Okay, but you'll need directions to my place."

"On second thought, I'm not sure I want to be seen driving away from a bachelor's apartment late at night. I have some steaks in the refrigerator. You get the wine, and I'll cook dinner. Is seven-thirty still okay?"

"You cook? I don't mean that the way it sounded," Seth added quickly. "I thought you had somebody to cook for you. With all the work you do on the farm, you can't have much time."

Courtney's smile was genuine. "Nell does all the cooking for the men, but I fix my own meals."

"Then, let me help. I toss a mean salad."

"Only if you promise not to use onions."

Seth's eyes grew wide with surprise.

"It's not what you're thinking," Courtney assured him quickly, but not before a tell tale blush crept up from under her collar. "I detest onions. It used to drive Grandpa crazy because he liked just about everything he ate smothered in them."

"Anything you want," Seth assured her. "I learned long ago never to argue with the cook."

Courtney knew inviting Seth to dinner was not a good idea, but she was glad he was coming. She had never fixed dinner for a man other than her grandfather. She wondered where she had found the nerve to offer to do so now. She was pretty good with tuna fish and hamburger, but if it couldn't be grilled, microwaved, or eaten raw, she had virtually eliminated it from her diet. It wasn't that she couldn't or didn't like to cook—actually she had never done enough cooking to know—she was simply lacking in experience. Nell cooked breakfast and lunch. There were always plenty of leftovers.

Crying on Seth's chest had dismantled another barrier, had undermined her determination to keep him at a distance. Now she wanted to enjoy his company, to bask in his admiration, to remember she was a desirable, feminine woman. She wanted to forget she was responsible for a huge farm that she had to pull out of debt.

For a moment she thought of casting aside her pride and calling her father. It would solve all her problems in one single step, but she knew she couldn't do it. It would be a betrayal of the almost twenty years her grandfather had spent struggling to recover what he had lost.

She would never forget her grandfather's last words. They hadn't been angry; they hadn't contained any emotion at all.

"If you need help, call your father. I made him sign a contract agreeing to repay the money if you ever needed it."

She had been too stunned to ask his whereabouts. For years her grandfather had told everyone he had lost contact with his son and assumed he was dead. Courtney had heard it so often she ceased to question it. It was easier to think of her father being dead than alive and not caring enough to contact her. She was crushed when she learned he had been living in Hong Kong for more than fifteen years.

Her mind had been filled with hundreds of questions, but her grandfather had lapsed into a coma and never regained consciousness. Months later she realized the pain she was still suffering came from knowing her father was alive, that his rejection of her was reinforced by all those years of silence.

It had been a worse blow than her grandfather's death. For years she had blunted the hurt of rejection by believing her father hadn't come for her because he was dead. By telling her he was still alive, her grandfather had destroyed her only protection against the knowledge that everyone in her life loved something else more than they loved her.

In the years since her grandfather's death, the burden of the farm had grown heavier each day. There had been times when she wanted to throw it all up, but knowing her father was alive had kept her going.

She had to succeed to prove she didn't need him, either.

It had been a grim struggle, one driven by anger, even hate. Each crisis, each step closer to failure, had increased her feeling of desperation, had made her more determined than ever to eliminate everything from her life except Gus and the farm.

But things had seemed much less desperate since Seth forced his way into her life. She could finally relax her guard. That didn't mean she would let him take over, but it was a relief to have someone to talk to. He always made her feel things would work out.

EIGHT

Courtney was unprepared for the churning sensation that started in the pit of her stomach the moment the doorbell rang. She felt positively girlish. She couldn't remember feeling like this when she was a girl.

"I like it," Seth said as soon as he got a good look at her outfit. "I definitely approve of you in a skirt."

Courtney knew her laugh was self-conscious in spite of a valiant effort to make it sound nonchalant. Remembering the fiasco of the gold dress, she had taken nearly an hour to pick out a skirt and blouse that flattered her without being a reminder of that terrible evening.

"I don't feel quite like myself," she confessed, taking the two bottles of wine from Seth so he could hang up his coat. "I wear a skirt so seldom I've almost forgotten what it's like."

"I like you in jeans, too," Seth said as he took the wine back. "Now lead me to the kitchen so I can work my magic with the salad."

He followed Courtney down the main hall, turned left down a narrow hall, then entered a third.

"Don't tell me. The kitchen is out back, and servants cook your fried chicken."

"Nell is our cook," Courtney replied with a grin over her shoulder, "but no ruler sits more securely on her throne. With the men up before dawn and sometimes having to stay up all night, Grandpa decided it would save time if they could eat on the place, so he built a new kitchen and added a dining room. If she were here now, Nell would kiss your hands for pushing all those horses off on me. The dining room is full again, and she's in seventh heaven."

"Then, call her up and introduce me this very minute. I could do with a little kissing from at least one Idle Hour female."

Courtney blushed furiously. "I invited you to dinner to show my appreciation for all the work you put into getting those stallion seasons, but I will not be blackmailed."

"Why not? It can be fun."

"You're too big, and much too mature, to be playing games."

"I don't know who told you that. The bigger and more mature you are, the more fun games can be. Children don't know what they're missing."

"Behave yourself or take your wine and go."

"Are you sure you want me to?"

Courtney eyed him as severely as she could, but it wasn't easy, especially with her belly acting peculiarly again. "Yes."

"Not even a little bit of backsliding?"

"You're the most impossible man," Courtney said with a burst of laughter that did nothing to relieve the uneasiness in her stomach or the tension she felt growing in all the muscles of her body. "I've often wondered how you could be so big and look so much like a teddy bear."

"You've tumbled my act."

"An act is just what it is. Do you know your eyes turn almost silver when you start to wheedle—"

"Then, you've noticed my eyes."

"Anyone who knows you can tell you're about to tell a whopper. But about that time you hit them with that stupid grin of yours, and they let you go right on and tell it anyway. No wonder you're such a successful salesman."

"I think I'd better get started on that salad. If you figure out any more of my secrets, I'm not going to be interesting enough to last through dinner."

His appeal had nothing to do with secrets. It was a powerful embrace, a comforting presence, and kisses she dreamed about. "I don't know," Courtney murmured over her shoulder as she delved into the refrigerator for the salad fixings. "I have a few odd jobs that might merit an occasional invitation."

"Can I pick out the ones I like?"

"Don't be absurd, and don't waste that little-boy look on me. First of all, it won't work, and second, it looks ridiculous on someone your size." It also looked absolutely adorable.

"My mother warned me about women like you," Seth replied good-naturedly, taking his coat off. "But I didn't listen to her, and look where it's landed me."

"And where exactly is that?" demanded Courtney.

"In the salad at the moment, but I fear it shall ultimately land me out the door and into the cold of night with nothing more than a sisterly peck on the cheek to keep me warm."

Courtney blushed again. That was exactly what she *had* planned, but she already knew she wanted something more. It seemed that since she had managed to confess most of her dark secrets to Seth, her barriers couldn't wait to come tumbling down. She wanted him to hold her and kiss her and never let her leave the comforting circle of his arms. Mumbling inaudible curses, she flung the marinated steaks on the hot grill.

"You've got fifteen minutes to fix that salad. How do you want your steak?"

"Medium-well to well."

Courtney looked up in surprise.

"I suppose you like yours dripping blood."

Courtney shivered involuntarily. "I like it barely pink." That was something else her grandfather couldn't understand.

"Then, I guess I can confess I cause Clay's wife fits every time she invites me over. They like their beef virtually on the hoof. After watching me try to avoid looking at their plates for a whole evening, she decided to serve me nothing but chicken or pasta."

"You like Italian food?" Courtney asked, trying to keep her mind on anything but Seth.

"How do you think I got to be this big?"

"I bet you were a godsend to the football team."

"I wasn't too bad once they got over the idea that just because I was large I couldn't play any position but defensive lineman. I don't look it, but I was pretty fast. And once I get under way, it's awfully hard to stop me. I made a few touchdowns in my day."

She knew he'd played football. With his stature and being raised in Kentucky, he couldn't escape it. "I suppose your mom and dad went to every game."

"Mom never liked football, but she died while I was in high school. Dad never missed a game, even after I went to college. He was certain I was going to have a great career in pro ball, but he died halfway through my senior year. It was pretty hard on me at the time, but at least he didn't know I turned down the offer."

"You were offered a professional contract?" Courtney sputtered, turning so quickly it brought a smile to Seth's face.

"Is that so hard to believe?"

"No, but . . ."

"I was drafted in the first round and offered a million-dollar bonus to sign."

"And you refused!" Courtney tried to control the squeak in her voice, but after all the lectures Seth had given her on fiscal responsibility, she couldn't believe he would turn down a chance to make that kind of money. "Why?"

"For the same reason you refuse to give up this farm. I wanted to be a horseman. Even though playing football would give me the cash to buy in at a higher level, it wouldn't have taught me anything about horses. And it would have kept me away from the business for five to ten years. There, the salad's finished," he said, looking into Courtney's eyes. "Then there was the matter of the farm," he added softly. "I guess I didn't feel I could wait that long."

Courtney had to drag her mind back to the steaks before they became charred rather than merely well done. "And?" she said as she dropped the meat onto plates and followed him to the table.

"I ended up making more money with horses than I would have with football. I have no crippling injuries, and I have nearly eight years of invaluable experience."

"Always the practical businessman."

"No, but sometimes knowing how to combine what you want with your natural talents works out rather well."

"Tell me about your mother," Courtney said as they sat down to the table. She had to get away from his never-ending success. There were times when its very magnitude scared her. She never felt so much like a failure as when she looked at what he had accomplished in so few years. She couldn't help feeling if Seth had inherited Idle

Hour, he would have figured out a way to stick to every one of her grandfather's principles and still make a profit.

Courtney shook off the depressing thought, took a sip of wine, and gave her whole attention to Seth's reminiscences of his childhood. There was nothing unusual about them, but out of the telling emerged a picture of the boy Courtney had seen in Seth all along, the serious, sometimes quiet child who knew how to keep his eyes on his goal, but who also knew how to make people like and trust him. Courtney found herself thinking about being the mother of a couple of boys exactly like that, and she nearly choked on her wine.

My God, had it gone that far?

If her subconscious had begun to think about bearing his children, she was probably already in love with him. When had it happened?

Courtney struggled to fight down the rising panic. She couldn't, she *wouldn't* allow herself to be in love.

"Aren't you going to tell me about yourself?" Seth asked. "Or are you going to sit there staring at me like I've got a pimple forming on the end of my nose."

Courtney realized she hadn't heard a word Seth had said for several minutes. Fighting back the confusion, she tried to pick up the thread of their conversation. "There's nothing to tell."

"There must be something."

"I told you the juicy bits this afternoon," Courtney said in a gruff defensive manner. "There's nothing else really. I lived with my grandfather from the time I was four. I always knew Idle Hour would be mine someday, so my whole life was geared to learning everything I could about horses and how to run a farm."

"No boyfriends, no proms, no shopping trips to Paris?"

"I had no time for boys, I turned down all invitations

to the prom, and what would I do with clothes from Paris? Gus wouldn't care if I turned up naked."

"Everybody else would."

"You know what I mean," Courtney responded crossly. "I never wanted fancy clothes."

"Where did you get that gold number you wore the other night, not to mention the outfit you're wearing tonight? You don't order that sort of thing out of a catalog."

"I do buy something occasionally," Courtney said, getting up from the table and taking her plate to the kitchen. Seth followed with his. "Actually, Marcia dragged me off shopping. She's convinced I'll never catch a man as long as I wear nothing but jeans."

"You caught me, and I didn't see you in anything else for months."

Courtney was breathless. What did he mean? This sounded like a lot more than friend helping friend, like he wanted to do more than offer her a comforting kiss.

"I didn't mean it that way," Courtney said, trying to calm her pulses so she could think. She had put the dishes in the dishwasher, and the only other way to play for time was to make the coffee. As luck would have it, the coffeemaker was already filled, and all she had to do was flip the switch.

"I did."

Courtney didn't want to face Seth, but she couldn't help herself. The sound of his voice was an invitation she couldn't resist. She turned and looked up into his eyes. She was no longer in any doubt as to what he meant. If ever a man's eyes gleamed with warmth and desire, Seth's did, and Courtney didn't really care which one might have the upper hand just now. Seth's eyes were an open window to his heart, and what she saw there was irresistible.

"You couldn't have learned to like me this quickly."

"I liked you from the very first. I think I'm crazy about you now."

"You think . . ." It was just as well one of them could think. She couldn't get out a whole sentence without grinding to a mental halt.

"You haven't given me a chance to try the idea on and see if it really fits, but if I were shopping, I'd pay cash for my chances and throw away the receipt."

"Why would you l-like me that much?" She even had difficulty saying the word.

"A lot of reasons," Seth said, firmly removing the coffee cups from Courtney's hands and drawing her toward him. "You're stubborn and hardheaded—"

"Those aren't reasons."

"And you're running away from something that scares you senseless. That brings out the protective instincts in me. A man likes to feel he's protecting his woman."

His woman! Courtney had never been called that before. She wasn't at all sure she liked it, but it didn't sound all that bad either.

"And then there are the obvious reasons. I don't share Marcia's dislike of jeans. On you they drive me crazy. I dream about the way your breasts stretch the nylon in your top and your hips pressure every seam. I like the way your nose turns up when you're about to give me the brush-off . . ."

"I never . . ."

". . . at least once a week. I like your eyes when they're blue, but I much prefer them when they start to turn green."

"My eyes are hazel. They don't turn green!"

"They're green right now. They started to turn the minute I took you in my arms. I like your hair, too. I've never seen hair quite that color. It's red, but it's got so much black in it, it's not really red at all. But I think I like your lips best, especially when I'm kissing you."

Having stated his preference, Seth kissed Courtney quite thoroughly. Rumbling sounds from the direction of the coffeemaker threatened to interrupt his demonstration. But being a resourceful man, Seth edged Courtney close enough to reach over and punch a button, immediately incapacitating the threat.

Courtney leaned into Seth, sending her temperature into triple digits. He took her lower lip between his teeth and nibbled his way across her mouth. The muted groan escaping Courtney seemed to increase his impatience. Placing his mouth firmly upon hers once more, his tongue plunged between Courtney's lips and past her teeth until it met her tongue, which she tentatively moved forward, lightly touching Seth's tongue before pushing into his mouth. Seth's arms tightened around Courtney until she was in danger of being crushed.

One of Seth's hands pressed the small of her back, holding her firmly against him until she became startlingly aware of the pressure of his loins. Hardly had her mind registered this when she became aware that his other hand had slipped forward until it cupped her breast. Both parts of her body were achingly sensitive and sending dangerous messages to every nerve ending. Courtney felt as though her entire body was ready for him.

Yet as much as Courtney wanted to remain in his arms, she was afraid if she lost control of herself, body and soul, she would never regain it. She couldn't risk that. Not yet. Not now. Gently but insistently she pushed him away.

"Do you like me at all?" he asked when they finally came up for air.

"Too much," she managed to mutter.

"What?" Seth held her at arm's length so he could look at her.

"I think I like you too much for my own good."

Seth looked stunned.

"I've had feelings for you for some time, but you kept pressing me until I got scared. Then you turned cool, and I thought you didn't care about me at all, that all along you were only interested in Gus and finding a place for your horses."

"You think I'd go to all that trouble for one sale?"

"How was I to know you were different from all those salesmen who hounded the life out of Grandpa?"

"And what do you think now?"

"I don't know. You're such a mass of contradictions. You're a smooth, successful salesman who never loses a chance to do business, yet you take the time to round up customers for me, search out stallion seasons, and turn up at midnight to deliver my foals. You drive a seventy-five-thousand-dollar car and dress like somebody out of *Town and Country,* yet you roll in the straw with Hamlet and prefer me in jeans. You advise billionaires on multimillion-dollar purchases, yet you ask me to pick out some bargain-priced brood mares for you." She smiled in a dazed sort of way. "You could probably wangle an invitation to any house within fifty miles of Lexington, yet you're spending your evening with me when you know I won't give you a sale and we'll probably fall into an argument before the night's out."

"Would it help you understand me better if I told you I loved you?"

"No!" Courtney broke from his arms.

"What's wrong?" Seth demanded, wondering why his words should cause such a terrified outburst.

"You can't. You can have a mad passion for me, you

can even make love to me, but don't ever say you love me."

Seth gazed at Courtney in bewilderment. She'd always backed away from becoming involved because it would interfere with devoting all her time to Gus and the farm, but now he saw naked fear in her eyes. "All right, I won't say it again, at least not now, but that won't change my feelings. Do you mind telling me what's wrong?"

"Nothing's wrong. I just don't want anybody to love me."

The mood was broken, and she moved away from him, poured their coffee, then sat down at the breakfast table, putting a solid object between them. "It never leads to anything and usually ends up hurting people." She wouldn't look at him, just stared down at her coffee.

"Not always."

"How do you know?"

"My mother and father." Courtney felt a lump in her throat. Obviously they hadn't been like her mother and father. "It won't work for me. Besides, I don't want it."

"Sometimes you can't stop things."

"Yes, you can. You told me yourself I ought to plan things out very carefully, look at the odds, and take the best possible choice, the one with the best chance of succeeding. Well, that's what I've done. I've seen what love can do to people's lives, and I don't like the odds."

"That's not what I meant."

"You can't pick and choose where to apply logic," Courtney flung at him. "If you're going to use it at all, you've got to use it consistently. That's right, isn't it? That's what you said."

"Look, Courtney," Seth began as he moved around the table toward her, but she leapt up from her seat.

"You're not going to change my mind. I don't want anyone to love me."

"People can't always help who they love. Sometimes it just happens."

He moved toward her again. She retreated just as quickly.

"You'd better go. It's getting late, and you know I have to be up at five."

"Courtney . . ."

"I'm really very tired. You should go."

Seth stared at Courtney, angered by the abrupt and unexpected twist their evening had taken. Where did she get off inviting him to dinner, cuddling in his embrace, then throwing him out the minute he said he loved her? If he thought she wouldn't refuse to see him for at least six months, he'd have forced her to thrash out the whole issue here and now. But he was too angry, too physically wrought up, to be objective.

"I'm not letting you off this easily," he said. "You may be able to convince yourself you don't care, but I won't let you lie to me."

"I'm not lying—"

Seth grabbed her roughly. "Look me in the eye and tell me you don't love me."

"I told you I liked you a lot, but I don't want to be in love with anybody."

"When will you figure out people don't fall in or out of love because they can fit it into their schedules or because it's the smart thing to do?"

"And what law says I have to love you just because you fell in love with me?" she demanded just as angrily.

"No law. With us it's just fact."

"Look, Seth, my feelings are stronger than I can afford just now. I've got so many things—"

"If you mention the farm or Gus one more time, I'm liable to become violent. I've had it up to here with your infernal obligations. Your grandfather is dead, and making Idle Hour the most successful stud farm in the world won't bring him back. What about your obligation to me?"

"I have no obligation to you."

"Then, what about yourself? I don't mean Gus or the farm," Seth said before Courtney could object. "I mean your obligations to you, to your feelings, desires, dreams? Surely they reach farther than a farm."

Courtney averted her gaze, and when she spoke it was in a voice that sounded dispirited. "I don't have time for myself yet."

"I won't let you sacrifice yourself to this—"

She turned back to face him. "It's not your choice to make."

The statement was irrefutable.

"Then, you don't have time for me, or us."

"I'm always glad when you come around. You've already made me tell you I like you very much."

"Is *like* enough for you? Because I'm warning you, Courtney Clonninger, it's not nearly enough for me."

"It's all I'm going to allow myself. Now, I think you'd better go," Courtney said when it was obvious Seth was going to continue the argument. "It's late, and being around you is dangerous."

"I'll go," he said, grabbing up his coat, "but we're not finished with this. You're going to tell me what's behind all this craziness."

"Look, Seth, I really don't—"

"Maybe this will help put some sense into your head." Without warning, he grabbed her and kissed her hard on the mouth, his tongue insistent, his arms crushing her helplessly against his huge frame. "There. Does that seem like something dangerous?"

"Yes," Courtney replied after the door closed behind him. "Lethal."

Then she burst into tears.

Seth sat in Clay's office waiting for his friend to join him, his mind engaged in replaying his evening with Courtney. He might have moved too fast, might have been too rough on her, but he couldn't regret it. She had barricaded herself against all human involvement, and he had to do something to force her out in the open. He didn't fool himself into thinking things were going to be easy just because she had admitted she liked him, but at least he had something to fight for. It had been impossible as long as she hid behind her barriers, out of reach and unaffected by his presence.

All of the anger and most of the frustration had drained away during the last week, and he waited for Clay with a growing sense of optimism that given time, he and Courtney would work things out between them. He was in no hurry. In fact, the next three or four months were going to be so busy he probably wouldn't be able to see Courtney more than a couple of times a month. That worried him. She already believed love caused nothing but pain. Unless he was mistaken, she was going to learn that denying love was more painful than accepting it.

And she did love him. After that night, he had no doubt. He had reeled when she made the comment about becoming his lover. He couldn't say it had been the farthest thing from his mind, but he'd never considered it a possibility. Now that it was, it was all the more crucial that Courtney realize her fears were standing in the way of her happiness.

He had lain awake every night since, a martyr to his body's insistent needs. He wasn't a philanderer or given to one-night stands, but he couldn't recall when he'd been without a woman for this long. There was no question about his putting pressure on Courtney, but the pressure inside himself was becoming more insistent. It wasn't merely a need to release the sexual tensions that had been gathering all these months. It was a need to fulfill his desire to make love to Courtney.

The feel of her body in his arms, the memory of her warmth and pliant surrender, only fanned the growing need within him. He didn't know how long he could wait. He only knew he must.

"It's taken quite a while, but we've managed to get old man Clonninger's debts reorganized," Clay told Seth when he finally got back from lunch. "Things don't look so bad now. You know, when Courtney first came in, I thought she was going to refuse to do anything I suggested, but she seemed to have made up her mind to do what was necessary. She's been most cooperative ever since. It's a shame her grandfather was such a financial mad hatter. That man scattered debts over half the world. I even turned up one in South America. We got that taken care of with the money the farm is bringing in from boarders, but I've got a couple more that are going to require attention."

"What did Courtney say about them?"

"I haven't told her. They're asking for immediate payment. While they're not large, at least not when compared to Courtney's assets, they're too big to settle out of the farm's present income."

"I'll pay them."

Clay looked at him hard. "You don't even know how much they're for."

"You said they weren't much. I'll pay them, and Courtney can pay me back."

"As your financial adviser, I can't recommend that. First, it's essential you protect your cash flow for the months ahead." Seth started to object, but Clay continued. "Secondly, if Courtney ever finds out, she'll never forgive you."

Seth's silence signified his agreement.

"You haven't taken me into your confidence about your relationship with Courtney, and I'm not asking you to, but I'm neither blind nor stupid. Anyone can see you've fallen in love with her. If you want to marry her, don't touch her debts."

"Suppose I cosign the loans, or offer to guarantee them if she defaults. Would that give her some time?"

"I don't recommend that either."

"Okay, you don't recommend it, but would it give her time?"

"Yes. Either your signature will be sufficient to extend the loan as is, or I can renegotiate it."

"That's all I wanted. Things are going well enough for her now, but she'll soon have stud fees and Gus's training costs. I think she can handle those if there are no extra demands on her for the next few months."

"Are you sure you want to do this? It could be a time bomb."

"I'd like to do a whole lot more. Her grandfather taught her everything there is to know about horses. Then instead of teaching her anything about finances, he filled her head with a lot of high-flown idealism. And if that weren't enough, he left her so guilt-ridden she can't think of anything but his damned farm."

"If Gus doesn't win big, she won't be able to continue without settling some of her debts, and that means selling some of her land."

"Have you tried to tell her that?"

"With exactly the same results you've had." Both men laughed, and Seth rose to leave.

"Just take care of those loans."

"Okay, but you'd better hope she never finds out your name is on them."

"If she does, I'm coming after your head."

"Some gratitude. You stick your neck out against my advice and then blame me. Maybe you and Courtney are better matched than I thought."

Clay ducked the cushion Seth sent whistling past his head and chuckled delightedly as his friend stalked out of his office.

"Okay, tell me why you called," Marcia ordered, abruptly ending their gossipy chat.

"I just called to talk."

"You've said exactly nothing for ten minutes. I know you're not paying for a transatlantic call to tell me the weather's perfect and Gus is growing like a bloody weed. What's wrong between you and Seth?"

"Nothing, I mean, there's nothing between Seth and me to go wrong."

"Then, I'm ashamed of you."

"What?"

"A woman who has a man like Seth Cameron knocking at her door would have to be crazy not to invite him in. Are you waiting for the man to tell you he loves you?"

"He already has."

Now it was Marcia's turn to scream an interrogatory, "What?"

"That's the trouble."

"Trouble? One of the best-looking men in Kentucky, not to mention one of the most successful, tells you he loves you, and you're crazy enough to tell me it's a problem! Bloody hell! You'd better lie down, girl. You've got a serious brain fever. You're probably already bloody delirious."

"Be serious," Courtney said, laughing in spite of herself.

"I *am* being serious, more bloody serious than I've been since Gerald asked me to marry him. You latch on to that man and hold on tight. You won't ever find one half as good again, especially not one who's willing to put up with all your foolishness about farms and horses."

"It's not foolishness," Courtney protested, half indignant, half defensive.

"Anything is foolish if it gets in the way of catching a husband like Seth Cameron. Run, I mean *run* to wherever he hides when he goes off to lick his wounds after an encounter with you, and beg him to forgive you. Bloody hell! I can't believe you would do this. You're a disgrace to the American female. If I weren't three thousand miles away, I'd go after him for you."

"I guess I can see how you'd feel like that, but you didn't have to put it in such explicit terms."

"I don't dare try to be subtle with you," replied Marcia, still incredulous. "If I thought Gerald would let me go, I'd fly out tonight. I just know you'll find some way to screw it up."

"I never have been able to see things as clearly as you, but I think I understand myself a little better now."

"You bloody well don't, and you probably never will," Marcia stated in disgust. "You've got enough crosses to bear and obligations to fulfill to qualify for a crusade all by yourself. I understand you, Seth understands you, half the state of Kentucky understands you, but you haven't a clue."

"I've got one clue," Courtney said, and a smile of self-satisfaction curved her lips. "Maybe if I think real hard, I can figure out the next step."

"I've already told you. Run and beg his forgiveness."

"I don't think I'll do that, but I will keep it in mind."

"Bloody hell," Marcia exclaimed. "I've got a terrible pain in my belly, and I don't know whether this child is going to come early or if it's just indigestion from listening to you talk like the biggest fool in the history of the world."

"Lie back. I'm sure it'll be gone five minutes after you hang up."

"No it won't," Marcia declared positively. "It'll take me at least an hour to stop wanting to hit you over the head for playing fast and loose with the best man you'll ever find."

"Remember me to Gerald, and call me the minute the baby's born."

"And you call me the minute Seth pops the question and you finally get the bloody good sense to answer yes."

Seth caught up with Courtney on her way to take Gus out for his morning exercise. She had been avoiding him again, but she didn't really mind being caught.

"He looks like he's thriving," Seth said. "When do you hope to start him?"

Courtney was glad Seth had decided to talk about Gus. After what had passed between them, she hardly knew how to start again. She knew she wanted him to like her, but she was scared he would start talking about love again. Between the two extremes was a fairly broad territory without the pressures and risks of either. That's where she wanted to stay.

"I've got to find a trainer first," she said. "Do you know anything about Barry Preston?"

"Sure. He's fairly young, but he's got a good reputation. How did you find him?"

"I went over to Keeneland a couple of mornings and watched all the horses work out. I liked his the best."

"You couldn't have made a better choice. You didn't ask anybody's advice?"

"No, but if I had, I would have asked you."

Seth took a moment to digest that. Clearly, there was something new in the air, and he didn't want to make a wrong step. "Would you take a piece of advice if I offered it as a friend?"

Courtney looked at the ground. "I would consider it that way."

Well, you can't have everything, Seth said to himself. "I'm glad you trusted me enough to tell me about your father." She continued to stare at the ground. "I know it still hurts, but it wouldn't be quite so bad if you could share it with someone else. I know, you've told me about it, but you haven't shared it. You're still trying to carry it alone."

"I know."

The long silence convinced him Courtney wasn't going to volunteer anything.

"But you're going to keep it to yourself anyway?"

"For a while longer."

"Why?"

"Because it hurts too much to talk about it."

She looked up at Seth as she replied, and he was shocked to see tears in her eyes. Even though she had cried on his chest once before, Seth thought of Courtney as one of the stiff-upper-lip kind. He didn't know quite how to take her glistening eyes, but he was glad for even this small chink in her armor. "It'll go on hurting until you drag it out and face it."

"I know, but I can't do it all at once. I've got to take it in little steps." They had reached the private training track, and to Seth's dismay, Barry Preston was waiting for Courtney. Damn, and just as she was beginning to open up again.

There was no hope of getting her to talk to him now. She and Barry were soon deep into a discussion of Gus's finer points, and Seth couldn't fool himself into thinking he came ahead of Gus. He had come to the conclusion she loved him, but between the farm and Gus and the incredible load of guilt and hurt she carried around twenty-four hours a day, he didn't have a snowball's chance in hell of claiming the major part of her attention. She might be getting in the way of his work, but Courtney was using her work as a shield against him.

Damn, he cursed again. He felt like a decathlon runner on an endless obstacle course. No matter how many obstacles he managed to clear, there was always one more staring him in the face. "I've got an appointment I can't miss," he said, interrupting their discussion on whether Gus's bones were hard enough to stand full training. "I'll get back to you as soon as I can."

Courtney nodded, and Seth walked off before he could say something rude.

Courtney watched him as he walked the entire distance across the meadow, a strong sense of sadness and loneliness inside her. For a moment she considered following Seth, but Barry's insistent voice reclaimed her attention.

"I'm sorry, I didn't catch what you said," Courtney said as she turned her eyes away from Seth's retreating form.

NINE

Courtney stood in front of the refrigerator trying to decide what to fix for supper. She didn't want any of the food she had in the house, but she had to eat something. So she stood there, feeling foolish and wondering why it was so difficult to make up her mind on the simplest things these days.

Of course, she knew it was all Seth's fault. Before he stepped out of that flashy Jaguar, she'd never had any difficulty making up her mind. Now she stood around like a nincompoop, dithering over everything she did. It was a wonder she could even get dressed in the morning. It had taken her an hour just to decide which lipstick to use the last time she went to a party. And it hadn't been for Mr. Hancock's benefit. She hadn't paid him any attention all night.

Except for quick visits, Courtney had seen Seth only three times during the last two months. Once he had invited her to dinner with one of his clients. The other two times he had taken her to one of the enormous parties given in conjunction with the Keeneland sales. He'd been a perfect date, but Courtney was aware of a strain between them. She knew it was her fault, but the longer Seth kept his distance, the more she wondered if she hadn't made too much of nothing. Wasn't it possible that when he said he "loved" her, he didn't mean he loved her in the eternal sense, in the sense that demanded commitment, the exchange of hearts, the deep, permanent feeling that left unending pain when it was ripped away?

There were lots of people who equated love with a less demanding relationship, and it was quite possible Seth was one of them. Courtney was irritated to find her heart beat faster at the thought they might be able to find some way to enjoy each other's company without getting hurt. A smart woman would know when to quit.

But she hadn't realized how lonely she was until Seth had descended on her like a whirlwind. Marcia had gotten married at a time when Courtney was too busy worrying about debts to have time to feel her isolation. She still might not have realized how she had isolated herself if Seth hadn't made her look beyond Gus and Idle Hour Farm. She wasn't totally sure she was glad he had done that. True, she had been lonesome, but her life had been well-ordered. She had known what she wanted to do.

She could have handled it alone, but it was nice to have the whole crew back again. And Ted was a lot happier, too. Since Christmas, the farm had been making enough money to meet its payroll. There was even a small profit. Now if she could just find the money to pay for the breeding seasons she needed. She would never accept a foal-sharing agreement, but she felt a warm tug at her heart that Seth had taken the trouble to hunt up the offer.

Courtney finally decided on tuna salad. She was tired of tuna, but she wasn't hungry enough to bother with anything else.

She had come to like his trying to take care of her. She didn't need his help and didn't want him to think she was depending on him, but it was nice nonetheless.

No one had done that in a long time. It was a nice dividend to being a woman.

She grinned. Wouldn't Marcia give her eyeteeth to hear Courtney admit that. She'd probably lose the rest of her teeth when Courtney told her she had grown inordinately fond of Seth's kisses. In fact, she had been disappointed when he had declined her invitation to come in after their last date. He had lingered willingly on the front porch, kissing her until she was so weak she had to lean against the wall, but he had refused to enter the house. In fact, he hadn't come in since that terrible night when she virtually chased him out. Courtney knew she had no one to blame but herself.

Her thoughts, as well as preparations for her salad, were interrupted by the insistent ringing of the front door chimes.

It took her by surprise.

She never had company, especially the kind that dropped in unannounced. As she walked to the door, she rehearsed what she would say, but the speech died unborn when she looked through the spy hole and saw Seth on the porch, a look of unholy glee on his face. With surprising alacrity, she undid both safety locks, turned off the burglar alarm, and threw open the door.

"Seth, what—"

"Kiss me, and I'll show you my surprise." He stood there on the porch, leaning down, his lips pursed, his hands behind him waiting for her kiss.

"I don't kiss anybody on the front porch."

"Okay, I'll come inside." He did. "Now kiss me."

"You've got to be kidding."

"Kiss me, or I promise I'll interfere with every loan you've got."

"You wouldn't dare."

"Clay is my best friend. I'll do anything for one of your kisses."

"Okay, but . . ." She leaned forward and gave him a hesitant peck.

"Pretty stingy," he said, straightening up, "but I'll give you your surprise anyway." His hands whipped forward, and Courtney let out a shriek. In each hand he held a large, live, squirming lobster.

"Dinner," he announced as he strode past her toward the kitchen. "I need your largest pot and lots of boiling water."

"What if I hadn't been home?" Courtney asked as she rushed to get ahead of him.

"You're always home."

"But what if I hadn't been?"

"I'd have left them for Hamlet, their dismembered bodies strewn across your steps," he said, dropping the squirming crustaceans into the sink. He took the ice tray from the ice maker and dumped half its contents on top of the lobsters. "Don't tell me you dislike lobster."

"I love it," Courtney said with a laugh. "I much prefer it to tuna."

"Is that what you were going to have?"

"Yes."

They both laughed.

"Oh, I almost forgot," Seth said and dashed out of the kitchen. In less than a minute he was back with a grocery bag. "The trimmings," he proclaimed, taking out French bread, the makings of a salad, wine, dessert, and two very large, red, shiny apples.

"You haven't by chance been reading Omar Khayyám lately, have you?"

Seth looked puzzled for a moment. "Aha," he said as

enlightenment struck, "a loaf of bread, a jug of wine, and an apple for the teacher."

"Something like that."

"Smart man, Omar. I should have listened to him earlier."

"You haven't done all that badly on your own."

"They do say persistence counts."

"If that's the case, you'll win salesman-of-the-year, or whatever they give people for steamrolling their way into other people's lives. I've never seen anyone with more determination."

"I have."

"Who?"

"You."

Courtney didn't need him to tell her what he meant by that. She busied herself with the salad while he salted the water to his satisfaction and waited for it to come to a boil. "I thought you might have given up on me." She didn't look up, but she could feel his gaze on her.

"I told you I was going to be working eighteen-hour days until the end of the summer."

"People still have to eat."

"Look, Courtney, the last time I was here, you all but threw me out. I thought what you said was utter nonsense, but you have a right to your opinion—even if I have taken at least a dozen sacred oaths to change it. I made myself scarce to give you a little time to think. Did I wait too long?"

"I didn't mean to sound like I had been counting the days."

"Were you?" He drew her into the circle of his arms and lifted her chin until she could no longer avoid his eyes. "Were you counting the days?" he repeated.

"Not exactly counting," she temporized, "but I knew an awful lot of them had gone by."

"You could have told me," Seth said and kissed her roughly.

"I wasn't sure you wanted me to, not after the way I treated you," she replied when she caught her breath.

"This is your chance to set things right," Seth said, kissing her again.

Courtney wanted to stay where she was, but the water was boiling and one lobster was threatening to climb out of the sink. The thought of those powerful claws anywhere near her ankles sent shivers up her spine. She was actually relieved when Seth released her to drop the critters into the steaming pot.

"I'll finish the salad if you'll set the table," Seth volunteered. "Fifteen minutes is all you get."

Courtney managed to do more with her fifteen minutes than set the table. The wine rested in a cooler of ice, the salad and dessert plates were within reach, the candles were lighted, and she had changed into a silk blouse and thin wool skirt that did nothing to disguise the slim, athletic body it covered.

"The garlic bread's in the microwave," Seth said as he set down the platter with the steaming lobsters. He was standing behind Courtney's chair when she returned. "I see you didn't forget anything," he said, indicating the bibs and towelettes.

"Just a precaution. Lobster should be eaten outdoors at a picnic table."

Dinner was somewhat subdued. Their conversation was easy and continuous, but Courtney's mind was not on what they were saying or on the food. She was more acutely aware of Seth's physical presence than ever before. She had admitted his attractiveness from the first, had enjoyed his kisses and embraces, but never had her whole body trembled with such excitement.

Then, just as unexpectedly, she knew what it was. She wanted him. She could hardly believe her own feelings. She had never wanted a man to touch her, a fact that had sometimes worried her, but she definitely wanted Seth.

As she busied herself extracting the last bit of succulent meat from a lobster claw, she tried to figure out what it was about Seth that made him so attractive to her where other men hadn't piqued her interest. She decided it was everything about him. He simply wasn't like anybody else. It was hard to determine just what was different or why it mattered so much, and after a little while she gave up trying. He was unique. It didn't matter why.

"If you'll take the wine into the den, I'll clear the table," she said when they had finished eating. "You probably ought to make up the fire, too."

"Let me help," Seth offered.

"It'll only take a minute," Courtney called over her shoulder.

"That was quick," Seth said when she joined him in the den almost immediately. "What did you do, pitch everything out the window?"

"Just about," Courtney admitted with a guilty grin as she settled into the opposite end of the sofa.

"None of that," Seth said, patting the cushion next to him. "This is your spot right here."

Courtney didn't need a second invitation. The soft glow of the fire and the satisfied feeling that came from a stomach filled with good food and wine made her languorous, and she nestled into his embrace.

"That wasn't so hard, was it?" Seth teased.

"No, and don't asked me why I took so long. I don't want to think about anything except how comfortable and content I am. I might even go to sleep."

The fire lent a soft glow to the room, but not enough warmth. Courtney reached for a down comforter she kept for the long evenings she spent studying pedigrees and pulled it over her legs.

"I can promise you won't go to sleep," Seth said.

Courtney laughed softly. "Too damaging to your ego?"

"Too much wasted time," he responded. "It's not often I find you in such a compliant mood."

"Fill me full of wine and lobster more often, and you never know what will happen."

"I'm putting in a standing order first thing tomorrow. But in the meantime . . ."

Courtney decided that being kissed as she cuddled in Seth's arms in front of a fire was about as close to heaven as she could get on this earth. Rather than feeling drugged by food and wine, her body was vibrantly alive, intensely aware of the vital, warm man next to her. Nestled in his embrace, she felt positively engulfed. She loved it.

"Do you know how long I've dreamed of doing this?"

"Too long?" she murmured.

"Much too long."

"There's something about forbearance making the wine taste all the sweeter."

"That's a lot of crap. All I can think of is all the wine we've spilled."

"Have you really been thinking of me all these months?"

"Obsessively. Why do you think I keep knocking my bruised head against the stone wall of your resistance?"

"A salesman's natural inability to believe he can't sell something, in this case, yourself."

"Heartless woman, do you still hold that against me?"

"No, not for a long time," Courtney said, and she

kissed him. It was the first time, and she felt unsure; but Seth's immediate response swept away any reluctance.

"Why don't you get comfortable?" Courtney suggested. "I don't think I've ever seen you without your coat and tie."

"They're like a second skin," Seth said, laying the discarded garments across a nearby chair.

"This is the first time I've felt like I could touch you," Courtney said, putting her arms around him and running her hands over his back. "Now I won't feel guilty if you get mussed."

"Oh, God, muss me. *Please* muss me," Seth groaned.

"Stop it," Courtney said, a little self-consciously, then mischievously tugged at the chest hair showing through his open collar.

"This is war," Seth declared and reached for the top button on Courtney's blouse.

"Don't you dare."

"Come here, gadfly," Seth said as he pulled Courtney to him and wrapped his arms about her once more. "You owe me something for that trick."

Courtney thought a kiss was a very pleasant price to pay until she became aware of his hand under her blouse, his fingers caressing the silk of her slip. She tried to pull away, but Seth's arms held her tight. Before she could protest, her body was electrified by a surge of energy that shattered her resistance and caused her to mold herself to his suddenly rigid body.

With an audible groan, Seth responded to her pressure. She felt the heat of his body's response. Her breasts, crushed against his hard chest, became firm and tender to the pressure. But where Courtney would have panicked a few weeks ago, tonight she felt only awakening desire.

She offered no protest as Seth's right hand moved forward to cup one of her aching breasts.

Her body was racked by sensations that made her yield further to Seth's embrace. Too weak with desire to remain upright, they gradually sank to the thick carpet. An incredible feeling invaded every part of her body, turning her senses into heat and pleasure. She unbuttoned Seth's shirt, slipped her hands inside, relieved at last to be able to touch the smooth skin and feel the taut muscles that gripped her so forcefully.

She hardly heard the words he whispered in her ear. When he unbuttoned her blouse, unhooked her bra, and took her breast in his large hand, she lost all awareness of anything except the delicious sensations that tugged in her belly, that arced from one end of her to the other. Her body ached from his touch. It tensed, then opened with desire. Her breath came in ever shorter gasps.

The smoldering flame she saw in Seth's eyes startled her. Only then did she realize he was in the grip of the same turbulence that had invaded every part of her being. His hand began to caress her breast, gently kneading it, turning her entire body into a tingling mass of sensations. She felt her muscles tense, her limbs stiffen, her breath slow then stop. Abruptly the tension fell away, leaving her weak and panting. Gently, he outlined the circle of her breast, first with his fingertip—then with his tongue. She heard herself groan, felt her body arch to meet his touch. Then his lips touched her swollen nipple, and Courtney thought she might explode.

No man had ever touched her. Her body was a virgin instrument, tightly strung but never played. Every sensation was unique, unprecedented, incendiary. With each new feeling she was sure she had reached the limit of her endurance. She was equally certain if Seth stopped now, she would surely die.

Seth took her nipple into his mouth and gently suckled it. Courtney literally rose off the floor. His lips moved to the hollow of her throat as he slipped her blouse from her shoulders. He eased her back down, his lips and tongue blazing a trail along her shoulder and back across her collarbone, then down the valley between her breasts. Courtney took his face in her hands and drew him up until she could kiss the lips that were subjecting her body to such delicious torture.

Seth's hand moved across her belly, his touch light and teasing. He began a gentle massage that sent currents of desire all through her. His other hand moved gently down the length of her back, the stroking of his fingers sending pleasant jolts through her. He moved across the plane of her back until he reached her shoulders, her neck, the back of her head. Their kiss deepened until Courtney felt as though she were being drawn into a bottomless well.

He broke their kiss, and she fell back to lie panting, her chest heaving.

His lips returned to their worship of her breasts, kissing, tasting, nipping, biting her swollen nipples until she wanted to scream from the delicious agony. When he unhooked her skirt, she automatically raised her hips to allow him to slip it from her body. She wanted nothing between her and the warmth of his skin.

Frantically her fingers fumbled with the buttons of his shirt. He took pity on her and removed it for her. She let her hands roam over every part of his chest, arms, and shoulders. Their size and power left her in awe. He was so splendidly huge, so absolutely perfect, it didn't seem possible that he could love only her. Her hands framed his face. The hunger she saw in his eyes made her feel like prey, pursued and about to be swallowed up. Yet it excited and thrilled her to know she had the ability to affect this man so powerfully.

She put her arms around him and snuggled close. She gasped as bare chest met bare breasts. His hands along the small of her back enfolded her, held her close. She wanted to move closer still, burrow inside him until she became a part of him. Seth responded with a kiss that sent his tongue plunging deep inside her mouth, plundering each secret recess for every drop of sweetness to be found there.

But the fire building inside Courtney didn't allow her to remain still for more than a moment. The same demon of desire seemed to be driving Seth. He pressed her against the length of his body, his hands on her bottom, holding her firmly against him. Heat from his inflamed body flowed into her, igniting a fire which scorched every nerve. She neither knew nor cared when he slipped the last of her clothing from her body. Nor when he removed his own. She only knew that she was moving toward something that drew her with irresistible power, something she suddenly realized she'd been created for, something fashioned by the gods just for her. She felt Seth's hands on her body, his lips locked with hers, his powerful limbs warming her entire length, and she moved willingly in his embrace.

His hands brushed over her soft skin, touching places no one had ever touched, exploring parts of her that had never been explored, becoming intimate with her in a way that left her breathless. Passion pounded the blood through her heart, chest, and head. Her body felt as if it were half ice, half flame. She breathed in deep, soul-drenching drafts as his touch sent her soaring to ever higher levels of ecstasy.

Yet as much as she wanted him, as wildly as her body clamored for the release that only he could provide, Courtney was hesitant to yield herself totally. Something inside her told her she was giving more than she suspected, that she was making a commitment greater than she wanted, that the love she had so long feared and shunned had at last captured her heart, but she wouldn't listen. The dormant sexuality of her body had been fully awakened. Her need of Seth was too insistent, her need of the comfort he provided too great, her need of physical release too long delayed. Desire for him overrode every warning, every impulse for caution, and she yielded to the searing need which had been building for months. Gradually her muscles relaxed, and she rose to meet him, turning an invasion into a homecoming.

Courtney gasped in sweet agony as she welcomed him into her body. Every feeling was new and shockingly intimate, yet it all felt so natural. Her mind knew nothing of what she would experience, yet her body seemed to have always known what to do. She molded herself to him until they moved as one being. Together they found a tempo that bound their bodies together, that allowed them to move in exquisite harmony with one another. Wave after wave of ecstasy throbbed through her. The pleasure was pure and explosive. Golden tremors of passion and love flowed between them. She wanted more of him, needed more, begged for more. Yet the more he gave, the more she required.

The world spun and careened on its axis. She cried out for release, but it didn't come. Instead the increasingly powerful waves of desire that repeatedly washed over her sent her soaring higher and higher, coming ever closer to the moment when she was certain she would explode into a million tiny bits of flame, burn, and evaporate into nothingness. Yet the need that held her in its grip was so powerful, so unrelenting, she willingly raced toward her own destruction. Surrendering completely, she felt herself hurled beyond the point of return.

Passion radiated from the soft core of Courtney's body, and she yielded herself to the burning sweetness that seemed to capture everything within her. Her body began to vibrate with liquid fire; a tremor inside heated her thighs and groin. She felt passion rising in her like fiery lava in a volcano. Then, in a moment of exultation, she soared to a wondrous, shuddering ecstasy.

Moments later she floated to earth in an exploding downpour of fiery sensations.

They lay for a time in each other's arms, covered with a down comforter, enjoying the contentment that came with surrender and release. But to Courtney's dismay, the nagging doubts from earlier in the evening had grown in importance. With them came the awful realization that she loved Seth, not in some transient way that could be enjoyed today and forgotten tomorrow, but with a constancy that would last for the rest of her life.

In spite of all her caution, she had been caught again. In spite of her effort to hold them back, tears welled up in her eyes. She gripped a trembling lip with her teeth. This wasn't the first time she had cried in front of Seth. It was bound to run him off, but she couldn't stop herself.

"What's wrong?" Seth asked, alarm in his voice. "I didn't hurt you, did I?"

"No."

"It was your first time?"

"Yes."

"What is it, then?"

"I love you."

"What did you say?" Seth asked, sitting up abruptly.

"I said I love you, dammit, and I don't want to."

"It's all right," Seth answered with a contented chuckle. "I love you, too."

"You don't understand," she protested, the tears still streaming down her face. "I don't want to love anybody, and I don't want anybody to love me. I tried so hard to keep it from happening. Dammit to hell, it's just not fair. I'm tired of being hurt. I don't think I can stand it again."

Seth was almost as startled by her curses as by her words of love. "I love you, Courtney. I won't let anything hurt you."

"You don't mean it. That's what they said, but they didn't mean it either."

"Who are you talking about?"

"My parents and my grandfather. They all said they loved me, but they lied." A sob shook Courtney's frame, but she pulled away and wrapped herself in the comforter when Seth tried to hold her.

"You've kept it bottled up far too long," Seth said softly. "Why don't you talk about it? It'll ease the pain."

"Nothing can erase twenty years of knowing everybody who should have loved you didn't," Courtney threw at him, but when he didn't say anything, she managed to calm herself. After a few minutes more she started to talk, staring into the fire as the words came haltingly from the deep recess where she had kept them for so many years.

"My mother hated staying home. I remember Nannie saying how miserable she was the months she was pregnant. When I was four, she left me with my nanny so she could travel abroad with my father. She died from some strange illness the doctors didn't know anything about. They never even let me see her."

"Maybe she was afraid you'd catch whatever it was," Seth suggested mildly.

"My father didn't see me either. He didn't have time, Nannie used to say. But when mother died and he had lots of time, he sold me to Grandpa."

"At least your grandfather loved you," said Seth, trying to salvage some love out of Courtney's life.

"No, not really. I told myself he did, but I was only a duty to him. He never told me he sacrificed everything he truly loved for me, but I knew it just the same. He never loved me as much as his horses," Courtney answered sadly. "He devoted all his time to getting to the top again. When he saw he wasn't going to make it, he trained me to do it for him. I don't think he meant to, but when he told me what I had cost him, it was the same thing as a guarantee I would do anything I could to pay him back, no matter the price." Courtney broke down again, still resistant of Seth's comforting arms. "Maybe now you can understand why I can't love anybody."

"Forget about your parents, your grandfather, even Gus and the farm, and concentrate on us. I love you, Courtney."

"For how long?" she asked, raising a tear-stained face to his.

"Forever."

"Nothing is forever. Tell me how long? Maybe I can stand it if I know when it's going to end."

"I'm not going to stop loving you," Seth repeated. "I don't know about your parents or your grandfather, but I'll never leave you."

"Everybody wants something. What do you want?" Courtney demanded angrily. "Are you still after Gus?"

"No, just you."

"Why should you be different from my own family?"

"Courtney, stop doing this to yourself. There's nothing wrong with you, and I'm not after anything. Try to forget what your father did. I'm sure he didn't mean it the way it happened. He must have been terribly unhappy himself."

"And Grandpa?"

"He must have loved you a great deal to do what he did." Surely he wouldn't have sacrificed everything just to spite his son. "But no matter how much he loved you, it had to hurt to give up everything he had worked a lifetime to achieve."

"But did he have to make me feel the weight of that sacrifice every time he looked at one of those empty fields?"

"I'm sure he didn't mean to, but it's over now. You can't change the past. Think about us."

"I can't forget Gus. He's the most important thing in my life."

"I guess that puts me in my place," Seth said as he reached for his clothes. "I had hoped you could forget that horse for just a few hours."

"I can never forget Gus. He's mine. I bred him. He and I are going to pay Grandpa back."

"I don't have four legs and a pedigree as long as your arm, but I could help."

"I have to do this by myself. Besides, everybody leaves me sooner or later." She had to drive him away so she could do this alone. Her tone was no longer argumentative, just fatalistic.

"I won't."

"I can't take that chance."

"Why did you make love to me just now?" Seth demanded angrily. "Was it just animal lust, or were you curious to find out what it was like?"

Courtney stared into space.

"I think you owe me an answer."

"Because I couldn't help myself," Courtney responded softly. "I love you."

"Then why . . . ?" Seth asked as he knelt beside her, his shirt still unbuttoned.

"I thought there might be some way we could love each other without pain. There ought to be," she said, looking up, anguish in her eyes. "Why does everything wonderful have to come with such a terrible price?"

"There's always risk—life is full of it—but not everything causes pain. Love can heal as well as hurt."

"When does it start?"

"As soon as you let it."

They remained still, looking at each other.

"You'd better go. There'll be questions if you stay any longer. I don't think I could stand that."

"All right," he said, kissing her gently, "but remember, I love you. Nothing can change that. Do you believe me?"

She nodded, and kissed him back.

Courtney didn't move when Seth finished dressing, nor did she move when he left. She didn't even move when Hamlet padded in—Seth must have let him in—and settled down next to her, his face resting on her silk blouse. She stared into the bleak landscape of her past, at twenty years of denying her need to be loved, and wondered if it could be different this time.

She hoped it would, but she was afraid it wouldn't be. Her mind and heart were in opposition, making her a battleground between hope and fear.

Courtney was in Ted's office pouring over cost projections trying to find the money to keep up her loan payments and breed her mares when the sound of Seth's

Jaguar barreling up the drive caused her to look up. She was surprised when he jumped out of the car and ran up to the office. Seth never ran. It wasn't part of his image.

"I've got another surprise," he announced as he bounded in the door, grinning from ear to ear. Courtney had never seen him act so unlike his normally calm, cool, controlled self.

"I can see your hands, so it can't be lobsters," Courtney said.

"Lobsters?" questioned Ted, looking up from his work.

"Seth brought lobsters by for dinner a couple of days ago." A look Courtney couldn't categorize passed over Ted's face; but it was quickly gone, and he found a reason to take himself off. "Now you've scared him away."

"Nothing like that. Ted just knows when he's needed at the other end of the farm."

Courtney couldn't suppress a grin.

"Guess what your surprise is."

"I have no earthly idea. Give me a hint."

"What do you want more than anything else right now?"

"Seth Cameron, if you've come here just to embarrass me . . ." Courtney began, her eyes narrowing at the thoughts that crossed her mind.

"No, that's what *I* want," Seth said, mercilessly teasing her. "What have you been worrying about for weeks?"

"Gus? The farm? How to pay off the loans?"

Seth shook his head at each answer.

"You?" Courtney asked in desperation, but Seth shook his head again. "I give up. What is it?"

"You've got to guess."

"Look, I can't stand here playing games with you. Somehow I've got to come up with the money for the stud fees for the mares—"

"That's it."

"What's it?"

"What you said, what you guessed."

"Seth, if you don't stop driving me crazy, I'm going . . ." Courtney froze, and her gaze locked with Seth's. "Do you mean the mares?"

"Yes," Seth replied with a satisfied sigh. "I've managed to find you two seasons to Unbridled." Courtney hesitated, waiting for the part of the agreement she couldn't accept. "The fee's the same, you will have full ownership of the foals, and you don't have to pay the second half of the fee until the foals stand and nurse." Courtney let out a whoop and leapt for Seth like he was a life raft in the midst of white water. He caught her effortlessly.

"That's perfect," she said, after giving him a spontaneous kiss. "I'll have won the Derby by then. Wait till I tell Ted."

"Wait a minute," Seth protested as she tried to remove herself from his arms. "Is one measly kiss all the thanks I get?"

"What more do you want? Let me rephrase that," Courtney added quickly. "What do you think would be a suitable reward? I think I'd better try one more time," Courtney said when Seth looked upon her with obvious intent. "Would you like to come to dinner sometime next week, say Tuesday night?"

"I'm ready for dinner right now," he growled.

"That's why I asked you for next week. Maybe you'll be calm enough by then to concentrate on food."

"You're a cruel woman, Courtney Clonninger."

"And you, Mr. Cameron, are the most persistent creature on earth."

* * *

"What are you thinking?" Courtney asked Seth. They were lying in bed after making love.

"I was just thinking about the first time I saw you, standing against that fence, your hair blowing in the breeze, and Gus showing off in the field. It seems like only yesterday."

"It was months ago."

"I know. You're a very difficult woman to catch."

"Have you pursued many?"

"Why is it I have a feeling the ground is about to open up underneath my feet?"

"Okay, that was an unfair question. I always seem to be doing that. I'll rephrase it. According to the many men you meet and compare notes with in your endless hobnobbing all over the world, did I take an inordinate amount of convincing?"

"I've never felt about any other woman the way I feel about you, so I've never pursued anyone like this before," Seth said, putting his verbal feet down very gingerly indeed. "But I would guess that some other men might think you were overly cautious before committing yourself."

Courtney's peal of laughter woke up Hamlet, who was lying outside the door. He gave a "woof" to protest being locked out of the bedroom.

"You ought to be a politician. You'd never be misquoted because you'd never say anything anyone could understand."

"I'm told that for a man to compare the woman he's with to any other woman on earth is to commit an act of the greatest folly. Setting my heart on catching you was folly enough for me."

"And do you think you've got me?"

"No. I wonder if I ever will. I sometimes feel our time together is borrowed, that any minute I'll be told it's up."

"People probably shouldn't stay together very long. Their lives are bound to get all snarled up."

"Don't you want something that lasts forever?"

"I don't even want to think about forever."

"Dammit, Courtney, you can't stick your head in the sand."

"I'm not. I just refuse to worry about any more than right now. Maybe, when I get everything here squared away. . . . Nothing is ever what it seems."

"Look at me," Seth demanded, forcing her to look squarely at him. "I love you. That's exactly what it sounds like. I love you and want to spend the rest of my life with you."

"I love you, too, but I don't want to talk about the rest of my life," Courtney protested. "Why can't we settle for what we have here and now?"

"I can't, and I don't think you can."

"But I can. I don't want to think of marriage and children and eternal commitment. I'm not sure it's for me."

Seth thought she sounded defensive. "I think you'd like it."

"You might not love me forever."

"Why?"

"My parents didn't. Grandpa didn't either. They're my family. If they couldn't love me, nobody can. There's something wrong with me. You'll find it, and then you'll leave, too."

"Courtney, you know there's nothing wrong with you."

"Then, why couldn't they love me?" she said.

The pain in her eyes convinced him she was not being coy. No matter how foolish he might think her fears, to Courtney they were at the core of the way she saw herself.

If he was going to convince her, he was going to have to show her, and she had already made it plain he couldn't earn her trust by helping her with the farm.

"I didn't know your parents or grandfather so I can't explain what happened, but I can promise you I'll never stop loving you. As long as you want me, I'll be here. I'll never go away unless you send me away."

"Don't talk about forever, and don't talk about me sending you away," Courtney pleaded. "Just hold me. Your arms are concrete, real, and when your love is no longer strong enough to keep me warm, I'll have something to remember." When Seth started to protest, Courtney kissed him into silence. "Don't make promises. Just hold me."

So Seth held her close, wondering all the while what it would take to convince Courtney she was worthy of love, that her family hadn't failed her through any fault of her own. He felt impotent to slay the dragon that stood between them, a dragon he had yet to find a way to reach.

Sometime later that evening the telephone rang, long and insistently, but it went unheeded. It rang again later that night, but Courtney was asleep by then and didn't hear it.

TEN

Courtney was surprised to see Clay Marchmont coming from the parking lot, but she was even more surprised to see Jerry Flanery right behind him. She couldn't stand the man; but he had been one of her grandfather's cronies, and she'd always been polite to him because of it.

He had made his money in real estate and stock market speculation, but he had a farm about two miles away where he raised horses. Over the years he had competed with her grandfather to see who could produce the best two-year-old, a competition her grandfather had always won until the last decade.

"Is Ted about?" Clay asked without his normal genial greeting. He looked so serious Courtney knew something was wrong.

"He's in his office. Can I help?"

"I sure as hell hope so," Clay said, giving Flanery a hard glare, "but I want Ted in on this, too."

They headed for the farm office in silence, another unusual circumstance. Courtney racked her brain for the possible cause of this surprise visit.

"It seems that another of your grandfather's loans has come to light," Clay said as soon as they were seated in Ted's office. "I'll let Mr. Flanery tell you what he told me less than an hour ago."

"I'm sorry to cause you distress," Flanery said, turning his hard, appraising gaze on Courtney. "When your grandfather asked for the money, I thought I'd be able to let him have it indefinitely—"

"But you've had recent financial reverses," Courtney interrupted, her tone cynical.

Flanery didn't look pleased. "Never that, Miss Clonninger," he said with a smile that didn't even pretend to be genuine. "I've just come across a business opportunity too good to pass up. As all my money is tied up at the moment, I thought of the million dollars you owe me."

"A million dollars!" Ted's face went as white as a sheet.

Outwardly, Courtney forced herself to remain calm, but her insides contracted into a double knot. Was there no end to her grandfather's loans? Even though the farm was making, a good profit at last, she didn't know how they could meet the demands, of this new obligation.

"What are your terms?" Courtney asked coldly.

"Well now, I wouldn't like to upset you with a whole lot of details your lawyer and I can handle."

"I have the final say on every decision made on this farm," Courtney said, her jaw too rigid for perfect enunciation. "What are your terms?"

"Your grandfather wanted the money immediately, and I had to take something in the way of a small loss to give it to him." Courtney didn't believe that. Judging by their expressions, Ted and Clay didn't, either. "Your grandfather didn't want to pay interest—he thought it was a short-term problem—so we finally agreed to six hundred thousand for the loan and two hundred thousand for each of the next two years if he hadn't repaid the loan. If he hadn't paid me back at the end of three years, the interest would be twenty-five percent a year."

"Twenty-five percent! That would make the interest alone a quarter of a million dollars."

"Not to mention thirty-three percent the first two years," Clay pointed out.

"If your grandfather had paid off the debt at the end of the first year, it wouldn't have cost him anything."

It was impossible for the farm to come up with one and a quarter million dollars in the next year. Even Gus's earnings probably wouldn't come to that.

"Okay, I'll pay you within the year," Courtney said as she started to rise. "If that's all . . ."

Flanery didn't move. "Actually, it's not all," he said with his hard smile. "You see, I need the money now."

"I'm sorry, but I don't have it. You'll have to wait."

"I'm afraid that's not possible. According to the terms of the contract, I can have my money *in cash* within ninety days of making the request. It's really quite generous."

Courtney felt like the wind had been knocked out of her. "I can't believe Grandpa would have entered into such an insane agreement, not even if he did think he could pay you back within three years."

Flanery glanced coldly at Clay.

"He has proof," Clay confirmed. "It's in my briefcase."

Courtney slumped black in her seat while Ted took the document from Clay. He would go over every clause, but Courtney had no doubt it would prove binding.

"I would have been content with a gentleman's agreement," Flanery said, "but your grandfather insisted it be official."

My grandfather my eye, Courtney said to herself. You corralled him, you old thief, and now you intend to take it out of my hide.

"That gives me until September second. I'll have the

money for you then." She didn't know how, but she just wanted to get rid of this old weasel so she could think.

"Clay has told me things are a little awkward for you just now," Flanery said, still showing no sign of rising. "I have an idea that might help you out a bit."

Courtney regarded him with narrowing eyes.

"As you know, I dabble in real estate from time to time. Well, I thought if you didn't have the cash, you might be willing to trade a few acres of land."

Courtney could almost see the sword pointed at her heart. "Just how many acres did you have in mind?"

"You must remember we're talking about farm land, so at twenty-five hundred an acre, and I'm being generous with that figure, I guess four hundred acres would just about cover it."

Ted almost rose out of his chair, but Courtney's gaze never wavered. She didn't flinch. "And just which four hundred of my acres did you have in mind?"

"I thought the land around the lake and along the creek would do." That land was in the center of Idle Hour. Even if Flanery used it for horses, the traffic would seriously disrupt the farm.

"And what did you intend to do with the land once you had it?"

"I haven't decided. I just thought of it."

"But you must have some ideas."

"Well naturally, that's only good business. I could use it for horses. That wouldn't require any additional investment."

"But that wouldn't make much money."

"I see you've inherited your grandfather's brains," Flanery said.

It's just as well since I've inherited his debts, Courtney thought.

"I could develop it. Maybe put in a golf course."

"Or a housing development, or a shopping center, or an office complex," Courtney said, rising. "You will have your money, Mr. Flanery, in cash, on September second. Now, if you will excuse us—"

"Now, don't be hasty, lass."

"Our business is finished. Good day."

Flanery heaved himself out of his seat. "I'll expect to hear from you by the end of the week," he barked at Clay.

Flanery left without even looking at Courtney.

"What are my options?" Courtney said, turning to Clay. She didn't want to think or feel the desperate fear that clutched at her heart. She had managed to get over all the other hurdles. She would get over this one, too.

"It's impossible to raise that much cash in three months without selling something."

"I mean to borrow."

"You can't borrow any more money, Courtney. The banks won't give you a cent."

"But my debts aren't that great. There's always the land as collateral."

"Your land is already encumbered. It's the only reason your grandfather got the loans."

"But I still have more money in land than debts."

"You're not considered a good risk. I've come across more loans, one of them from Argentina."

"But you've said nothing about payments . . ."

Clay looked embarrassed. "I was able to delay the payments for right now, but they must begin next year."

"How much do they come to?"

Clay told her.

"Then, there's no way I could borrow the money?"

"None at all, at least not until the farm is able to generate a greater income. No one is going to lend you money until you've proved you're capable of reducing your debt, not even with Gus's future earnings as a consideration."

"Then, he'll just have to wait."

"He won't. If you don't pay him by September second, he will take you to court."

Later, several hours of brain-cracking thought still hadn't produced an answer. Courtney was convinced she could manage the debt if Flanery would just give her time, even at his usurious twenty-five percent. It was the September deadline that terrified her.

"I'm in a real bind this time," Courtney told Seth when she saw him that afternoon.

"I'd give you the cash if I had it," Seth said, "but I don't have that kind of money lying around, not during the sales season."

"I wouldn't take it if you offered it to me," Courtney said, a little stiffly. "Letting you find boarders for me is one thing. Accepting a million dollars is quite another."

"Then, how are you going to get it?"

"I don't know," Courtney said. "Do you have any ideas?"

"Several, but you won't like any of them."

"I rarely do," Courtney said, making a half-hearted attempt to smile, "but that's no reason not to listen."

"Okay, first sell some of your least useful land. Let me finish," Seth said when Courtney started to interrupt him. "You can get a better price than Flanery's offering. You could choose which acreage to sell, who you sold it to, and put some controls on what they could do with it."

Courtney shook her head. "Right now my land is the only way I have to make money. I can't cut into it."

"Then, try a combination sale. Sell the house, one mare and foal, and only enough land to make up the difference."

Courtney shook her head again. "I've got to have somewhere to live, even though I don't need a place this big," she added when Seth glanced toward the sprawling mansion and cocked an eyebrow. "And I need the mare and foal for the future."

"I've saved the best option for last," Seth said dryly. "It also has the virtue of being the easiest one to complete before the deadline."

Courtney didn't dare allow herself hope. This was his last suggestion, and he still hadn't mentioned Gus.

"You could syndicate Gus, selling only enough to raise the money."

Courtney stiffened.

"You could retain enough shares to keep complete control, but you'd have the cash. Gus hasn't even started yet, but Barry tells me he's been attracting a lot of attention. People are dropping by all the time to talk, but they always end up in front of Gus's stall. I know I could get you a million for a third ownership. If things work out just right, I might even get it for a quarter."

"I'll never sell Gus," Courtney repeated, but for the first time she felt her resolution weakening. She needed every acre for the income it would bring if she was to keep up her payments on the farm debt. The mares and foals would be a drain on her for the next few years—especially when it came to paying stud fees—but she needed them for future income. Selling the house wasn't much different from having a development in the middle of the farm. She wouldn't get top dollar if she put on restrictions. But without them, the buyer could do anything he wanted, including tear down the house and put up condominiums.

But not Gus. He was at the center of everything she had worked for since her grandfather's death. His earnings were going to give her the means to restore the farm to its former glory, not just pay its debts. She couldn't do that if she started selling pieces of him.

"I can't sell Gus," she said with a heavy sigh, "not even part of him."

"Courtney, I hate to be the one to tell you this—it really ought to have come from Clay—but if you don't make up your mind to sell something, you're going to lose everything."

"That can't happen as long as I keep up my loan payments."

"If Flanery sues, your other creditors will probably file as well. With your present financial situation, the only way you could keep the farm would be to file for bankruptcy. If that happens, you risk losing control of the farm and the horses. If Flanery or anyone else can convince the judge you won't be able to pay your debts, the judge can decide to sell your horses and land if he thinks it's the best way to satisfy your creditors."

Courtney felt like she was being sucked into a black void. No matter which way she turned, things got worse. Neither Ted nor Clay nor Seth could figure a way out that didn't involve selling something. How did she think she was going to succeed? Yet she couldn't agree to sell Gus, not even a part of him.

"I'll have to think about it," she said. She could tell from the look on Seth's face he was surprised. "I'm not stupid. I know I'm boxed in, but I haven't given up yet. I'll let you know in a couple of days."

"You'd better have your answer ready by the end of

the week." He paused. "I wish there was something else
I could suggest. I know how much Gus means to you."

"Nobody knows what Gus means to me," Courtney said
through gritted teeth. "It'll be like tearing out my heart."

"Okay, have it your way. I'll call you tonight."

"I won't have decided."

"I know. I'll call you anyway." He gave her a quick kiss
and was gone.

Courtney walked to the house in such a daze she almost
closed the door on Hamlet. She placed a quick phone
call to Gus's trainer. As she had expected, he wasn't in,
but she left word he was to call her the minute he returned. She wandered about the huge house, and as
usual, whenever she came to a crisis, she ended up before
the portrait of her grandfather.

"Don't you ever let up?" she asked aloud. "You let me
think I'm going to make it; then you hit me with another
loan." She turned angrily to the portrait across the room.
"You hated this place," she flung at her father. "You told
Grandpa you'd like to see it in ashes. Well, it looks like
you're about to get your wish."

Even though she'd tried to make herself and everyone
else believe otherwise, all she'd ever wanted her whole
life was someone to love her, someone to hold her when
things went wrong, someone to stand behind her when
she had to make tough decisions. But she drove people
away. Every time she found herself at a crisis point, she
ended up standing in an empty room facing the future
alone, haunted by the past.

Her father seemed to stare down at her, his faint smile
tinged with melancholy.

Ever since her grandfather died, Courtney had looked
upon Idle Hour and then Gus as all she had left in the
world, but this unending struggle just to hold on was tear-

ing the heart out of her. Now it looked like she was going to lose everything just before Gus could race and start the farm on the long climb back. The jarring ring of the phone interrupted her thoughts.

"Barry? Courtney Clonninger . . . I'm glad Gus is doing so well . . . Yes, I get your reports every week. Look, I know we talked about going slowly with him, but something has come up and I've got to come up with some cash quickly . . . A million dollars . . . You don't have to tell me it's a lot. Can you push up his schedule? . . . No, I don't want you to run him before he's ready, but there must be some easy races . . . As many as you can . . . That few? But that won't even be half of what I need . . . Are you sure that's all? I never realized how many races it took to win a million dollars . . . Well, plan on the two big ones and keep your eye open for something else . . . I know, but three races in two months is not a lot . . . I'm coming to the track next week. We can talk more then . . . Yeah, you, too. Bye."

Courtney had been pacing the floor while she spoke on the phone, too tense to sit down, but now that another option had been taken away from her, she felt too weak to stand and sank into the sofa. She sat for so long without moving that Hamlet gave up and went to sleep.

She had been driven to her last option. She had to call her father.

Her whole body shook at the thought of speaking to him. For several months after her grandfather's death, she had lived in fear he might show up and she would be forced to deal with that part of her life.

But he was alive, he was still her father, and her grandfather had said he was very rich. Up until now she hadn't considered talking to him. How could she call him up and ask for money?

But it took only a moment for Courtney to realize it came down to a matter of sacrificing her pride or everything she had worked for. This was the only solution that remained. She had to call him.

With unsteady fingers Courtney dialed the number. She made a mistake and had to begin again, but finally the phone started to ring. This can't possibly be Hong Kong, she thought to herself. It's loud enough to be next door. Suddenly, the phone stopped ringing. Someone had picked it up. Courtney waited breathlessly to hear the sound of her father's voice for the first time in twenty years.

"Hello," said a feminine voice with a subtle accent. "This is Mrs. Stephen Clonninger. May I help you?"

His wife! He was married.

Courtney slammed down the receiver.

"You can syndicate Gus," Courtney snapped at Seth when he came by two days later, "but I won't sell more than a quarter of him."

She was in a savage mood and didn't care if she sounded ungrateful. She had tried to call her father two more times. Once there had been no answer. The second time the same woman answered, this time in Chinese—at least it sounded liked that—and Courtney had hung up. She didn't know why, but talking to the woman who had taken her mother's place was worse than talking to her father. In the end she decided she couldn't talk to him at all, much less ask him for money.

"I can't guarantee anything, but I ought to be able to get that much."

"You're supposed to be the hotshot salesman," Courtney said sarcastically. "Prove it." The fact that Seth was taking extraordinary pains to be gentle with her only made her angrier.

"A lot depends on what Gus does in his most recent workout, the gossip along the back stretch, and whether I can find two buyers willing to bid against each other."

"So now they're having to *overbid*, are they?" she rasped angrily, pointing an accusing finger. "Are you trying to tell me you don't think Gus is worth the money or that you can't sell him for the price? Maybe I should find myself another horse merchant."

"I'm trying to tell you not to tie my hands," Seth replied quietly. "Let me talk to Barry first. We'll pick the best time for the sale. It's best to sell after a big race, but sometimes it works just as well to sell just before."

"Just do it."

"Taxes will take a big bite out of the sale price. We're going to have to sell for about two hundred thousand extra. That means selling more of the colt."

Courtney exploded. Seth listened quietly, but when she got around to personal observations, his patience snapped.

"Stop right there."

The coldness in his gray eyes caused Courtney to pause on the verge of another intemperate outburst.

"This situation may be none of your doing, but it's none of mine either. If indulging in childish tantrums would change anything, I'd let you raise all the hell you want. But it won't and you know it. You need money, and you have to sell something to get it. These are facts, and you've got to live with them. You don't have to like them, but I do expect you to face them like an adult."

"I know," Courtney said, but she remembered Seth had first come to Idle Hour because he wanted to sell Gus. Well, now he was going to get his chance. The question

Courtney wouldn't let herself ask, but which wouldn't leave her brain, was would he continue to come back after Gus was sold? Courtney knew her fear was prompted by her old feelings of being unlovable, but she couldn't help it. Seth's saying he loved her didn't wipe all that away. His love hadn't survived a crisis yet. "I'm not putting the blame on you, but I can't take this calmly. Let me know everything that's happening. I don't want to be kept in the dark about anything."

But when she went to see her colt two days later, she wasn't sure it wouldn't be easier if she were kept in the dark. Gus was looking gorgeous and training exceptionally well.

"He's a good horse," Barry said, "but he's even better because of your work with him." He grinned. "I've been telling everybody about the great job you did. Don't be surprised if you find yourself swamped with yearlings this fall."

When she watched Gus on the track, it almost broke her heart to know she had to sell a part of him.

"The Sapling Stakes is still three weeks away, but he's ready now."

"Do you think he'll win?" Courtney couldn't believe she was asking that question, not after the times she had insisted he would be a great champion.

"By a mile," Barry assured her. "There's nothing to give him a race except Flanery's horse."

Courtney felt the muscles in her throat constrict. "Flanery's horse?"

"Didn't you know? He's got himself a good one this time. He's undefeated in five races."

"He won't be in the Sapling?"

"No, but we'll meet him in the Hopeful."

"And?"

"My money says Gus will beat the pants off him."

Courtney tried to take comfort in Barry's confidence, but to be beaten by Flanery's horse would be a bitter, bitter defeat.

"Barry and I agree we ought to schedule the sale for the day after the Sapling," Seth said a week later. "We can take him up to Saratoga. All the buyers will be there for the yearling sales. It couldn't be a more perfect setup."

"I'm serious about not selling more than twenty-five percent."

"The way things are shaping up, we won't have to."

Two weeks later Courtney stood in the winner's circle accepting congratulations for Gus's easy victory in the Sapling Stakes. Even before she could leave her box, the TV announcer was talking about the possible match-up with Flanery's Pride in next month's Hopeful Stakes.

"We always knew he was a good horse," Courtney said to the announcer. "We just didn't know how good until today."

"Your trainer tells me he's going to run in the Hopeful. You know Flanery's Pride will be in the same race. No horse has been closer than five lengths to him at the wire."

"We're looking forward to meeting Flanery's horse," Barry answered when the words stuck in Courtney's throat.

"He and my grandfather had a friendly rivalry for years," Courtney managed to say. "I mean to carry on the tradition."

* * *

"It's scheduled for the tenth," Seth said over the phone. He had been flying all over the country.

Courtney would have given half the money Gus won to have him close enough to hold her in his arms. "I'll be there."

"I see he's running in the Saratoga Special the previous day."

"We decided he needed an extra race to be ready for the Hopeful. Who are the buyers?"

"You won't know them," Seth said, "but I didn't invite anyone who wouldn't agree to your complete control of the horse. I've been telling everyone all they're buying is the honor of paying one quarter of his bills and standing in the winner's circle next to you. You'd be surprised what an inducement that has turned out to be. I miss you."

"Me, too," Courtney said. "You know I didn't mean any of the things I said, don't you?"

"I never thought you did, though the language you used was a bit of a shock."

"I could start saying *bloody* like Marcia."

"I like it better when you cuss in English. How are you holding up? Are the reporters still bothering you?"

"They didn't follow me back to Lexington." She paused briefly. "I'll be coming up before the race. Will you be there?"

"I won't get in until the morning of the tenth. Save dinner for me."

"Spoils to the victor?"

"Something like that."

But Courtney didn't feel like a victor. She had put Gus's winnings in the bank with the hope of buying a brood mare in the fall. But knowing she was making the first step toward putting the farm back into the top ranks of thoroughbred racing farms didn't give her the feeling of satisfaction and happiness she had expected. It couldn't, not with Gus's sale hanging over her head. She would never get used to anyone else owning part of him. It would be the same as owning part of her.

"Do they pester you?" Courtney asked Barry after she sent the last quote-hungry reporter away. She hadn't had a minute to herself since Gus's win in the Saratoga Special the day before.

"All the time. He's the only horse they think can give Flanery's Pride some competition. They've been playing it up for a month. But Gus is getting better every day. When I think of how good he could be, it scares me. If I were a betting man, I'd put some big money on him in Vegas. Gus is certain to go off at a very long price for the Hopeful Stakes. Nobody thinks he can beat Flanery's Pride."

"I've never bet either," Courtney replied absently, "not even when I had the money."

"Here comes Seth with his money merchants," Barry muttered. "Time to give Fate's old roulette wheel a spin, but I wish we didn't have to put any part of Gus on the block."

"You can't wish it any more than I do," Courtney said bitterly and turned to face the potential buyers.

"I have to give him credit for finding buyers who're truly interested in racing," Barry whispered. "Ali Haiam is the most successful of the Arabs. What he spends on horses in one year would make your grandfather's head spin. The Englishman is Barry Hite-Wilkins. He inherited half an English county and seems determined to cover it with horses. The other man is Ito Suzo. I don't know what he does, but he buys horses by the van load."

Much to her surprise, Courtney found she was not expected to participate in the discussion. The groom led Gus out of his stall, and the buyers directed their questions to Seth or Barry. Whether it was due to English reserve or Eastern disdain, no one paid her any attention. She didn't mind. She was sure if she opened her mouth it would be to say the wrong thing.

Seth didn't say much either, just asked a question now and then which served to keep everyone talking. Finally, after about twenty minutes, Seth said it was time to start bidding.

"The price is fixed at one million, two hundred thousand American dollars," he said. "You'll be bidding on how much of the horse you can buy for that amount."

"Is there no chance I can buy the horse outright?" Mr. Suzo asked.

"None."

"I'll bid forty percent," said Hite-Wilkins.

"Thirty-five," replied Haiam, but before anyone could bid further, a small crowd of people came around the corner of the barn and bore down on them with angry determination.

"This guy tells us you're about to sell Red Phoenix abroad," one of the men demanded of Seth. "Why don't you give the Americans a chance to keep him here?"

"We're only selling a percentage of him," Seth replied. "I thought the price tag might be a little too steep."

"What is the price?"

"One point two million. The question is how much that will buy."

"Sounds like a forced sale to raise cash."

"Control of the horse remains with his owner," Seth told them.

"I bid thirty percent."

"Twenty-nine."

"And America bids twenty-eight," the outspoken, angry man said.

"You cannot bid," stated Mr. Suzo. "You were not invited."

"Our money's as good as anybody else's."

"But whose money is it?" asked Hite-Wilkins. "Is it a private offer or do you represent a syndicate?"

"I'm sorry I didn't inform you of the sale," Seth said soothingly, "but as you haven't been bonded, Mr. Firestone, I can't allow—"

"I'm bonded," announced Andre duPont. "I can write you a personal check for the whole amount."

"I will top your bid at twenty-seven percent," said Hite-Wilkins.

"Twenty-six," responded Haiam.

"Twenty-five," Firestone and duPont countered simultaneously.

"Mr. Cameron, I must protest the presence of these men. You assured me—"

"That you wouldn't have any competition but an English farmer and a desert sheik," interrupted Firestone. "You won't steal this horse that easily."

Courtney listened in stunned amazement as the argument continued to escalate despite Seth's efforts to mediate. Within minutes everyone was furiously shouting insults at everyone else. The reporters, scenting a good story, were pointing their microphones as close to the mouths of the enraged combatants as they dared.

Courtney cringed at the thought of the headlines the next day.

"The sale is off," she blurted out. Instantly the microphones were aimed at her. "I'm sorry if you've been put to any trouble, but the sale is canceled."

"But you assured me the horse would definitely be sold," Mr. Haiam complained to Seth.

"Mr. Cameron has nothing to do with this," Courtney said. "Red Phoenix is my horse, and I'm not selling him."

The Americans and the reporters seemed pleased. Seth was angry, but the three buyers were furious.

"You assured us of a sale," repeated a livid Mr. Haiam. "It is not acceptable that you go back on your word."

"I am sorry, but Miss Clonninger does own the horse."

"She is a woman," Haiam said just as if it would make Courtney disappear.

"An irrational woman, but she is still the owner," snapped Hite-Wilkins. "You should chose your clients more carefully, Mr. Cameron, or in the future you may find your buyers greatly reduced in number."

"Do not call me when you change your mind," Haiam said to Seth, blandly ignoring Courtney. "I will not be interested."

"I am gravely displeased," Mr. Suzo said quietly as he left.

"I'm sorry," Courtney said to Seth after everyone had gone, "but I just couldn't let them have Gus, not with all the fighting."

"Don't you understand anything about selling horses?" Seth exploded. "Have you been hiding away on that farm for so long your brain is incapable of assimilating anything more complicated than breeding rights and sore muscles? That *fighting,* as you call it, was going to be the factor that would get your money for a twenty percent share, or less. Do you think I chose buyers from three different countries by accident? How do you think five of the richest Americans at Saratoga just *happened* to find out about this sale and just *happened* to turn up as the bidding started? And who do you think tipped off the reporters so the buyers would be spurred on by national pride?

"Dammit to hell, Courtney, I worked on this sale for a month, planning everything down to the last detail, and you blow the whole thing wide open with your blind determination to own every hair on that damned horse's hide. Well, you've got him, at least for as long as Flanery and the courts will let you keep him, but don't come to me next time. You'll have to get out of this one alone. But then, you've always wanted to do everything by yourself, haven't you?"

"Seth, please, I didn't understand—"

"You'll have to excuse me. You've just driven off three of my best buyers. I've got to see if I can mollify them, or I may find myself in bankruptcy court alongside you."

"Seth, I'm so sorry. I didn't mean . . ."

But Seth didn't hear her. He was gone.

Seth was so furious he didn't dare go after his enraged buyers right then. He couldn't calm them down when he was so angry himself. He had always known Courtney didn't have a good grip on reality, that her fanatical devotion to the farm and Gus got in the way of her seeing things clearly, but he had thought she had enough sense to let him run the sale. Didn't she have any confidence in his ability to get the most money for the smallest share of Gus? She told him she thought he was the best horse merchant in Kentucky. But when he finally had a chance to prove it, she pulled the rug out from under him.

He knew how much Gus meant to her. That's why he'd really put himself out to organize this particular sale. And it had been working even better than he dared hope. He probably could have gotten the money for as little as fifteen percent of Gus. Everybody would have sworn he was a genius.

Now they were more likely think he was a fool to endanger his professional stature in an attempt to rescue a woman who seemed determined to propel herself into bankruptcy court.

Why couldn't Courtney trust him? He knew more about the business world than she did. More about the horse business, too. He was more adept at making hard judgments, critical decisions. He only wanted to use his knowledge and expertise to help her, to protect her. If she would only let him, he'd have that farm making money hand over fist in less than a year. And he wouldn't mind the work. He loved her. He'd do anything for her.

You're better off out of this mess, the little voice whispered. It had been nagging at him for days, warning him to beware of loving Courtney, that giving his heart to a woman like her would get it thrown back at him again. He had pointed out to the little pest more than once that it was too late for preventive measures, that he'd already lost his heart. Then be thankful you've been given a second chance to escape, the voice urged. Run.

Seth had no intentions of running. He loved Courtney. Nothing could change that. He didn't want to change it, but he thought it might be best if he kept his distance until he could think through the situation calmly. Besides, that might give Courtney time to decide she'd been foolish to turn her back on his help.

ELEVEN

They hadn't spoken in more than a week. Seth hadn't called her, and she didn't have the courage to call him. She had gone over every word and action of that horrible sale, but she couldn't figure out how she was supposed to know it was a setup. She supposed if she could have guessed, the buyers would have, too. Barry said Saratoga was still buzzing about the sale, and that Seth's buyers were still keeping their distance. Courtney felt terribly guilty every time she even thought about Seth, which was almost all the time.

She forced herself to stop pacing up and down the library. She picked up the latest issue of the *Daily Racing Form*, then threw it back down. A picture of Flanery's Pride covered half the front page. He had won the Sanford by fifteen lengths and was the odds-on favorite for the Hopeful Stakes. Some bookmakers were already quoting odds on him for next year's Kentucky Derby. Articles predicting he would be the two-year-old champion appeared in the paper almost every day. Everyone seemed to have forgotten Gus was undefeated, too.

I hope Barry does decide to put a bet on Gus, Courtney thought as she pushed aside the booth she'd been studying. He could really clean up.

A thought struck her that was so shocking she sank

down into her chair with a plop. She immediately dismissed it, but it wouldn't go away. She studied it from every angle for fifteen minutes, then, dismissing it again, headed outside to finish her chores. She managed to forget the crazy notion in the rush to get through the second half of the day, but the minute she came back to the house the idea burst on her again.

No matter what she did, she couldn't get it out of her head. Through a restless evening and a sleepless night it gnawed away at her. It was a crazy gamble, but it wasn't impossible. And if it worked, she would be free of Flanery's threat and his debt. If it didn't, well, she wouldn't be much worse off than she was now. She would still have to call her father.

But every time she decided she couldn't do anything so completely against her nature, against everything she'd been taught, she remembered Seth's wrathful expression. She couldn't face him until she figured out a way to pay off Flanery. She had not only refused his help. She had flung it back in his face in front of several reporters and some of the wealthiest men in the world. She had exposed him to backstretch gossip and public jibes from newspaper columnists. After a morning of stomach-churning indecision, she made up her mind. Calling her father would destroy her pride, and she had very little left. Another failure couldn't make things much worse.

Hovering indecisively between driving over to see Flanery or using the phone, Courtney ultimately decided it would be best to call. She had to be in complete command of the situation. She doubted she could control her expression—she disliked Flanery too much and the success of her plan was too important to her—but she could control her voice.

She sat down and carefully planned out every word she

intended to say, thought through every possible response. Only when she was certain she had covered every eventuality did she pick up the phone. If Seth could plan his sale in minute detail, so could she.

Flanery was out, but he called back before Courtney's nerves completely unraveled. She very carefully positioned the microphone of a portable tape recorder next to the mouthpiece of the extension phone.

"This is Courtney Clonninger. I called to congratulate you on Flanery's Pride's victory in the Sanford." She used the la-dee-da accent she and Marcia had perfected years ago when they were children and would pretend to be society matrons. "It must have been quite spectacular . . ." She tried to keep her voice casual, but it was all she could do to keep it from shaking. ". . . Grandpa always said you'd breed a really good horse someday . . . Yes, I know his bloodlines, and I must admit that has me worried just the tiniest bit. Don't you think he's a little short on stamina? . . . Oh, goodness me, I don't mean to imply some ordinary horse could beat him, but what will happen when he comes up against a really good horse with sound distance ability, a horse like Red Phoenix, for instance. Well, Flanery's Pride just might find the assignment a little too tough . . . Mr. Flanery, I'm not trying to disparage your horse, but my trainer says Red Phoenix is going to win in a cakewalk . . ." Barry hadn't said anything of the kind, but Courtney couldn't quibble at a lie now. ". . . I know how proud you are of your horse, and that's really why I called. I thought rather than see him embarrassed by Red Phoenix you might want to enter him in some other race . . . Mr. Flanery! There's no call to use that kind of language. I was just trying to be helpful. If you don't care whether Red Phoenix beats your horse to flinders in front of the entire membership of

the Jockey Club, then I don't . . . Of course I'm willing
to put my money where my mouth is . . . You know I
can't do that, but there is something else I might consider. If Red Phoenix wins, you won't demand cash for
my loan, but will allow me to pay it off, without interest,
as quickly as I can . . . Of course, I wouldn't think of
pressuring you. If you're not sure Flanery's Pride can beat
Red Phoenix . . . I don't know why I should pay a penalty
if I lose. You'll be getting your money either way . . . Well,
suppose I agree not to tell everyone you took advantage
of a dying man to lend him six hundred thousand dollars
at thirty-three percent interest. Horsemen stick together,
Mr. Flanery, and you'd be run out of Lexington if that
ever got around . . . You should be ashamed to use such
language to a lady . . . Not all women are stupid even if
they are ladies, but I still don't think you want this
known . . . It would be impolite to call a lady a liar, and
not particularly wise, since I have the whole conversation
on tape . . . Mr. Flanery! I blush to hear you talk so. I
fear I shall have to hang up . . . Just remember our little
bet, and my tape recorder."

Courtney hung up the phone and collapsed on the
sofa. Her heart was beating so fast her chest hurt. She
forced herself to get up and walk slowly around the room
and take deep, slow breaths. She wasn't done yet. The
riskiest part of her plan was yet to come.

Five minutes later Courtney was on the phone again,
but this time she was making a transatlantic call to Marcia
Ribbesdale's husband in England.

"Hello, Gerald? This is Courtney. No, don't call Marcia," she said quickly. "I've already talked to her about
the baby this week. I wanted to speak to you . . . Thanks,
I always knew he was a good horse. Look, I hate to impose
on you, but I don't know who else to ask. There's some-

thing I must have done, but it's got to be done in absolute secrecy." In spite of a dozen explosive "bloody hells," Courtney managed to tell Gerald what she wanted and agreed to wait by the phone until he called back. She was chewing her last fingernail down to the quick when the phone rang.

"I got several different quotes, but the odds average out to about six-to-one. Courtney, are you bloody sure you want to do this?"

"I'm absolutely bloody sure I *don't* want to do it, but I have no choice. I want two hundred thousand dollars placed with as many bookmakers as it takes. I've got to make a million dollars."

"What happens if this bloody horse of yours doesn't win? He could be left at the gate, step on a nail, or come down with a fever. English bookmakers don't refund money once it's bet, not for any reason."

"I know. And American banks don't make loans to horse farms overly burdened by debts. I'll have the bank transfer the money immediately."

"Why don't you do this in America? You can probably get the same bloody odds at the track."

"You know if I bet that much money on Gus at the track or in Vegas, it would ruin the odds. If I tried to bet that much with bookies, I'd probably be arrested. Besides, it's absolutely essential that no one guess what I'm doing. The minute I withdraw the money from the bank, it's going to be all over Lexington. It won't stampede my creditors if they know I've transferred the money to you. They'll assume I'm buying a horse."

Courtney's last call was to the bank. As she put the phone down again, she murmured a fervent prayer that neither Ted nor Clay would find out what she had done until her nerves recovered, hopefully after the Hopeful

Stakes. She didn't think she could face either one of them now.

As for Seth, she didn't dare think about what he was going to say. As for what he would do! Well, she didn't particularly want to think about that either.

Two weeks later Courtney still hadn't seen Seth, but she had talked to him by phone. She decided, however, not to tell him what she intended to do about Flanery. When his questioning became too insistent, she told him she had until a week after the Hopeful to decide.

"You're not leaving me much time to arrange a sale."

"I'm going to do it myself," Courtney told him. "I jeopardized your reputation the last time. I won't do that again."

Seth insisted he wasn't worried about his reputation, but Courtney held firm.

"What have you got in mind?" he asked.

"It's my secret."

"Nothing harebrained, I hope."

She wasn't sure he believed her, but she couldn't trust anyone with her secret. Not even Ted. "You'll find out."

During the days that followed, Courtney tried to act as though she hadn't a worry in the world, but she couldn't keep her mind off her bets. At least a dozen times a day she wondered how she could have done anything so insane. She, who had never wagered so much as a nickel in her life, had bet virtually every cent she had on the outcome of a horse race. She didn't need to remember her grandfather's words to know she had done a foolish thing, but every time she went over her line of reasoning, she came up with the same solution. There was nothing else she could have done.

Hoping to avoid as much of the prerace tension as possible, she stayed in Lexington until the last minute. When she finally did arrive in Saratoga, the knowledge that she would soon see Seth and know the outcome of the race kept her too agitated to think straight. She decided that in her present state it would probably be best not to meet Seth at all. She didn't want to go to the barn and talk to Barry about Gus, either. She didn't want to see anyone she knew. She actually considered watching the race from her hotel room.

But once she arrived at her hotel, she changed her mind. She was scared silly and as nervous as a cat, but she wasn't a coward. She took a cab to the racetrack shortly after midmorning.

Courtney arrived at the track wearing a stunning green dress chosen especially to complement her eyes and hair. She hoped the fact that it emphasized her figure as well wouldn't go unnoticed. She wore a straw hat with a huge, floppy brim that provided her some small protection from the sun and prying eyes. She had no sooner entered the guests' clubhouse than she was hailed from across the huge room by Catherine Offill, probably the one female in the world she most disliked. It was impossible to escape, so Courtney pinned a smile to her face and walked forward.

"Courtney, Courtney Clonninger," Catherine trilled at the top of her lungs, thereby informing everyone in the clubhouse that the owner of Red Phoenix had arrived. "I was wondering when you would get here. You certainly are cutting things a little close. But then, maybe you're not overly anxious to find out how Red Phoenix measures up against Flanery's Pride."

"I'm quite confident," Courtney replied. *Liar. You're scared to death.*

Catherine gave Courtney's outfit a careful and jealous

scrutiny. "Things can't be going too badly with the farm if you can afford an outfit like that."

Cat, Courtney thought.

"I wonder who it's for?"

"To impress you, of course," said Courtney in a brittle voice.

"You can't fool me. Seth has already been here looking for you."

"Thank you," Courtney said, more than ready to move on.

"If you'd take a piece of advice from me," Catherine said in a falsely confidential tone, "you'd watch out for Mr. Cameron. Big barracuda gobble up little fish. And from what I hear, Seth has all but swallowed you whole."

Courtney stopped dead in her tracks. "I hope there's something other than malice behind that remark."

"I'm not trying to be mean," Catherine assured her with hollow sincerity, "but I know you've been hidden away on that farm of yours for so long you can't possibly know what goes on in the outside world. Seth Cameron is a handsome man, but he is also very clever. Not that he would do anything that was actually illegal, but he does things every day you'd never think of. I think it's a crime no one has bothered to warn you."

"Warn me?"

"About his buying up your loans."

Courtney had been feeling rather tired from the strain of the last two weeks, but her adrenaline glands immediately started pumping massive doses of stimulant into her veins. She was instantly alert, her body tense, and her fingers gripping her purse until the leather creaked in protest. "Seth is not buying up my loans."

"I *knew* they hadn't told you," Catherine said, spurious concern competing for triumph in her eyes. "It's all very hush-hush," she whispered confidentially, "but my father drew up some of the agreements. He says Seth has been buying up every loan he could get his hands on for the last year. He doesn't know what he means to do with all that land, but it's common knowledge he can't wait to get his hands on Red Phoenix, especially after the way you pulled the rug out from under him a few weeks ago."

"This is nothing but rumor," Courtney snapped.

"If you'd ever set foot off that farm of yours, you'd realize everybody in Lexington knows he's always wanted to sell your colt. He's being seen with those buyers again, the ones you made so angry when you called off the sale. Well, I mean, you figure it."

"I don't know what Seth is doing. I don't keep track of who he sees or what he does," Courtney said with icy disdain, "but I have complete faith in his integrity."

"Well, of course I could be wrong, but at least now you can't say nobody told you. Ta-ta," Catherine trilled and vanished almost as quickly as she had appeared.

Courtney stood glued to the spot, her mind racing. She didn't notice Gerald Ribbesdale's approach.

"How are your nerves holding out? Not very well, I see," Gerald said when Courtney jumped nearly a foot.

"You startled me," Courtney said, sighing with relief.

"If I had nearly a quarter of a million dollars riding on this race, I'd be worried, too. I don't imagine Catherine's spurious concern helps."

"You heard?"

"Yes, along with at least twenty other people."

"She doesn't like me any more than I like her, but I can't imagine why she should want to make up lies about Seth."

"I have no idea what you and Seth have been doing—Marcia keeps me remarkably ill-informed—but Seth has a reputation for being exceptionally ethical in his dealings with his clients. He's also a man who never let's sentiment get in the way of making money."

"I have complete faith in Seth's word and his intentions."

"Good." Gerald seemed to take her word for it. "Now, let's see about getting you a glass of wine. The strain on your nerves must be something awful."

It was, and after Gerald had caught her up on Marcia and the baby and then drifted away to talk with other friends, Courtney decided to go back to the hotel until just before the race. Her mind was in an uproar. She needed time to think, and the members' clubhouse at Saratoga wasn't the place to do it. Too many people wanted to talk to her about Gus and the farm. She didn't want to talk to anybody about anything.

She told herself over and over again she trusted Seth, that he'd never do anything to hurt her. After all he'd tried to do for her, it would be insulting and demeaning to give Catherine's lies one ounce of credence.

But she couldn't stop herself from asking what she'd do if Catherine were right.

Moments later she was in a cab headed back to her hotel.

She knew Seth wasn't trying to sabotage her—she really did—but the knowledge he had bought up her loans angered her. He had no right to interfere. They were her loans, and she was going to pay them off by herself. She couldn't understand why he kept trying to meddle, especially after she'd made it clear she didn't want his help.

The more she thought about it, the angrier she got. She told herself it was just one more proof of his love. She told herself a man didn't shell out that kind of money if his heart wasn't involved. She told herself it didn't matter that everyone in Lexington knew about the mess her grandfather had created. She told herself she was over-reacting because she was upset and nervous and almost beside herself with anxiety over the bet. She told herself all these things over and over, and she got even angrier.

Seth had no right to take on her obligations, especially behind her back. She had explained why she had to do this herself, but he just couldn't seem to understand. Didn't he think she could to anything by herself? Was he afraid she would lose everything if he didn't take over?

The nagging feeling of inferiority, of unworthiness, reared its ugly head. Courtney felt like taking the first plane home, but she knew that wouldn't solve anything. It would actually make things worse. She told herself she would head for the track as soon as she had a few hours of quiet.

Courtney hadn't been in her room twenty minutes when there was a terrific banging at the door and Seth's voice penetrated the barrier between them. Without thought, plan, or preparation, she leapt to her feet, threw open the door, and rushed into his arms.

"Good lord, I've missed you," Seth said as soon as their lips parted.

"I missed you, too," Courtney said, allowing herself to be maneuvered back into the room and the door closed.

"I came as soon as I heard what Catherine said. I've threatened to guillotine her at the finish line if she opens her mouth again."

"It doesn't matter," Courtney said, realizing, to her sur-prise, it really didn't matter. "Not as long as I'm in your arms."

"Do you mean that?" Seth asked.

"Yes. I've wanted to tell you for days, but I was afraid to call."

"I was afraid you were still angry with me," Seth murmured as he kissed her neck and ears.

"I'm not angry now."

Passion and deep desire overcame the need for more words. Their hands moved frantically over each other, racing against the passing seconds to remove each other's clothes. Moments later they fell into bed, their bodies joined in lovemaking that was intensified by the emotions that had kept them apart. There was nothing gentle or tender about their coupling. It was rough, hard, and fast.

A short while later they collapsed, their bodies momentarily drained of energy and emotion.

Seth was the first to speak. "I didn't buy up your loans. And I have no intention of taking over Idle Hour Farm or Gus." He rolled on his side to face Courtney. "I did cosign a few so Clay could renegotiate them to give you a little more time."

Courtney sat up in the bed and pulled the sheet up to cover her breasts. "Do you mean Clay is in on this, too?"

"I did it against his advice."

"Well, all your scheming came to naught when Flanery popped up with his loan," Courtney said, unable to keep an edge off her voice.

"What are you doing about Flanery?"

She averted her gaze. "Don't worry about that."

"You can't keep putting off the inevitable."

"I've told you I'd take care of it." At Seth's skeptical look, so chock full of male superiority, she couldn't hold her tongue. "I may have taken care of the whole thing already."

"What have you done?"

Immediately Courtney wished she'd kept her mouth

shut. She felt particularly vulnerable lying next to him, naked.

"You haven't gotten another loan, have you?"

Well, maybe she could tell him part of it. "It occurred to me that I might to be able take advantage of Flanery's pride in his horse. I got him to agree that if Gus wins today, he will let me repay the loan in a regular way, without his godless twenty-five percent or demand for full payment in cash."

"Did you get him to sign a paper to that effect?" Seth asked. Courtney was pleased to see he was impressed for a change.

"There was no chance of that."

Seth's expression indicated he thought the agreement was worthless. "And what will you do if he wins?"

"I promised never to reveal how he took advantage of my grandfather."

"You can't make that stick. All he has to do is deny it."

"I got the whole conversation on tape."

Seth let out a long whistle. "And if you don't win?"

"I'm still working on that."

"Mind telling me?"

"As a matter of fact, I do."

Seth looked mulish.

"It's really none of your business," Courtney said. "I told you from the beginning I would handle my own debts. I'm trying very hard not to be angry with you for cosigning those loans. I could have died when Catherine announced you had bought them, and I couldn't categorically deny it."

"You could have."

Holding the sheet tightly against her breasts, she turned to Seth, prodding him in the center of his chest to punctuate her words. "Seth Cameron, you know damned well you're always doing things I don't want you to do. You intentionally forget to tell me. I never know what I'm going to find out."

"I only do it because I love you."

"I know that, and it's the only reason I didn't close the door on you."

"You mean that, don't you?"

"I've never put up with so much interference from anybody in my life as I have with you."

"Do you regret it?"

"No."

"Prove it."

She leaned forward to kiss him and was swallowed up in his embrace. His pulled the sheet from her limp grasp, and his hands slipped up to her breast.

"No," she murmured, breaking the kiss abruptly. "I've got to go back to the track."

"There's plenty of time."

"I'll never get dressed."

"I'll help you." Seth's hand was on Courtney's warm flesh, and his touch destroyed all her resistance.

For a short while she completely forgot about Gus and the race and Flanery's Pride.

Courtney looked at her watch for the tenth time. She was certain she was going to be late. She shouldn't have let Seth make love to her a second time, but she couldn't help it. Then the big brute had had the effrontery to tell her he couldn't watch the race with her.

"Mr. Suzo insisted he had only a single half hour available all week, today, precisely during the running of the Hopeful. He knows my client has a colt running and wouldn't be able to keep his mind on what he's doing."

"Rather clever of him."

"Not as clever as he thinks. I'm empowered to act as agent for the owner. He'll be able to watch the race while the groom and I show the horse. Mr. Suzo won't get him for a penny less than he's worth."

Courtney was disappointed Seth couldn't watch the race with her, but she saw the eagerness in Seth's eyes and finally understood this was the kind of excitement he loved. He thrived on the battle of wits, the maneuvering to get ahead of the other man. She understood more fully what a terrible thing she had done when she called off the sale. It must have been harder for him to see his carefully constructed plans come to naught than to miss out on the commission.

The taxi skidded to a halt, and having already paid the fare, Courtney sprinted for the box seats reserved for owners. The horses were only just coming on the track. She was relieved to see Gerald Ribbesdale already in her box.

"I thought you might need some moral support," he said. "And a little something to calm your nerves," he added as he handed her a glass of white wine.

Courtney wished it had been Seth.

She didn't know how nervous she was until she saw Gus step onto the track. All at once she realized how much was depending on the results of this race, and her stomach turned over. She set the glass of wine down. She was shaking too badly to hold it. The race wouldn't start for another fifteen minutes. She didn't know how she was going to stand the wait.

"I was in Hong Kong for a couple of weeks last year," Gerald said unexpectedly. Courtney whipped around to face him, all thought of the race wiped from her mind. One look and she knew what he was going to say. "I met a man there by the name of Stephen Clonninger. Courtney, why does everyone think your father is dead?"

Coming on top of the tension of the race and her bet, the shock was almost too much for Courtney. She didn't want anyone to know about her father. She felt humiliated.

"Grandpa wanted everybody to believe he was dead. He didn't even tell me until just before he died."

"Then, you've never tried to find him?"

"I told you, I thought he was dead. Afterward I didn't know if I should. He had made no effort to find me in twenty years."

"I think you ought to call him."

"Why should I want to find a man who would sell his only child?"

"Who told you that?"

"Grandpa."

"Call your father."

"I tried, but I can't." The pain in her voice was so great Gerald put his arm around her. He was guiding her to one of the chairs when Seth burst into the box, breathless from his sprint from the stables. Courtney went for the comfort of his nearness like a wounded fox to earth.

"I thought you had a horse to sell."

"I gave Suzo a flat price and told him to take it or leave it. He knew I had called his bluff. He accepted the price, and we were done in two minutes. The groom didn't even have time to take the horse out of the stall."

The blared voice of the announcer penetrated Courtney's consciousness. The horses were approaching the gate for the race that would determine her whole future. Struggling to put all the stunning disclosures of the day out of her mind, Courtney shushed Seth and directed his attention to Gus.

"He looks magnificent," Seth said, studying her colt through powerful binoculars. "Barry has done a superb job with him."

"Flanery's Pride looks good, too," Gerald said. "It ought to be a good race."

Courtney kept her eyes on Gus. Even a glance at Flanery's colt would be a betrayal. In the field of all bays, Gus's red chestnut coat stood out clearly. It was easy to see that he got a good start. It was even easier to see Flanery's Pride got away first, soon building up a lead of six lengths. Courtney felt her stomach begin to tie itself into knots. The Hopeful was a relatively short race. Gus couldn't afford to give Flanery's Pride a long lead and still win, but as the horses continued down the long backstretch, Flanery's Pride still held an easy lead.

"Your jockey had better make his move soon," Gerald said.

Courtney couldn't help but glance over at the box where Flanery was beaming with so much pride and confidence it made her sick with fear. He was probably already picking out the exact piece of land he planned to take from her.

Flanery's Pride increased his lead to eight lengths by the time the horses reached the final turn. For most of the crowd, the race was over. They were quiet, some of them were even looking away from the track, but Courtney knew Gus hadn't started to run.

"Come on, Gus," she said in a hoarse whisper. "It's now or never."

Almost as though they heard her, the jockey dropped his hands, and Gus laid back his ears and lengthened his stride. Not until the horses had come off the final turn and swung into the home stretch did the crowd realize the full extent of what had happened in a mere twelve seconds. Flanery's Pride's lead had been slashed to three lengths, and Gus was cutting into the gap between them with ground-devouring strides. At first the crowd couldn't believe what they were seeing. Gus wasn't merely getting closer; he was running so fast each stride brought him perceptibly nearer to the overwhelming favorite. Halfway through the stretch he caught Flanery's Pride. He swept by him with such a prodigal display of power that the crowd watched in near silence as his lead stretched to two lengths, five lengths, then nine lengths as he rocketed over the finish line.

Not since Secretariat had a two-year-old won a Hopeful Stakes like that. The crowd exploded with a roar, and Saratoga went wild.

Courtney wanted nothing more than to collapse into her seat, but Seth caught her up in a bear hug that threatened to deprive her of breath and gave her a kiss that bruised her lips. Then tucking her arm into his, he headed her in the direction of the winner's circle.

"This is one celebration I intend to see you enjoy to the fullest," he said as they hurried past people shouting their congratulations. "For two years you've been telling everybody this colt was something very special. A lot of people are going to be eating crow."

Courtney was beyond the power of rational thought. After years of worry and planning, of denying herself and thinking only of the farm, everything had been put right in less than a minute and fifteen seconds. Gus was every bit as good as she knew he would be, and she had won the money to pay off Flanery. She had turned the corner, and she had done it by herself.

Suddenly she was running toward the winner's circle, running toward the colt she had nursed from a newborn foal to the threshold of a championship. She threw her arms around his neck, and he started to show off just as he had done so many times in the field back at home. For a brief moment she could almost believe she was alone with him. It didn't matter that Seth and Barry and the governor were waiting while TV news cameras ground away. The bond was still there. He was still her horse.

Gus pranced around her, then reared and walked toward her on his hind legs. As the crowd held its collective breaths, Courtney backed away to leave him standing alone. He dropped on all fours and shoved his head against her chest so hard she stumbled against Seth. When she kissed him on his muzzle, he nuzzled her pocket, looking for the sugar she always carried there. She realized she hadn't thought to bring any, but Seth dropped several cubes into her palm. Gus gobbled them up, and a nervous Barry, grateful the show was over, reclaimed his charge. The crowd loudly applauded Courtney and Gus, and the governor remarked on the close bond between owner and horse.

"She was with him every day from the moment he was foaled until he came to me," Barry told a TV interviewer. "She's really the one who's responsible for what he is today. I've only tried to continue what she began."

It was some time before Courtney could leave the winner's circle, but Flanery was waiting for her when she returned to her box. She stiffened and grabbed for Seth's hand.

"You won your bet fair and square." He seemed to be quite sincere in spite of his obvious disappointment at having his horse shown up as another early bloomer.

"I wish you were as gracious in business as you are in losing," Courtney said.

"If I were gracious in business, I couldn't afford to be

a gracious loser. Take as long as you want to repay the loan."

"You'll have your money in a few days. I'll deliver the check myself."

Flanery gave her a startled look.

"How on earth . . ." Seth began.

"I'll tell you after you've had a very strong drink," Courtney whispered as she headed for the clerk's office and her winner's check. "You're not going to like it at all."

TWELVE

It was almost two hours before Courtney was free of the last reporter. She retired gratefully to the clubhouse. Most of the members had left, but there were still a few having drinks. She had to run the gauntlet of their congratulations before Seth could settle her at a table and order her a glass of wine, a bourbon on the rocks for himself.

"Now, I want you to come clean about everything," Seth said, taking a generous swallow of his drink. "I don't know why you wouldn't let me help. You know horses, but I know the business."

"You know, that's been part of our trouble all along," Courtney said, forgetting for a moment what she had intended to say. "You feel, and you try to make me feel, like you're the only one who can do anything. I don't think you do it intentionally, but ever since I met you, you've been trying to manage me, nudge me in the right direction, make sure nothing bad happens to me."

"Good Lord, Courtney, I love you. Of course I want to make sure nothing bad happens to you. What's a husband for?"

"Since I don't have one, I don't know. But we're not talking about marriage, so that doesn't come into the discussion. Just for once, I'd like to feel you think I can handle a situation on my own, that you could stand back and let me take over, being confident all the while that I will do the job just as well as you would have done it."

"But you're so damned idealistic. I've had a lot more experience than you."

"Which reminds me." Courtney took out the check Gus had won in the Hopeful. She turned it over, endorsed it, and handed it to Seth.

"What am I supposed to do with that?"

"I'm not entirely sure. I suppose I should give it to Clay, but since cosigning my loans was your idea, it's only fair that you deal with it."

"Now look here, I was just trying to keep people off your back. No one is pressing you for the money, least of all me." He handed the check back to her, but she pushed his hand away.

"I've been trying to tell you for nearly a year I have to do this on my own. I consider this business with the loans a high-handed piece of meddling, another sign you have no faith in my abilities. I want your name off those loans now. Maybe Clay can put them back the way they were and use this money for the payments. I don't know, but if you can't handle it, I will as soon as I get back to Lexington."

"You do that," Seth said in clipped tones as he handed the check back.

Courtney knew he didn't understand and was hurt, but she didn't know what else she could say to make him appreciate how she felt.

"Now, tell me how you came up with the money to pay Flanery," Seth said. "I thought your bet with him showed a good understanding of his character."

"I doubt you're going to admire the rest of it," Courtney confessed, keeping her eyes lowered. "I won the money."

"What?" It wasn't an exclamation of horror, rage, or condemnation. He just didn't understand what she had said.

"I said I won the money."

"How?" He was beginning to suspect what she meant, but he couldn't believe it.

"I had Gerald place some bets for me."

"With whom and how much?" He knew how, but he still couldn't believe it.

"Two hundred and twenty-seven thousand dollars with just about every bookmaker in England and Ireland. I got a little better than six-to-one, and I won over one point three million." She said it all in a rush, the words coming as fast as she could get them out.

"Are you crazy? You could have lost everything!"

"Lower your voice," Courtney hissed. "There's no need to tell the whole world about it."

"But to bet every cent you had!"

"I bet only the money Gus won in his first two races. If I had lost it, I wouldn't have been much worse off than I was before. I'm not a gambler. If I ever had any doubts, the last week would have removed them. But after canceling your sale, it was my only chance to get out from under that debt without losing part of my land or part of Gus."

"I'm happy you can repay your debt, really I am, but I can't believe you would risk all your money."

"What was two hundred thousand dollars when I stood to lose millions? It was an awful gamble—I admit that—and I was scared to death; but I had to do something. You can't know what I've been through these last two weeks."

"Whatever you suffered, earning an average of a hundred thousand dollars a day should deaden the pain considerably."

He still didn't understand. He thought she was a scatterbrained female who had taken an insane chance and been lucky. "Nevertheless," she added a trifle defiantly, "I can pay off the debt and be done with Flanery. I've got my two hundred and twenty-seven thousand back to buy a brood mare this fall. With the farm earning enough to pay its way, I can use Gus's winnings to pay off some loans and buy stallion seasons for the brood mares. After the close calls I've had this year, I'm absolutely cock-a-hoop. Now I can begin to concentrate on building up my stock. I've been studying pedigrees for years, waiting for this day."

Courtney couldn't understand why Seth wasn't sharing her happiness. Even though she had kept asking him not to, he'd worked just about as hard as she had to the keep the farm from going under.

"As soon as I can afford it, I'm going to cut back on the number of boarders. I want the pastures filled with my own mares and Gus's foals."

"What about us?" Seth asked.

"I hoped we could go on as before, but that's not what you want, is it?"

"No. I love you, Courtney. I want you to be my wife."

Courtney felt the butterflies begin to dance in her stomach again. They did every time Seth mentioned marriage.

"I told you I wasn't looking for a long commitment," Courtney said, dropping her eyes from Seth's gaze. "I'm happy to go on just as we are. I've got the farm to run."

"It's about time you put Gus and the farm aside and thought of yourself. Everything you do is for the farm.

Now that it looks like you're out of the woods, you're still thinking of the farm. What about you? What about your future?"

"But the farm *is* my future," Courtney insisted. "I've spent twenty years getting ready for this day. Now I have a chance to prove I know what I'm doing."

"And what about me?"

"I love you. That hasn't changed."

"No, it hasn't. Apparently your love is just as shallow as ever."

Courtney was shocked by his words. A physical blow could hardly have affected her more cruelly.

"You seem to expect me to continue hovering around, to sit quietly out of the way when I'm not needed, but to be handy in case an emergency arises or you want to have dinner and spend the night together."

"That's not the way I meant it." It sounded ugly when he put it that way. "I do love you. It's just I'm not ready for marriage. Why can't we go on like we have been?"

"I want a home and children and a wife I can see every day, a wife who will worry about me instead of whether the yearlings have enough hay or the brood mares' pasture is getting too dry."

"I want to get married someday, too, but not right now. It scares me when I think of it, but it scares me even more to think of being without you."

"What are you waiting for, Courtney?"

"A lot of things. I have to get the farm back on a sound footing. It will take a lot of work, though the way Gus ran today, it should take only two or three more years, less if he wins the Triple Crown."

"Ever since I've known you, I've had to play second fiddle to Gus. Everything I did, I did so you'd notice me, not to benefit that blasted farm. Well, I'm not doing it anymore. I want you to forget the farm. Think of us. Don't you want anything for yourself? You're always telling me you need to do this next or you have to get things to a certain stage. What are you, Courtney, a computer program that must be worked through to the end? Don't you have any feelings, any dreams of your own that don't center around the farm?"

"I've never thought of myself separate from the farm."

"My God, that's it! I've been staring at it for months and never seen it. You have no identity except through Gus or Idle Hour."

"That's not true," Courtney replied hotly. "It's not fair, either. I think of the farm because Grandpa loved it so much." Her voice sounded tired, and she realized she no longer felt her all-consuming zeal about the farm. In fact, at this moment, it seemed more of a burden than anything else.

"That was his choice, Courtney. You don't owe him anything."

"But I do. He might not have loved me, but he gave up everything for me. Can't you see this is the only way I can repay him? Can't you see I've got to repay him? Can't you wait a little longer?"

"I don't owe him anything."

"I owe him everything," Courtney replied angrily. "I've tried to explain it to you over and over again. You don't understand."

"No, I don't. If your grandfather loved you enough to sacrifice his place for you, I can't believe he would want you to let it ruin your life."

"It's not ruining my life," Courtney replied indignantly. "I love Idle Hour Farm, and I love Gus. I can't wait to go to work in the mornings. I hate to leave the library at night. I like everything about what I do and can't imagine doing anything else. I've always felt sorry for people who had to go to work in an office or work with machines. Everything here is so alive, so exciting, so full of promise."

"Maybe we're both wrong. Maybe there isn't room in your heart for both the farm and me."

"You know that's not true. I've been in love with you for months."

"I wonder if you really love me, Courtney. In fact, I begin to wonder if you're capable of loving anybody. You've let your fear of rejection and feelings of inadequacy work on your heart until it's no more than a shriveled-up, hard knot. It's turned you into an emotional cripple. You'll never be able to love until you stop being afraid of being unloved."

"I'm not afraid," Courtney almost shouted, "but I don't have time to prove it to you now. All I've done is ask you to wait a little longer."

"I think the time has come for you to decide. I would never ask you to give up Gus, but I won't take a backseat to a whole lot of barns and pastures."

Courtney felt shocked and fearful. Inside her there was a gradual drawing away.

"How much longer do you intend to make me stand around, hands clasped behind my back, patiently waiting to be needed? One year, three years, or will it continue to stretch on indefinitely because you're waiting for one more horse to win a race? I can't live with your obligations hanging over my head for the rest of my life. You won't let me help you, but you won't let go either. You're going to have to decide, Courtney, and you might as well do it now."

Courtney's brain refused to work. With Gerald knowing her father was alive, Gus winning the race and her million-dollar bet, and Seth practically forcing her to choose between him and Idle Hour, too much had happened for her to be able to make rational decisions. Somewhere mixed in with her feelings for the farm, her fears of her own inadequacy, and her love for Seth, somewhere in that swirling whirlpool of feelings was Courtney Clonninger. But right now she couldn't separate herself from all the rest.

Faced with the question of what Courtney Clonninger wanted, she couldn't answer, and she couldn't decide on the spur of the moment. This was probably the most important decision of her life. She couldn't get it wrong.

"I can't decide right now," she said at last, her voice a plea for his understanding. "I need some time to think."

"Take all the time you need," Seth said, getting up and tossing some money on the table to pay for the drinks. "You can call me when you make up your mind."

Courtney watched him go with tears in her eyes. She knew he didn't understand. She doubted she could make him understand, but she would not be stampeded into giving up when success was within reach, when the freedom from guilt was in sight. It wasn't fair of Seth, and it wasn't what she wanted.

It wasn't, was it?

"I don't think five races will be too much. That'll make a total of eight with the three he's already won. I've checked the dates, and he'll have plenty of time to rest in between."

Courtney was talking to Barry about Gus's race schedule for the rest of the year. After Seth had left her, she had laid out a plan whereby Red Phoenix would run in the five richest races in the country for his age group. If he won all five, she would be able to pay off the loans

Seth had cosigned. She hadn't been able to make up her mind about her future, but she knew she wouldn't be able to think with that debt hanging over her head. With everything else on her mind, that was just too much.

"It looks all right to me," Barry agreed. "He's strong and fresh. But you don't have to do this. Seth would never press you for the money."

Courtney's gaze flew to Barry's face. "Is there anybody in Lexington who doesn't know Seth was determined to keep my farm afloat, single-handedly if necessary?" she asked angrily.

"Things have a way of getting around," Barry said noncommittally.

"Well, you can let this *get around*," Courtney snapped. "I am paying my own bills, I'm making my own decisions, and I'm taking responsibility for what happens. My success or failure has nothing to do with Seth Cameron, and I refuse to do business with people who look over my shoulder for Seth's approval."

"No one's doing that."

"Yes, they are. I feel like a little girl everyone is trying to protect."

"You should be glad Seth is interested in you instead of throwing his help in his face."

"Good God," Courtney exclaimed. "Is nothing I do private?"

"Not when you have a screaming match in the clubhouse. Everybody at Saratoga knew what you two said before the night was out. You're big news right now."

"But not so big I don't need Seth, right?"

"He's a fine man, one of the best in this business. Nobody's telling you what to do, but there's no point in cutting off your nose to spite your face."

"You don't understand," Courtney groaned. "Nobody understands."

"The general feeling is you're the one who doesn't understand."

The weeks following the Hopeful Stakes were the most eventful of Courtney's life. Gus won the Washington-Arlington Futurity by fifteen lengths, and offers to buy him, to syndicate him, to stand him at stud, even requests for breeding rights, poured in so fast she couldn't deal with them. Clay had orders to refuse to discuss selling, syndication, or standing him at stud. She instructed Ted to tell anyone wanting breeding information to call back in two years.

Idle Hour took on boarders for two new clients, Courtney had contracts to break all the yearlings she thought they could handle, and Ted had an offer to stand two stallions.

Everything was going so well Courtney was shocked one afternoon when she realized she wasn't happy. It may have been that she was leaning on the fence, watching her two weanlings play in the same field where Gus had played the day she met Seth. It may have been that she hadn't stopped thinking about him. Whatever the reason, it didn't take her long to pinpoint the cause. Putting Idle Hour Farm on the road to recovery had relieved her load of guilt and eased some of her feelings of inadequacy, but it had done nothing to fill the void in her life left by Seth's departure.

Nowadays she could hardly think of anything except Seth. She kept remembering little things she hadn't been aware she knew about him: how his clothes were so much a part of him he didn't look like himself when they were in bed; the way his huge body unfolded from his low-slung Jaguar; how his eyes turned almost silver when they made love. She found herself quoting him, thinking like him, planning like him as though she didn't have a mind of her own.

That's when she realized she didn't.

Her whole life had been shaped by two things: her grandfather's sacrifice and her parents' rejection. Outside of that, there was no Courtney Clonninger.

That forced her to take her mind off the weanlings long enough to take a good hard look at herself, and she didn't like what she saw. Wanting nothing to distract her, she turned away from the field.

She had never had time for Seth or anybody else because of the farm, but what had the farm actually given her? Her grandfather had loved his horses and his land more than he loved her. Maybe he also hated her father more than he loved her. If not, why had he lied about his death? Then Courtney realized her grandfather had told her about her father not because he was sorry he had kept the secret from her or because she needed to know she had someone else in the world she could depend on.

He had told her so she would have the money to save Idle Hour from destruction. He hadn't thought she could save it by herself. He had expected her to fail.

A wave of anger such as Courtney had never known swept through her. It was for her grandfather's farm she let Seth leave. She hadn't heard from him since he walked out of the clubhouse at Saratoga. She had been certain he would call before the end of the first week, but when she'd entered into the second week without a word from him, she had given up and called his office. His secretary had said she didn't know where he was and promised she would tell him Courtney had called. But he hadn't returned her call. Ted hadn't heard from Seth, and Clay knew nothing about his schedule.

She thought of all the things Seth had done for her and the number of times she had been ungrateful or reluctant to accept his help. Finally she understood he had helped her in secret to spare her pride, that he had done everything he could to help her make her own way rather than make the way for her. He might not have done what she wanted, but at least he had tried to do what was best for her.

The thought of his small farm plagued her. All she had to do was think of what Idle Hour meant to her, and she could imagine what it must have meant to him to make a start toward getting back the place where he had been born and had grown up. And she had consistently refused to give him credit for wanting to do anything with horses except sell them. That was almost like saying she didn't like breeding horses because she wanted to race them, or the reverse, and she knew how foolish that was. Why couldn't she see the same thing in Seth?

She desperately wanted to see him, to have him hold her.

When the second week passed without a word, she called the secretary again, but the woman still couldn't help. A third call elicited the information that she thought Seth was in Europe. When she heard he had been in Kentucky for the September weanling sales, she realized his secretary was being intentionally vague.

Seth wasn't going to call her.

The shock was devastating.

She was back at the fence watching her two weanlings— she seemed to be spending all her time there these days— when Gerald Ribbesdale drove up. She hadn't seen him since Saratoga. Since she hadn't taken his advice, she wasn't anxious to see him now.

"Thought I would come around with my goodbyes before I shoved off," he said. He gave her a careful scrutiny. "I must say, you don't look any bloody happier than Seth did when I saw him."

Gerald believed in getting to the heart of the matter right off the bat. It had the effect of administering a very nasty shock nearly every time he opened his mouth.

"We had a slight disagreement," Courtney said stiffly.

"From the looks of you, it must have been a bloody row."

So much for the English finesse. He was about as subtle as a fist to the jaw. "It was more in the nature of a difference of opinion."

"You were probably raising hell with him again for trying to help you tow this bloody farm of yours out of the river tick."

Courtney swelled with indignation, but there was nothing she could say.

"You should be glad he took an interest in your white elephant. Don't know what I'd do with the bloody thing if I had it in England."

"Probably sell it down the *bloody* river for the *bloody* taxes," Courtney snapped back.

Gerald grinned. "Marcia told me you were rather hardheaded, as well as fanatically devoted to the place. The pater's, was it?"

"No. Grandfather's."

"Much the same thing. All bloody oppressive, these inherited baronial estates. Believe me, after wrestling with one for five years, I know. I should have sold the bloody thing the day I reached my majority. Marcia and I would be a deal more comfortable in a decent cottage than in that monstrous place. Full of damp and ancestors best forgotten. Oh well, you don't want to hear about my problems. Just remember, none of us gets through this bloody world alone, and the sooner we learn that, the easier we make it on ourselves, not to mention those we love."

He was as direct as a charging bull, but now that she had recovered from the initial shock of his brutal frankness, she could see the concern in his eyes. Clearly all his mindless rambling wasn't mindless at all. No wonder Marcia was so stuck on him.

"Did you call your father?"

Courtney's stare didn't change.

"Thought you wouldn't. A mistake, just like giving old Seth the heave-ho. Call."

"Which one?"

"Both."

Courtney did call Seth's office again, and finally his secretary knew where he was. He had gone to Europe for the major sales and wouldn't be back for two months. A transatlantic call three days later was no more successful. The sales officials didn't know where Seth was—he could be in France, England, or Ireland—and they didn't know where he was going to be. As far as Courtney was concerned, he might as well have dropped off the edge of the earth.

Courtney sat staring at the huge gold trophy on the mantel in her den. Gus had just won the Champagne Stakes over the best horses in the East and was now the overwhelming favorite for the Kentucky Derby. Yet all she could see was Seth's face staring back at her from the shining surface and hear his accusing words ringing in her ears.

I begin to wonder if you're capable of loving anybody, Court-

ney. You've let your fear of rejection and feelings of inadequacy work on your heart until it's nothing more than a shriveled-up, hard knot. You'll never be able to love until you stop being afraid of being unloved.

All her life she had been running from anything that had to do with her family. During the last weeks, when she had finally come to accept the fact that Seth was not going to return her calls, she realized she was still running. She had been doing so ever since her grandfather had told her that her father was still alive.

It was finally time to come to grips with her past.

She had been able to forgive her father until she found out he was alive. It was then her anger grew almost into a hatred. She was angry not just because he had rejected her, but because he was alive and still rejecting her.

Why hadn't she figured this out before? Why had she allowed it to eat away at her for so long? Because you ran from your fears, something inside told her. You never wanted to analyze them. You were afraid to face anything. You're still running away, but Seth's leaving has finally forced you to look at yourself.

Realizing her love for Seth was greater than her fears was a shock to Courtney. She never had any doubt about loving him, but until now she had been willing to risk losing Seth rather than do battle with her own monsters. It took her no time at all to conclude that her fear and bitterness over her father's rejection were about to cost her the one thing she wanted most. It remained only for her to decide what she was going to do about it.

She had conquered her guilt over the farm. Now it was time to face her father.

Without a second thought, Courtney got up, walked to the phone and started to dial. She had dialed it only a few times, but her father's number was engraved in her mind. As the phone rang, she realized that though she was cold with apprehension, she wasn't shaking.

"Hello." It was the woman's voice again.

"This is Courtney Clonninger. May I speak to my father?" There was an audible gasp on the other end, followed by a moment of silence.

"I beg your pardon, but this is something of a shock. I'm Kazuyo Clonninger. I married your father seventeen years ago."

"I didn't know. My grandfather never told me. Where is my father? May I speak to him?"

"He's dead, Courtney. He died three months ago."

Courtney wanted desperately to say something, to quickly explain why she had called; but her throat constricted, and the words remained locked inside. Tears welled up in her eyes.

"It was a heart attack. We all knew he was working too hard, but he never learned to slow down. I tried to reach you when he first got sick, but I never got an answer. I admit I forgot after that."

"I wish I had known."

"I wish *we* had known. You see, we never heard from you. I was afraid you wouldn't care."

"Grandpa told me he was dead."

"I knew of the bitterness between my husband and his father. There was nothing I could do to change that, but it was his estrangement from you that worried me most."

"Why? Didn't he think he got enough money for me?" Courtney demanded, bitterness making her careless of the hurt her words might inflict.

"I cannot excuse what he did to you. Your father was an angry man. I do not think he ever regretted taking his father's money. He always said his father had nothing to give but money, but I do think he came to regret that he had cut himself off from you."

"Then, why didn't he write me?"

"I begged him to, but he always refused. He was too proud to admit he had made a mistake."

"But he spent the rest of his life paying for it."

"That is often the price people are forced to pay for their stubbornness."

The words hit Courtney like an exploding shell. Was she making the same mistake with Seth? Would she spend the rest of her life paying for her stubborn pride?

In a flash of understanding she realized that she wanted to marry Seth, that she wanted him for her husband forever, that she wanted to bear his children. She didn't know when or how it had all come about, but it was all in place in her mind now. She must have gradually come to that way of thinking over the last six months, probably about the time they first made love.

She knew now she loved him as deeply as she could ever love anyone. She was only kidding herself when she thought they could take what they had with no promises for tomorrow. The kind of love they shared, the kind of love that kept him coming back to her and kept her looking for him no matter how many times they argued, that kind of love didn't recognize barriers of time or place. She loved him now just as much as she had when she 'was in his arms, and she imagined she would love him just as much when she died as she did this minute.

But most important of all, she knew he still loved her. If not, there would have been no reason not to return her calls or messages. He was running away from her just as she had been trying to escape the knowledge that she was hopelessly in love with him.

"Why did you call?"

Courtney swallowed hard. "That's not easy to explain. I've spent years hating my father and feeling guilty for the sacrifice he forced my grandfather to make for me. I became so bound up in those feelings I didn't know who I was or what I wanted. When I found it was threatening to destroy my own chance for happiness, I had to do something."

"You must understand that my husband was an unhappy man. He felt his father loved his horses more than he loved his son, and he hated him for that. He always wanted to go into business, but your grandfather wouldn't let him. Shortly after we were married, I asked your grandfather to let us see you—Stephen and I had a terrible fight when he found out what I had done—but he refused. He swore he would have Stephen arrested if he ever set foot in Kentucky."

"When was that?"

"You must have been about eight or nine."

Courtney thought of the years that might possibly have been salvaged, and she felt like crying all over again,

"I never knew."

"I didn't suppose you did."

"I'm glad I finally got to talk to you. I called before, but I couldn't get the courage to say anything. Thank you for telling me. I guess I'd better let you go."

"Wait a minute. I had intended to wait until everything was settled, but I must talk with you about your father's estate."

"What estate?"

"The money he left you."

"But he should have left everything to you."

"I have quite enough money of my own. The bulk of his estate goes to you."

"Estate! Why . . . but . . . God almighty!" Courtney finally exclaimed.

Kazuyo Clonninger laughed. "Your father was a very successful businessman. I don't know how much it will come to after taxes, but you will inherit much more than he got from your grandfather."

Courtney dropped the phone.

"Are you still there?" Kazuyo Clonninger was asking when Courtney retrieved the receiver.

"Yes." Even that one word was an effort.

"There are many details we will need to go over together. I will be in the States in November. Could we meet with your lawyer then?"

"I would like that very much," Courtney said.

"I'm looking forward to meeting you. There are many things I want to tell you about your father. Maybe if you were to know a little more about him, you would not hate him so much."

For a long while after she hung up, Courtney sat in a state of shock. Her whole life had taken an abrupt and unexpected turn. She didn't know what to make of it, but she did know she had to see Seth. She didn't know just what she was going to say to him, but she would figure that out later. What she wanted more than anything else in the world was to feel his arms around her once again.

THIRTEEN

"I'm sorry you couldn't find Seth, but I'm delighted you came to England," Marcia said to Courtney.

Courtney had traveled to Europe to tell him she would marry him under any conditions, but a week of calling every place Gerald thought he might be in England, Ireland, or anywhere on the Continent had failed to locate him. She had intended to stay in a hotel—she thought it would give her more freedom in searching for Seth— but Marcia and Gerald had insisted she stay with them as long as she was in England. Now she was glad of the emotional support.

"I didn't know when I was going to be able to show you the baby," Marcia said.

"She's beautiful," Courtney replied, thinking of Marcia's daughter with only half her mind, "but you didn't have to make me a godmother."

"With all that red hair, I couldn't not," Marcia said as she handed the baby to its nurse, "but you don't want to talk about my child, or the depressing fact that I'm already pregnant again."

"Did you want to be pregnant?"

"Don't talk like a bloody fool. I was crazy enough to believe my mother-in-law when she said nursing mothers couldn't get pregnant. Oh well, if this one's a boy, at least

I'll have the bloody succession taken care of." She gave Courtney a searching look. "Is my lighthearted chatter failing to vanquish the blues?"

Courtney shook her head with a sad smile. "I'm afraid so. I don't want you to think I'm not glad to see you, but I desperately want to see Seth."

"And the bloody bounder has gone to earth somewhere between here and the Russian border and doesn't mean to come to light until you clear off."

"It looks like it. He told me to call him when I made up my mind, but how can I do that if I can't find him?"

"Well, the word's out now. Surely it won't be long before he realizes you didn't come all the way to England just to turn him down again."

"After turning him down for the better part of a year, he probably thinks it's an ingrained habit."

"The major sales will be over soon, so he's bound to turn up. I promise to rout him out and send him straight home. Now quick, before you have to leave to catch your plane, tell me about your father. Gerald says he was positively rolling in money."

"You should have seen Ted when I told him we had all those millions to spend on the farm. The man danced on his desk. I mean *literally* on his desk. He still hadn't gotten the office straight when I left."

"So you're debt free and rich to boot."

"It looks that way."

"Poor little rich girl, huh?"

"I know this sounds trite, but I was happier when I had all those debts hanging over my head and Seth coming by the farm every day. I've paid off every cent, the place positively gleams with new paint, and I'm cleaning out barns for the brood mares I plan to buy during the coming year. Gus is winning everything in sight and getting better every day. It's a dream come true. It's more than I could have hoped for, and all I can think about is Seth."

Courtney tried unsuccessfully to fight off the tears. "Why won't he return my calls? I used to think he didn't answer because he still loved me. I'm not so sure now."

"I don't know. I wish I did. I'll give the bloody bastard a piece of my mind when I see him, but I know he'll call you before long. I just know he will."

But as Courtney made her way into the airport several hours later, she hadn't found any reason to think Seth would change his mind. From the looks she had seen passing between Gerald and Marcia, she guessed they didn't believe he would change his mind either.

She didn't claim to have acted with brilliance or intelligence. In fact, she was quite ready to admit she had been a complete fool, but he owed her a chance to tell him she had been wrong. He had said call. Well, she had spent hundreds of dollars calling over half the world, making a nuisance of herself, and probably an object of pity as well, and he hadn't even bothered to pick up a phone. The least he could do was say he was still mad as hell and didn't want to be bothered with her just yet.

Or ever.

She wasn't sure that not knowing if he would ever come back wasn't just as bad as knowing he definitely wouldn't. Either way, she'd never been more miserable in her life.

Suddenly Courtney's gaze focused on the back of a man about fifty yards in front of her, and she lost her train of thought. Even before she had time for conscious thought, she *knew* it was Seth. She didn't stop to consider that the odds were enormous against finding him at the airport or that it was virtually impossible to recognize anyone from the back. She knew it was Seth, and oblivious to the shocked stares and cold indignation of the people she bumped into, she started running through the crowd calling his name. The one thought in her mind was that Seth was walking away from her. If she didn't reach him soon, he might disappear forever.

She was drawing closer, but the crowds between them were thicker. Then she came to a point where the lines for boarding two different planes crossed the aisle, and she was certain she would never get around the mounds of luggage and tight knots of people. In desperation she almost screamed his name.

Half the heads in the airport turned in her direction, but she didn't care. One of them was Seth. There was no one else in the whole world who was so big, so immaculately dressed, and who stared at her with eyes filled with such cold anger. Her steps slowed as she neared him. His gaze did not transform into a warm smile of recognition, and his arms did not reach out to fold her in a crushing embrace. Courtney felt like she had come face-to-face with an iceberg.

"What do you want?"

"To see you. You said to call. I called dozens of times, but you never answered."

"Wasn't it enough that I made a fool of myself in front of half the horsemen in America? Did you scream my name for fun, or are you trying to make sure I can't show my face in England either?"

"I had to see you. Why haven't you answered my calls? Why have you been hiding from me?" She was totally unaware of the angry crowds that streamed around them as they stood blocking the busiest aisle in Heathrow airport. All she saw was Seth and his anger.

"Why should I? You made it quite clear where I stood."

"But I was wrong. I know that now. I love you, Seth."

"You don't need me."

"Yes, I do. I thought I didn't, but I was wrong about that, too. I thought everything in the world, including myself, had to take a backseat to the farm, but now I know that isn't true. You're the most important thing in my life, Seth. I want to be with you. I want to be your wife."

"Until a week ago I actually believed—fervently hoped—you would come to that conclusion."

"I came to it a long time ago," Courtney told him, "almost the minute you left. I found I didn't enjoy things as much when you weren't around. I didn't even enjoy Gus winning, not like I did at the Hopeful. The farm is important to me, Seth. It's in my blood. I suppose it always will be. It's my inheritance. But it's not the center of my life now, and it never will be again." Courtney stopped suddenly. "A week ago? What happened a week ago?"

"I went to Kentucky," Seth said, the blaze in his eyes suddenly growing brighter. "I thought maybe all those messages meant you had finally changed your mind. Anyway, I hoped you had. But just before I left, I got this very official letter from Clay telling me all my obligations for your loans had been canceled because they had been paid in full. That confused me, so I stopped by Clay's office on my way to Idle Hour. It's a good thing I did. It probably saved me from making a bigger fool of myself than ever, but then all that new paint would have told me something was different."

"What are you talking about?" Courtney asked, bewildered.

"Your father and all his goddamned millions, Courtney. Why didn't you tell me about your father?"

"I didn't know. I mean, I did know, but I didn't *know*."

"That cryptic statement may say exactly what you want

it to say, but I have no idea what the hell you're talking about."

"I didn't know anything about him. Like everybody else, I had thought he was dead. Just before he died, Grandpa told me he was alive, to call him if I ever needed money."

"Did he tell you how much?"

"At least fifteen million."

Seth's gaze would have frozen an erupting volcano. "So you let me run over half of Kentucky drumming up customers for your damned farm, racking my brain for ways to help you handle your debts, proving to every Tom, Dick, and Harry I was crazy in love with you, and all the while you sat there in your air-conditioned mansion pleading poverty and an uncrushable spirit, telling me everything had to take second place to your crusade to return the farm to its former glory, how you were afraid of love and felt unworthy—"

"Seth, please—"

"You let me blather on about your unquenchable spirit in the face of insurmountable odds, your pluck, your heart; and all the while you knew you could call up daddy, and all the money you needed would come pouring through the telephone. You must have had a great time watching me perform like a dancing bear. That was what you called me, wasn't it, a big teddy bear?"

"Seth, please. It was never like that."

"Then, what was it like? You tell me, since I obviously can't see what's in front of my face."

"It's true. I did know I could call my father if I was ever absolutely up against it, but the rest of it is also true. I did intend to make it on my own without anybody's help."

"Then, why didn't you tell me? Why did you let me make a fool of myself?"

"I couldn't. I didn't want anybody to know. But I did tell you not to help me, that I could make it on my own.

"Telling me you could make it on your own when there wasn't a single person in Lexington who thought you could last out the year isn't the same as telling me you've got a father tucked away ready to drop fifteen million any time you decide to pick up the phone."

"If you're so determined to keep quoting figures, you might as well get it right. It'll be ninety-one million after all the taxes are paid."

Seth blanched. "My God, and I had the audacity to think you needed me to help you escape Flanery's evil clutches. I can see now why you were willing to risk the paltry sum of two hundred thousand. And to think of all the work I put in on that deal. I don't think I've ever set up anything quite as complicated, and it would have worked perfectly, too, but of course you had no intention of going through with it, not with all those millions ready to drop into your palm."

"Seth, that's not the way it was."

"I'm surprised you even bothered with Gus. Unless he's as good as Secretariat, he'll never be worth half that much."

"Stop it," Courtney screamed, totally unaware that she had brought passenger traffic to a dead stop for the second time in an hour. "I did try to call my father, but I couldn't. I did mean to go through with the sale, but I couldn't."

"You're a regular weather vane, twisting about with every breeze."

"It was all your own fault," Courtney shouted, her accumulated frustrations boiling over. "I never wanted you to come out to the farm. I never wanted you to sell Gus or to find boarders or yearlings for me to break or show me your damned farm or cosign my loans or fall in love with me or make me fall in love with you or make love to me or any of the other things you were always doing. But you wouldn't listen. You always knew better than I did. You scorned the reasons I gave you without wondering if I didn't have reasons *that were private* that would explain what I had done."

"You never really listened to anything I said. Even when I found you the best bargain in the whole Keeneland bloodstock sale, you would have let it get away because you didn't believe I could possibly be right. Is it any wonder I fought so hard against your dragging me by the nose wherever you wanted me to go?

"You didn't understand me, and you didn't try very hard, Seth. You don't know what it's like not to be well-loved, popular, and successful. Your father may have lost his farm, but the rest of your life has been one success story after another. I was deserted by my parents when I was four, bought by my grandfather out of anger, and saddled with an enormous farm, a huge debt, and an even larger load of guilt. Sometimes it was all I could do to face the next day. But you'll never understand that, not with your masculine superiority and your *if I can't see it, it doesn't exist* attitude. But you couldn't take me on faith either. Just what the hell was it you fell in love with, Seth, the idea of playing Sir Galahad to my cringing Lady Guinevere or my too-willing body? It certainly couldn't have been for the poor, quivering fool inside. You didn't like anything about her."

"I fell in love with something I thought was there. Only I discovered it was an illusion."

"Seth, look at me, really look at me. Do you really *see* me?"

"I don't know who you are. You may have slain your

dragons and laid your burdens to rest, but you also shed the girl I knew. I've got to go, Courtney. I have to catch my plane."

"Are you coming back? Don't you even want to give yourself a chance to get to know me?"

"I don't know. I don't know much of anything anymore."

Courtney looked down, unable to meet his unflinching gaze. "I never would have been able to call my father if it hadn't been for you. I mustered the courage to do that only when I realized I might lose you. I never imagined it would drive you away. Please, Seth . . ."

But when she looked up he had vanished as completely as if the floor had opened up and swallowed him.

Courtney tried to concentrate on the present instead of the past or the future. She had hidden herself away in the den, her only refuge these days from Gus's overwhelming success. He had won the Breeder's Cup Juvenile four days earlier, and Ted had already received two offers to syndicate him for sums in excess of fifteen million dollars. Her father's wife, a lovely Japanese woman, had spent the week with her at Idle Hour, and many of the misunderstandings of twenty years had finally been sorted out. It was impossible to make up for all that lost time, but Kazuyo Clonninger had invited Courtney to visit her in Hong Kong next year after the Triple Crown.

"After the tension of those weeks, you will need a long rest far away from everyone who wants to share a success they did nothing to earn."

Courtney's thoughts couldn't help but go to Seth—they had been on little else since that harrowing meeting at the London airport—wondering if he would ever want to share her success. He had done a lot to help her achieve it, but it seemed they had been able to find more happiness in failure than in success.

Courtney had shamelessly used her stepmother's presence as an excuse not to go out. The racing community, anxious to welcome her back into their midst, had showered her with invitations to dinners, parties, charity gatherings. People her father had grown up with as well as those who had worked with him wanted to know all about him and his success. Absolute strangers hounded her with causes and charities to the point she stopped answering the phone herself.

She sighed. She had been doing that a lot lately, but taking herself to task didn't do any good. In fact, nothing much did. She didn't seem to care about anything these days. Oh, she could still make herself go to work each day and make decisions about the farm and show enough of her previous enthusiasm that people didn't ask questions, but she didn't care passionately, not like she had when she met Seth.

How odd. Every fiber of her being had cared about the farm and Gus in the beginning, but now that she had all the success she could want, it didn't give her the happiness she craved so desperately. She hadn't wanted Seth in the beginning when she couldn't get rid of him. But now that she would have been willing to trade the farm for him, she couldn't have him.

She had always known she was a little out of step with her peers. That hadn't bothered her, not much anyway, but now she was out of sync with her own life. The misunderstandings and fears and anger and denied truths of the last twenty years had so disoriented her thinking, she couldn't seem to get anything right. She didn't know how she was going to get Seth back, but she knew she must.

For four years she had devoted her entire life to the

farm, only to find that while it released her from the chains of suffocating obligation, it offered no fulfillment, no real happiness. The only thing she truly loved was Gus, and she would hardly see him for the next two years. When he came back to Idle Hour, if he came back, he wouldn't really be her horse any longer.

She repeated her vow to win Seth back. Everything she had ever wanted, *really wanted,* could be found in his arms. She knew it was the one place she wanted to be, and if wanting and hard work would bring him back, then Seth Cameron was going to be hers someday.

Courtney slipped out the library door, reached her car without anyone seeing her. and drove away. She needed time to think. For the last several months, ever since Gus's success had turned the farm into a seething mass of activity, all of it seeming to need her constant attention, she had fallen into the habit of going out to Seth's farm. He'd laugh at her if he knew, but she didn't care. It was quiet there, no one bothered her, and she felt closer to him than anywhere else. He had left something of himself there he couldn't pack into a suitcase and take to England, or France, or Japan, or Australia, or South America, or any of the other places he went to buy and sell horses.

As Courtney pulled her car to a stop under the spreading limbs of a hundred-year-old oak, her gaze automatically went to Seth's Jaguar parked under the shed. She could never see that car without expecting to see Seth climb out and head straight toward her, his enormous frame dwarfing everyone in sight, his smile of happy anticipation making her forget anyone else was around. Now it brought a lump to her throat and reminded her much too forcefully of everything she had let slip away.

She wandered down behind the house to the pasture where Seth's mares were kept, the three mares she had helped him buy last year. They were alone in the pasture; their foals had been weaned some weeks earlier. It made her feel closer to him. It was the one thing she had done for him, maybe the only thing she would ever be able to do for him. Somehow the mares and the foals they had produced represented a future for him that she would always have a small part of. It wasn't much, but it was all she had right now.

Seth tossed the *Daily Racing Form* aside. In the three months since he left Courtney at Saratoga, he had buried himself in work. He had attended more sales, attracted more clients, and made more money than ever before, but he had never been able to get Courtney out of his mind for more than a few hours at a time. He would be talking to a client, even in the process of bidding on a horse, and any one of a thousand things would trigger a memory, and it would all come flooding back.

After Courtney's tremendous success, he tried to convince himself she didn't need or want him anymore. He had read hundreds of articles, literally hundreds of thousands of words, about her and Gus and her enormous inheritance, but it only made the ache worse. Nothing filled the void or erased the pain.

It seemed so long ago when he had insisted he be first on her list, maybe even the only one on it. Now he would have settled for being at the bottom. Three months had proved to him that even though half a loaf might be terribly painful, it was still better than no loaf at all.

That woman has certainly made you swallow a lot of pride, his inner voice nagged. He silenced the inner voice with a pithy oath. It was that damned little voice that had gotten him into this mess, first by telling him Courtney would appreciate his doing things for her, and then by telling him she was an ungrateful tease when she had resisted his offers of help. Somewhere inside Seth's head there was an irrational, spiteful impulse. He had been so hurt after Saratoga that he had let his own anger keep him away. Let her see what it's like without me, he had thought, and she'd change her tune.

He had thought he was coming home to an ardent welcome when he had headed to Kentucky. That letter from Clay had confused him for only a minute, but it was nothing compared to the shock of finding Courtney was rolling in money and Idle Hour was thriving. The insidious little voice had shouted that she had made a fool of him, that she had let him jump through one hoop after another, all the while knowing she could have millions just by picking up the phone. She must have been laughing at him the whole time, the voice said, delighted to see what she could make a grown man do.

He had flown back to England in a rage that had not abated by the time Courtney ran him down in the middle of Heathrow airport. Hundreds of people had stared, incredulous, as they stood arguing at the top of their lungs in the middle of the most crowded concourse during the busiest part of the day. You might as well have had the argument in the middle of Newmarket Heath, the little voice had said. She could hardly have mortified you any more completely.

He had listened to his little voice and stalked off to catch his plane. He had kept listening to that voice for another two weeks until he felt the first tremor of doubt. The voice shrieked all the more loudly; but he couldn't block out Courtney's words forever, and once he allowed himself to think of what she had said, he was forced to reevaluate his actions. From that moment on, his little voice had steadily lost ground until Seth would have strangled the little bastard if he could only have gotten his hands on him. Knowing that the voice was actually part of him did nothing to improve his mood.

He had been guilty of every charge Courtney leveled at him. Even worse, he had clothed his deeds with the self-righteous conviction he was helping the woman he loved. He hadn't been able to see what he was doing even when she pointed it out to him, which she had done quite often. Egotistical bastard. He wondered if that was why Cynthia had left. It certainly would have helped if she had told him, though he doubted he would have seen it then either. He needed a thick armor of self-confidence, aggressive energy, and unflagging bonhomie to be a good salesman, and he had done a spectacular job in the last few months. But the same characteristics had kept him from the one thing he wanted most. Courtney.

Irritable, he got up and walked over to the window. He didn't know why he had come to the farm. It represented so much that seemed unimportant now, but it gave him the only feeling of peace he had been able to find in the last months. It made him feel closer to Courtney somehow. It was only here that he was able to feel that he might someday be able to win her back.

Why he thought that, he didn't know. After the way he had acted in the airport, she probably didn't want to see him again. Despite what Marcia said. Oh, yes, Marcia had given him pure mortal hell more than once; that was half the reason he had returned to Kentucky the first time. Marcia had assured him Courtney was pining for him, but there had been no more messages from Courtney. Marcia insisted Courtney was still in love with him, but he wondered. Marcia hadn't been left standing in the middle of the airport, humiliated and abandoned.

Out of the corner of his eye Seth noticed someone

moving down by the pasture. Damn, it was impossible to keep the tourists off of farms these days, but he couldn't figure out why anyone would want to trespass on his land. There were no famous horses here, and he had no reputation outside the industry.

That's Courtney, his mind screamed at him. But what was she doing here? His mind seemed to be unable to decide what to do, but his body had no such doubts. In a moment he was outside and running down the path that led from the house to the pasture. He slowed to a walk only when he neared Courtney.

She appeared to be lost in thought, unaware anyone was approaching, completely wrapped up in watching the horses. Strange how it felt so right to see her here. He didn't know how much he had longed to have her here until now. He vowed right then he would never let her leave again.

He didn't know what to say. He was afraid the sound of his voice would drive her away. Should he apologize? Should he avoid mentioning what he'd done and hope she would forget it? As usual, he acted on instinct and did something else entirely.

"You don't have enough horses at Idle Hour, so now you're casting covetous eyes on my measly trio?"

With a strangled cry, Courtney whipped around at the first sound of his voice. One look at his face—an instant too short for conscious thought—laid bare the deep hunger, the aching need in his heart, and she flung herself at him. He ran toward her, his outstretched arms welcoming her once again.

Courtney had never known that anything could be so wonderful as the feel of Seth's arms around her, the relief of being held tightly in his embrace, the bruising kisses that he planted on her mouth. After months of missing him, of wondering where he was, of fearing he would never again hold her in his arms, the relief was almost an unbearable ache.

"Are you sure you want me back?" she asked.

"Positive," Seth murmured into the ear he was teasing with his lips. "Are you still afraid?"

"Petrified."

For a long while they stood quietly, watching the horses together. They didn't need to speak of the past, for it truly *was* the past and no longer a part of their lives. It only remained to face the future. Maybe it was a sign of the future that she wore a dress and he had come out without a coat and tie.

"Why did you come here?" Seth finally asked.

"It makes me feel less unhappy," Courtney replied, holding Seth a little tighter. "Idle Hour represents all that kept us apart. This is yours. I always feel closer to you here."

"Do you feel close enough to marry me?"

She looked up into his face. "If you still want me."

"I never stopped."

"After you walked away from me at the airport, I wasn't sure."

"And I wasn't sure you wanted me, either, not after what you said."

"What changed your mind?"

"Nothing changed it. I have always wanted to marry you. What changed yours?"

"Realizing I was happier when I had lots of problems and you were coming around, all the time. Why didn't you call?"

"A misguided sense of personal injury. You might say a bruised ego. At first I was angry you wouldn't turn your back on everything for me. I guess I never understood your need to work off the debt. I couldn't understand why you couldn't change your priorities, especially after all I had tried to do for you." Courtney started to protest, but Seth kissed her into silence. "Then I came to Kentucky, learned about your inheritance, and I felt I'd been made to look a fool. After what you said in the airport, well, I couldn't imagine you were really in love with me. It took a while for me to begin to see just what I'd been doing."

"Not as long as it took me. But that's over now." She looked up apprehensively. "It *is* over, isn't it?"

"Yes," Seth assured her.

"Good. I want you to syndicate Gus." Courtney felt Seth stiffen, but she went ahead. "Everybody has been driving me crazy about him."

"Are you sure you want to syndicate him?"

"Of course."

But Seth had not missed the split second of hesitation. "I think you ought to retain sole ownership," he said, "though I will insist you insure him."

"I already have. I always knew you were right about that, but why shouldn't I syndicate him?"

"Because he's yours, and you shouldn't share him with anybody else. Be selfish. Take all the credit, all the money, all the glory."

Courtney chuckled happily. "But think of the huge commission you'll lose."

Seth had relaxed again, but he stiffened even more alarmingly at those words.

"I'm sorry. I didn't mean it like that."

"Courtney, you've got to be sure my marrying you has nothing to do with running Idle Hour or selling horses. It wouldn't work if you thought I was just looking forward to the next commission."

"I'm sure. It was just a thoughtless joke. After all the

times I really accused you of hanging around only for commissions, I thought it was funny that now you could have them all."

"I guess I'm just sensitive on the subject. You'll have to get someone else to sell your horses for you."

"I have an even better solution. I'll keep all of them." They both laughed.

Abruptly Seth's expression became serious. "Could we begin here?"

Courtney studied him closely. "You're not still afraid I'll put the farm first, are you?"

"No, but I doubt the farm will show you the same consideration. I know we'll probably move to Idle Hour in a few years. This place is too small for many horses or children, but I'd like to have you to myself for as long as possible. I don't want Ted or anyone else coming up to the house every hour of the day or night asking questions."

"Okay, as long as you keep your office in Lexington."

"It's a deal." They were quiet for a while. "Did you know the Nijinsky mare had a filly?" he asked.

"No. What's she like?"

"A little beauty. I think I just might race her myself and then breed her to Gus when she retires."

A bubble of laughter started building in Courtney's throat. When she looked up, Seth's eyes were like dancing devils, and she let loose a peal of laughter. She tried to speak, but she only laughed harder. Even as she leaned against his wonderfully comforting chest, she realized she was going to be able to spend the rest of her life with this man, and she kept on laughing.

But her laugh was no longer one of amusement. She was laughing from pure joy.